SoulShares
DEEP PLUNGE
BOOK THREE

Rory Ni Coileain

For more information contact:
Riverdale Avenue Books
5676 Riverdale Avenue
Riverdale, NY 10471.

www.riverdaleavebooks.com

Design by www.formatting4U.com
Cover by Insatiable Fantasy Designs Inc.

Digital ISBN 9781626012066
Print ISBN 9781626012073

Second Edition June 2015
First Edition August 2013 Ravenous Romance

Prologue

The Realm
2,327 years ago

If this is what a saved world looks like, deliver me from a fallen one.

Lochlann stumbled, went to one knee on the uneven, charred ground. He'd almost forgotten the luxury of riding, at this point. Of course, he'd been lucky to find a horse at all, when the three days of lightning and terror had ended and he'd emerged from his *dolmain* deep within the hollow hill and the world itself had been warped and twisted around him. The horse was luckier than he was, really; he'd left it at the last stream he'd forded before crossing the border formed by fire and storm and the spending of magick.

How many leagues he'd crossed on foot since then, he had no idea, but the length of silk he'd torn from his shirt to wrap around mouth and nose was black with soot, and he'd long since forgotten his last sighting of anything green or growing. If not for the pull of the Summoning he followed, it would be simple to wander this blasted land in circles for a lifetime.

The dark-haired Fae staggered to his feet, brushed

1

the soot off his leathers—though why he bothered was a mystery, their brown had long since gone black—and turned, shading his eyes with one hand and scanning the horizon. The channeling was drawing him toward a nearby rise. *Maybe I'll be able to see him from there. Or at least get some idea of what happened.*

As Lochlann approached the hill, instinct sent his magickal sense questing for energy to heal his rasping throat, his parched lungs. But the land around him was bereft of magick, and he was forced to turn within, drawing on the living magick of which he was formed. *Shit. Everything's drained. Everything.* He shuddered, suddenly cold. *Were they able to defeat it? Or am I being Summoned into a trap?*

The Fae sighed with relief as magick, unbound and unexpected, coursed through him. He breathed it in, let it fill throat and lungs and eyes and every other part of him, and then Shaped the magick into health. This was the gift of the Demesne of Water, the only Fae healing that could be accomplished without causing more pain than it eased.

He crested the rise, and stopped short with a whispered curse.

He stood, not at the top of a hill, but on the edge of a low cliff, overlooking a broad, flat valley. The skeletons of trees broke up the monotony of the landscape, and small eddies of blown soot chased each other across the barren ground.

And a few minutes' walk from the base of the cliff, a perfect circle was set into the ground, of a black so utter it both drew the gaze and repelled it. Around the circle were knots of muted color.

Fae, clustered together, in clothing that might

once have been finery. Some were wounded, and some of those were being tended to by others; some paced, arms wrapped tightly around themselves; some sat and stared, and even at this distance a Fae's keen senses could make out their stunned, dazed expressions.

I made it. But where's Cuinn?

Almost on the thought, the air stirred beside him, and an outline formed. A familiar outline, sandy blond hair, strong shoulders, lean hips, and pale green eyes gazing out sharply from the sketched-in face. Gradually, the rest of the figure filled in, and Lochlann could see that his one close friend was as battered and weary as any of the Fae gathered around the black circle.

"Did you win, or lose?"

Cuinn rolled his eyes. "If we'd lost, trust me, we wouldn't be having this conversation." He looked Lochlann up and down, his gaze measuring. "I take it the *dolmain* kept you adequately protected?"

Lochlann nodded. "It's an old one. It goes all the way back under the hill. But even so, I don't think it would have lasted through some of what I was hearing without the ward you put up." His body was going to remember the way the ground trembled all around him for a very long time. "Just out of curiosity, if my part in this is so important, why did you send me off alone, instead of letting me go with the four thousand Rovilin and Aine sheltered? You knew they'd be safe."

The shorter Fae opened his mouth to reply, then closed it again firmly, rubbing the back of his neck as if something there pained him. "They're safe. Yes. But they aren't what they were. And we need you the way you are."

"You lost me." Lochlann's gaze flickered to the

3

black circle, and to the host of Fae around it. Some of them were growing restive; a few, the more mobile and the less patient, were wandering westward, looking off toward the horizon. "What happened to them?"

Cuinn raked a hand through his hair, apparently oblivious to the trails of soot he left through the length of it. "Living magick is going to be in short supply in the Realm. At least for a while."

"You told me that was going to happen, if you won." Every living thing in the Realm was formed of living magick, the energy that went into each channeling a Fae performed. But the source of that energy lay within the human world. And the battle that had just been fought had ended with the sundering of the two worlds, Fae and human, and the sealing away of everything in the human world. Along with the most ancient and evil enemy of the Fae race.

"Those of us who are left are going to have to make do with less, until we figure something out." Cuinn kicked at a stone, sent it tumbling down over the cliff, watched it fall. "We worked out a way to help the whole race use less living magick. What's left of the race, anyway." He stared out across the valley, nearly expressionless.

Lochlann knew the truth. Fae didn't love, not the way humans did. And while friendships—such as the one he himself shared with the prickly Loremaster— were not unheard of, most Fae considered altruism to be a purely human pastime. But the Loremasters were not most Fae; they knew the safety of the Fae race was in their charge, and their failure to stop the *Marfach* before it wreaked the devastation surrounding them was bitter. Especially for Cuinn. "What did you do?"

Cuinn's features twisted in what could almost have been a smirk, except Lochlann knew better. "Kept them safe, as many as we could. Sent as many Loremasters as we could spare from the fight off with them. Rovilin and Aine put them all into a deep sleep, and while they were sleeping, the two of them completely remade what's left of the race." Cuinn, too, was looking off westward, to where the sun burned orange in a soot-laden sky. "Fortunately, they got it done before we had to seal the portal, so they could tap into the ley energy to do it."

"Remade how?"

Cuinn laughed, a short, harsh sound that was almost a cough and definitely without humor. "The Fae have Royals, now. And Nobles. The ones who can channel elemental magick are going to wake up as nobility, and they'll interbreed and keep their precious bloodlines pure to keep their status. Elemental magick doesn't drain the Realm. And the freaks of nature who are the Fae Elementals are going to be Royals. As long as they keep breeding, there will always be more elemental magick."

"Would I have been a Noble?" Lochlann was intrigued despite himself. The thought of Fae accepting rulers would have made him laugh, if his friend hadn't been so bitterly serious. Things were going to be interesting in the Realm while the Fae got used to this new way of life. Not that it mattered to him.

"I doubt it." Cuinn's half-smile was the first Lochlann had seen on him since he'd Faded in. "Healing is the gift of the Demesne of Water, but you draw on pure magick to do it, not elemental. No, *chara*, you'd be a commoner—there they are!"

5

Cuinn was looking past him, off westward, to where two figures on horseback were sending up clouds of soot and dust all out of proportion to their size. "There who are?"

"Aine and Rovilin. Now we can start."

The Loremasters clustered around the black circle were stirring now, the wounded struggling to rise, pushing away the helping hands of their fellows. Even at this distance, Lochlann could feel the pain of the injured, the exhaustion of the more intact. A curse that went along with the gift of Water. Fae, as a general rule, were short on empathy, but healers were something of an exception. "Two more will make that much of a difference?" Shading his eyes, he studied the crowd around the circle. "There must be a thousand Loremasters down there."

"One thousand, two hundred and eight. If we haven't lost anyone since the battle ended. And we're going to need every one of them."

Cuinn's voice was tight, controlled; Lochlann turned back, and was astonished by the anger he saw on his friend's face. "What is it?" He rested a hand on the blond Fae's shoulder. "How many did you lose?"

"It's not that." Cuinn shook his head sharply. "Though we lost too damned many. Killed in battle, dead by their own hands to stop the *Marfach* from warping them, spent to nothingness banishing the bastard."

"Then what is it?"

"Every one of them is needed so desperately, and there are Fae down there clinging to life solely so they can let go of it where it will feed the last channeling." Cuinn spoke through clenched teeth, avoiding

Lochlann's gaze. "They're all needed. Every one but me."

Lochlann's own chest was tight with Cuinn's unmistakable anger. An anger he didn't understand. "You told me you had your own part to play."

"I do." More anger, if anything. "And they won't tell me what it is." He glared down at the ink-black circle, as if it somehow collaborated with the Loremasters to hide the secret from him.

Lochlann followed the direction of Cuinn's gaze, focusing on the circle, rather than the Fae gathered around it. "What is that?"

"It's everywhere in the Realm."

He started to laugh, but Cuinn looked serious enough that he turned the laugh into a cough. Not difficult, given the soot and ash that hung in the air. "You lost me again."

Cuinn sighed, but Lochlann suspected he welcomed the distraction. "There's a very real sense in which space and time don't exist when you're dealing with pure magick."

"That much I follow." Magick was a paradox, both real and not, visible and invisible, permeating everything but with no form of its own. And any magick touched all other magick, in some way that gave most Fae who weren't mages at or near the level of the Loremasters headaches to contemplate. That was how Fading worked, a thing Fae accomplished instinctively once they came into their birthright of power, moving from magick to magick, becoming magick themselves for the barest instant.

"That circle—" Cuinn gestured with a jerk of his chin—"is a barrier between magicks. Not just a ward.

The magick on the far side of it can't touch the magick on this side of it."

Lochlann stared at the blackness. "I thought there wasn't any magick left on the far side of it." The preparation for the last battle with the *Marfach* had taken years, to hear Cuinn tell it, gathering together every remnant of living magick from the world humans and Fae had shared, to keep it away from the ancient enemy that inhabited that magick, fed on it, and twisted it into its own image of pure, unadulterated evil.

Cuinn coughed into his hand, "Damned soot." He rubbed at his eyes, reddened by smoke, their pale green even more vivid because of the blood hue. "The *Marfach* is there. And the energy in the ley lines. The ley power isn't living magick, strictly speaking, but no one wants to wager on the *Marfach* being unable to figure out how to use it somehow."

"I see your point." One look at the utter destruction around them was more than enough to remind him of the cost of that particular error. "So that thing is the only window between the two worlds?"

"It's not a window at all. It's a magickal representation of everyplace in the Realm. Every place where the *Marfach* could cross back. And that image, that representation, has been locked down, tempered, warded, sealed. Every protective channeling any of us knew." Cuinn's brows drew together again; the respite answering questions had given him was apparently over. "But it's still not going to be enough. Not until it's finished—oh, damn." Just that quickly, frustration yielded to a hushed sorrow. "They're starting."

Lochlann watched, fighting to breathe against a hollow sensation in his chest, as two critically injured

Fae were carried out onto the gleaming black surface of the circle. If they were still injured, if they hadn't healed this long after the final battle with the *Marfach*, then their wounds were mortal. Yet they had refused to die.

"What are they going to do?"

"Watch." Cuinn's gaze was fixed on the circle, on the two Fae that lay there alone, their bearers having melted back into the onlooking throng.

Lochlann was about to reply, but bit back the words as spindles of silver-blue light rose up from the circle around each of the injured Loremasters. Spindles that bent, and wove themselves into intricate webs over each recumbent form, until the two were all but lost to sight, shrouded in dancing light. And then the webs started to tighten, to draw the two Fae down into the substance of the circle. As Lochlann stared, transfixed, they slowly gave up their substance to the light-sucking blackness of the circle.

"*Slántai a'váil*," Cuinn whispered. *Farewell*, as the webs gave back their light to the circle, silver-blue sparks chasing each other across the surface before being swallowed up in the darkness. That darkness was not entirely featureless, though; at the very limits of his vision, Lochlann made out—or thought he did—two fine lines of silver-blue, curving just under the black surface. And the brilliant green of new grass limned the circumference of the circle.

Before Lochlann could find his voice, two more Loremasters were helped out onto the ebon surface. These were able to sit, and did; the eyes of the male were closed as he struggled with pain, but the female saw, and gasped, as the light shot up around her.

His gift, or curse, of empathy allowed him to feel

her heart race with the touch of the net of lights; her terror nearly overwhelmed him as the net began to pull her down. Yet under the terror lay iron determination, and she barely flinched as the first of her substance disappeared.

"*Shit*—Lochlann, damn it, don't go with her!"

Cuinn's voice was like a dousing with cold water; Lochlann gasped, shook himself, and tried to make his eyes focus on his friend's face. "Where is she going? —where are *they* going?"

Cuinn didn't seem to hear him. "*Eiscréid*, I thought this would be far enough away that you wouldn't be drawn in—"

"I don't have to be drawn in. I won't let myself." Yet he had to fight to keep from looking back toward the circle, to ignore the movement he could see at the edge of his vision, to keep his attention on his agitated friend. "What are they doing?"

"Two things. Neither of which we can afford to have you caught up in." Cuinn took Lochlann by the arm and firmly turned him away from the view below. "Their souls are becoming a part of the portal. They'll see to the protection of any Fae that passes through into the human world, now that we've sealed the humans off from us, and hold the portal against the *Marfach*, if it tries to return here from the human world."

"That's one."

The blond Fae seemed to have trouble finding his voice. "They're giving the magick they're formed of back to the Realm," he managed at last.

Now Lochlann *had* to look. He turned on his heel, and saw two more Fae being assisted into the empty circle. Not quite empty; two more lines, finer than hairs and detectable only by their bluish-silver glow, arced through the blackness. And the green rim he had seen around the circle after the first two Fae departed was now a greensward extending maybe thirty paces from the circle's edge in all directions.

Resolutely, he kept his eyes on that swath of green, even when the flare of light told him the circle was about to claim two more wounded mages. This time, he saw the life suffuse the charred and barren ground, saw it go green from within, in an ever-widening circle under the feet of the Loremasters who awaited their turn in the black.

"You *want* to do what they're doing?" Lochlann risked a look back at Cuinn, who was watching the scene below with a predatory intensity, unhampered by Lochlann's gift.

Cuinn nodded tightly. "I know how badly they need magick, and souls, to make this work. But they won't let me be a part of it. Other than to seal the channeling off when the last of them go into the Pattern." A muscle jumped in the sensual male's jaw—and even burned and exhausted and black with grime, 'sensual' was one of the first words anyone would use to describe him. "Do they really expect me to be content with that?"

"At least you'll be there to help me, when it's my turn." There were four Fae, now, two males, two females, taking their places on the circle; Lochlann carefully kept his gaze fixed on the empty center of the circle and focused on not sensing the emotions swirling around the black expanse. "After seeing this..." He shook his head slowly. "I could never do what you asked of me alone."

"You could if you had to. But I'll help you."

The two Fae fell silent, watching the dance that went on below them. It *was* a dance, slow and stately and possessed of a terrible beauty. Four by four, now, the Loremasters came, kneeling on the hard black surface, the females surrounded by swirls of skirts blackened with smoke, the males by cloaks rent and stained with blood. Lochlann saw faces he knew, males and females he had shared a night with, sometimes more, and in those moments he had to look away. Four by four the nets of light took them, and the life they poured into the land pushed back the devastation. Silver-blue tracing slowly filled the darkness, bright points of light racing along arcs and whorls that grew more and more intricate with every vanished Fae.

The sun sank, and the moon rose, and by the time the last few Loremasters entered the circle, it was almost as if they knelt on a piece of the night sky itself. Cuinn cleared his throat and turned to Lochlann. "Do you think you can be close to them and not be drawn in? I should say good-bye, but you don't have to come with me if it would put you at risk."

"I can manage." Lochlann's own voice, unused for hours, was gruff and choked. "Hurry, before the lights take them."

Cuinn nodded, and Faded; Lochlann followed, taking form at the very edge of the black circle beside his friend.

This close, the beauty of the portal took his breath. Midnight blackness was set with icy silver-blue light, a magnificently complex net of glittering diamond. The four Fae who knelt in the midst of it were equally beautiful, though each bore scars from the battle they had endured. Only one of the four was known to Lochlann, and that by reputation only— Dúlánc, the leader of the Loremasters, the strongest of them, and nearly a thousand years old. So ancient that his age had begun to show, his black hair was frosted with white. And from him, Lochlann sensed no fear at all; apprehension, yes, but it was nearly lost in fierce excitement.

"We will be enough." Dúlánc's deep voice seemed to come from the very depths of exhaustion as he addressed Cuinn, yet it trembled with that same excitement. "If you seal the Pattern well behind us, we will be enough to hold the portal against anything less than one of our own, wielding the magick of a whole world."

"I won't fail you." Cuinn stood, feet shoulders'-width apart and arms crossed, his jaw set in what might have been determination and might have been anger. Both, probably. "But I should be with you."

Dúlánc sighed. "One had to remain behind. And none of us are capable of doing what you will one day do."

"Do I get to know what that is?" If anything, his friend grew even more pugnacious in the face of the senior Loremaster's formality.

"Not yet." The hint of a smile touched the elderly Fae's lips. "One of the things you have to do is figure it out."

"I would feel better about that if I didn't know for a fact you don't actually know everything."

Now Dúlánc laughed outright. "Fortunately for all of us, stubbornness is essential to your task."

The older Loremaster was still smiling as he turned to Lochlann. "Brother of Water, I should have thanked you before now, but believe me when I say that we are grateful for what you are about to do. This work—" Dúlánc's gesture took in the whole of the circle—"is far from finished. And without you, it could never *be* finished."

"I don't understand." Lochlann felt his cheeks warm, at being addressed as 'brother' by a male already a legend. "But I'll do as Cuinn's explained to me."

"We can ask no more." The smile, the laughter in the eyes faded. "From tonight, you will no longer be Lochlann, but Lochlann Doran." Lochlann the Stranger, Lochlann the Exile. "Until you find the one destined for you on the other side."

"What about me?" Cuinn put in, one eyebrow nearly disappearing into the sandy blond locks that fell over his forehead. "Am I to be renamed as well?"

"Oh, yes." Dúlánc chuckled dryly. "Several of your fellow Loremasters had suggestions for a new name. I chose to ignore them. From now on, you will be Cuinn an Dearmad. Wisdom of the Forgotten. For forgotten we will all surely be. None of the four thousand were told the truth of the portal, and they will wake to a world without Loremasters."

"Dúlánc." The woman who knelt behind the elder mage spoke softly. "The Pattern remains unfinished until we enter it."

"Thank you, Aine." Dúlánc took a deep, cleansing breath. "Cuinn, Lochlann, you might want to step back."

Lochlann obeyed, and as a precaution averted his eyes. But even looking off into the magickally restored forest bordering the portal site, he saw the light. Saw it build, saw it flare. And heard his *chara*'s long, unsteady sigh when darkness returned.

"Cuinn, I'm sorry—"

"Stand back." Cuinn's eyes were a sharp green glint in the darkness, reflecting Pattern-light. "All the magick for this is going to have to come from me—I don't want to drain you accidentally."

Again Lochlann gave way, but this time he watched. Cuinn closed his eyes, bowed his head. His hands clenched into fists, then relaxed. And he began to glow. At first, it was as if his skin was suffused with fire, the way a child's hand looked clutching a light-orb crafted by a doting parent. The light swiftly brightened, though, and in a matter of moments his friend was engulfed in white and green fire, subtly patterned. *Yes, he told me, his father was Air and his mother was Earth.*

He closed his eyes, briefly, to let the searing after-images clear.

When he opened them again, Cuinn still blazed as brightly, but knelt beside the circle, reaching for the matte-black surface. The green and the white raced out from where he touched it, like oil touched with a spark, or like frost etching itself on glass; the circle flared up brilliantly, then faded once again to blackness. This was a different sort of blackness, though. The circle now gave back the starlight like a mirror, and when Lochlann edged closer to look, he saw the brilliant silver-blue tracery faded to the thinness of a hair, nearly invisible.

"Are you ready?" Cuinn spoke quietly, from behind him.

15

So soon? Lochlann's heart raced as he turned. But, then, why wait? "If the portal's ready, yes."

The magickal glow hadn't faded entirely from Cuinn yet, and Lochlann caught his breath at his friend's beauty, his features edged in shifting light. He had never bedded Cuinn—their sort of friendship was a rarity among the Fae, and would never have survived the kind of sexual collision he knew the Loremaster favored—but it was easy to see why males and females alike vied, and sometimes even dueled, for his attention.

"It's ready, though I'll probably have to help you through. One of my first jobs come morning is to trigger the wards the others crafted for this place, and figure a way to open the portal when necessary without me having to spend magick to do it directly." Cuinn shifted his weight uncomfortably. "Do me a favor? Be careful, once you're over there. If things went as we planned, nothing physical can harm you. Look around, find out what the Sundering has done to the human world. And then when you find the human with the other half of your soul, you shouldn't need the invulnerability any more, because with his help you'll be able to tap directly into the raw magick that's left on that side."

"Slow down, *chara*. Breathe." Lochlann managed a smile. "You told me most of this already." Cuinn had first approached him, tentatively, several years ago, not long after the Loremasters had started their planning. "And I agreed to do it. I'm a volunteer, remember?"

"I know." Cuinn took a deep breath, and let it out in a sigh. "I'd feel better if we were able to be more certain. We tried to control as much as we could, but there are aspects of this that are beyond anyone's ability to foresee or control. And no one has been able to test the system."

"That's my job. And I trust you." Words rarer even than 'I love you' among the Fae, and never spoken lightly.

"Maybe you shouldn't." The gaze Cuinn turned on him was haunted, his emotional aura that of a male pushed to his limits and past them, and facing a task that demanded everything he had left.

Lochlann shook his head. "Send me through, *chara*."

Cuinn stared at him a moment longer, then nodded. "All right. Go."

Lochlann stepped tentatively onto the circle, not sure what sort of surface would greet him. It was solid, and as smooth as it looked; he moved out to the center, the small space of darkness in the tracery of light, and knelt as he had seen so many other Fae do in the course of the endless day just past. He looked down at the gleaming surface, and fought down dizzying vertigo. The silver-blue Pattern gleamed in the circle below him, its lines finer than spun silk. And past the lines, he saw a sky full of stars. "*Cho'hálan*," he whispered. *So beautiful.*

One swirl of light, directly in front of him, caught his attention.

Dúlánc, it said, in the curves and angles of *d'aos'Faein* shaping. Beside it, another skein of lines shaped *Aine*. There were other names as well, all subtly shifting, rearranging themselves. As if their bearers were trying to find their places in a new reality.

Cuinn gestured, whispered, and the mirrored surface vanished.

The brilliant glory of the lines revived, and for an instant longer Lochlann was enthralled by beauty.

But the lines were blades, keener than any knife. Lochlann fell through them, between them, the blades cutting deep and bloodless.

But not deep enough.

He dropped through the Pattern to the bottom of the cage of his ribs, before he stuck. He tried to lunge for Cuinn, sought his hand, nearly blinded by the pain. His wordless screams rent the night air, one after another. *It's gone wrong, no one could survive this!*

Cuinn, as pale as his own revenant, stared at what was left of Lochlann in shock. Then he gestured, and a whirlwind sprang up around him. He pointed at the center of the circle.

The merciless wind hammered at Lochlann the Exile like a great fist. His scream went ahead of him, opening the way into his new world.

Chapter One

Garrett pushed open the dressing room door. Or he tried to. Someone was using the mirror behind it, so the door wouldn't open all the way. "Incoming," he called out, wondering where the hell the cheery tone was coming from. "Suck it up, Buttercup."

"Oh, for Christ's sake."

Garrett thought he heard a shuffling of feet, and the next time he tried, he could get the door open wide enough to get through, shoving his bag in ahead of him. The door closed again behind him, as Leandro took a step back to continue running a comb through his thick black hair. "You're early." The Brazilian flashed him a quick smile in the mirror.

"Yeah, I know, I need to have something to eat before I go on." Garrett tossed his bag in the corner, shrugged out of his coat, draped it over the tiny dressing room's single chair, and sat down in the chair, facing a lit makeup mirror and a table littered with more powders and creams than the cosmetics counter at Saks. Not that he needed that shit. At least, not yet. *Maybe soon. But not yet.*

"Take your time." Leandro settled one last stray lock in place, then set down the comb with a satisfied nod. "I'm going out early, we have a full house. Maybe I'll pick up enough to take Antonio out for drinks after I get off."

"Good luck." Garrett didn't take his eyes off the old, discolored mirror as the door opened and closed behind him, the persistent bass thrum of the music from the dance floor swelling for a moment and then fading. Sound insulation on the dressing room door. One of the decent things Tiernan Guaire had done since he took over Purgatory. That, and furniture for the dancers' dressing room. And lights.

And paying a respectable enough wage that Leandro didn't really have to do his dollar dance if he wanted to take his boyfriend and former business partner out on the town. Garrett grimaced and reached into his bag, digging out a wrapped sandwich and a bottle of water. It hadn't always been that way. For most of his time at Purgatory, he'd gotten by only by turning tricks. Sometimes even in this very room, back when the lighting sucked and the ceiling and the walls were nothing but stained grey cement.

Did it happen in here, I wonder?

Working by touch, he reached back into the bag and took out two bottles of pills, one large, one smaller, and set them carefully on the edge of the table. Checked his watch, slowly, ritualistically. Five minutes to ten. Plenty of time to eat. Even a few bites of his sandwich would be enough to let this newest protease inhibitor do its thing.

Why the HELL am I bothering?

He glared at his reflection, pissed off at it for looking like nothing had happened today. Same mop of blond curls, same dark amber eyes, dimpled chin, and bow-shaped mouth. Same body that men he'd never met and never would were going to be getting hard at the sight of in about half an hour. At least now he didn't have to let them fuck him to pay for food.

Shit. He grabbed the sandwich, unwrapped it, and forced himself to start eating. Not that he had much of an appetite. That was what had set off this whole latest round of doctor's visits over a month ago. Blood tests. Waiting for results. Change of meds. More blood tests. More waiting. And then, today...

"I don't understand it, Mr. Templar." Dr. Terwillar's scowl didn't sit well on her usually cheerful features, and she glared at the computer screen as if she wanted to put one of her thrift store Doc Martens through it. "Your viral load is literally off the charts. It's worse than it was before we switched you to the Fosamprenavir. And there is no way that's supposed to happen." She kept pushing the same stubborn strand of graying hair out of her eyes, a mechanical tidiness that was starting to irritate the shit out of him. Better than being angry at the fucking virus that was going to kill him. The virus that didn't realize the magic pills were supposed to keep it in the background of his life until someone somewhere came up with a cure. The virus didn't care what he felt.

Ten o'clock. He reached for bottle with the larger of the two pills. Damned if he was going to give up.

***

The plastic water bottle bounced off the rim of the wastebasket and clattered to the floor. Garrett grimaced, but didn't bother going back for it. *I'll get it when I come back.* No turning back now; he'd let himself hear the beat and the music was calling him. Ten years he'd been doing this, and the music still called him. He'd always told himself the day it stopped was the day he was going to quit. *Looks like my schedule might be changing.*

He let himself out of the dressing room and started down the hall, his bare feet cold against the cement, adjusting himself as he went, his gloved fingers only a little clumsy. Some of the customers complained about the coverage of the thong he wore when he danced, but it protected him against the worst pole burns, and anyone who really wanted a look at his package just had to wait for him to do a corkscrew around the pole.

Shit, Leandro wasn't kidding. The noise from the dance floor hit him like a padded hammer as he let himself out of the back hallway into the front of the house. Over and over, with every bass beat from the speakers. Friday night, and the dance floor was jammed nearly to the walls, or at least as far as he could see on tiptoes, with men in various states of dress. And various states of undress. Everyone was still dressed, though, at least a little. Well, the night was young.

Two of the poles were occupied, the ones toward the back. Leandro's jock was already pretty well stuffed with green, from what he could see as he made his way through the crowd, and if there were a couple of baggies in with the cash, Garrett very carefully wasn't seeing them. And Frederic was rapturously being Frederic, Christ, the guy should have been a contortionist.

They'd left the front pole for him, they always did. He was the one who brought the audience in. He was the one who made them forget everyone else and jam the dance floor to watch and then stand back in awe, hands dropping to groins, groaning softly. A line from an old song skittered through his head: ... *'cause he knows that it's me they've been coming to see, to forget about life for a while.* Yeah, that was it. He gave them that. But where did he go, to forget about his?

Right here. Garrett gripped the pole, testing the rubber surfaces that covered his palms, then swung himself up, legs scissoring, to wrap one leg around the pole over his head and extend the other as he slowly spiraled down.

It was starting already, he could hear the exclamations, a few squeals, some of the regulars calling his name. The rush. He hit bottom, did a long slow sweep around the pole with legs extended as the bass beat kicked his ass, then swung his legs back in and shimmied up the pole. Hugged it, his mop of blond curls nearly brushing the ceiling. Worked it, all the way down, fucking the long gleaming hard length of it, slowly spinning to make sure every guy on the floor got the view he liked best.

Garrett had never been a gymnast, and though he'd studied dance off and on, it sure wasn't anything like this. There were probably names for some of the things he did with his body, but he didn't know what they were, and didn't care. He made himself happy when he danced, and the fact he made others happy when he did it was just what his Grand'Mere Toinette had called lagniappe. A little something extra, thrown in for free.

A sharp prickle ran down the back of his neck as he hand-over-handed it back up to the driving beat. *What the hell?* He'd always been intuitive—he hated the word "sensitive," it was the word his mother used to describe him because she couldn't make herself say the word "gay"— ever since he could remember, he'd had an acute sixth sense. But why was it acting up now? *Someone's watching me?* No shit. About a hundred someones.

Hooking a knee around the pole, he corkscrewed halfway down in a graceful arabesque; his legs were longer than they had any right to be on a guy who was only five foot nine, and he knew how to use them. With a grin, he spread his legs wide, grabbing the pole in between them and letting the pole stand in for the world's longest, hardest cock. Which every man in the room probably figured he had right now. Spinning around, working his ass against the cool slick metal.

Viral load. The thought was like a physical blow. *Shit. They're going to have to use Lysol on the pole.*

A wave of revulsion, dizziness hit him. Hard. He let go of the pole. He fell. His head hit the floor, and the music and the lights all went away.

"Hey."

Garrett's head was being cradled. In someone's lap, probably, from the feel of it. A hand was touching his face. He opened his eyes, and looked up into the most stunning, sensual blue eyes he had ever seen. Eyes that peered at him anxiously, dark hair falling around them.

The man's fingers brushed Garrett's cheek. "Are you all right, *scair-anam*?"

Chapter Two

I cannot believe I just said that.

Lochlann brushed the dancer's curly blond hair back from his face, his hand perfectly happy to acknowledge the truth his mind was running in circles trying to avoid. *Garrett.* A few of the spectators had been calling that name, even chanting it, a minute ago. Now those spectators were crowded around, their murmuring barely audible over the driving music. They'd been quick. But he'd been quicker.

Soul-share. He'd known it the moment he'd seen the male undulating up the pole. The shock when he'd felt the subtle whisper of magick within him had taken his breath. Magick. After what, six hundred years, give or take? He'd pushed his way through the crowd, captivated by the male's grace and enthusiasm. And beauty. *Damn.*

But then Garrett had fallen. And Lochlann, who hadn't been a healer for 600 years and had last given a damn about any living soul, Fae or human, long before that, had raced to his side and lifted his bleeding head into his lap.

"Huh?" The male shook his head, as if to clear it, and winced. "Shit. What happened?"

"I'm not sure. You fell." Lochlann kept his face impassive with an effort, as the healer he had once been tried to reach out, enter into Garrett to assess his injury. Tried in vain, of course. "Maybe you should just lie here for a minute."

"I..." The male looked up at him, confused. "Yeah. I'd like that."

The dark-haired Fae moved to settle the human more comfortably. It was as if the onlookers had vanished, for all he cared they could be on the moon, or in the Realm. "Take your time." His fingers moved almost of themselves, stroking Garrett's forehead, toying with the curls that fell over it, meeting eyes of an amazing warm brown that was almost gold.

And he stared, stunned, as the human's aura shimmered into view. This *had* to be some effect of soul-sharing. His inner magicks had been the last to go. He'd held on to those for almost a century after he had lost the ability to channel, but he hadn't been able to read an aura for half a millennium.

Maybe I've forgotten how to do it. Because what he was seeing didn't make any sense. The quiescent male in his lap had an aura spiking with panic and despair; the beautiful body that enchanted him swirled with the dull gray ashen hue that denoted a terminal illness in a human. Not possible.

Garrett's gloved hand clutched at his, startling him. "Who are you?" The human's eyes were intense, almost fevered.

"I'm Lochlann." The Fae turned his hand in the human's, holding it more gently than he'd held anything in the last few thousand years. "You'll be all right—"

26

"What the fuck happened?"

Lochlann looked up, a growl starting, as someone pushed through the hushed circle of onlookers. A male, tall, blond, hair falling in waves over his shoulders. Ring in one eyebrow, leather jacket over a plain white T-shirt.

Eyes of a clear, faceted blue, like gem-quality topaz. The eyes of another Fae.

"Tiernan." Garrett tried to sit up, and for the first time Lochlann saw the bloodstains on his jeans. "Sorry, I don't know what happened. I fell."

Gently, Lochlann urged Garrett back down. He kept his face carefully impassive, doing his best not to reel under the impact of the one-two punch he'd received. First his SoulShare, after more than two millennia. And now, for the first time since coming through the Pattern, he was seeing another member of his own race in the flesh. Coincidence?

"You never fall." The other Fae's eyes narrowed. "Are you all right? You're bleeding."

Lochlann was totally unprepared for Garrett's reaction. The human's eyes went wide, his aura flared with alarm. No, panic. He scrambled to his knees, looking back at Lochlann's bloodstained jeans. "Fuck. Get home. Get those washed. Shower." His gaze went back to the blond Fae. "You're going to need to get someone out here with Lysol, or bleach, or some damn thing. The floor, and the pole."

Garrett started to get to his feet, but hesitated, turning back to Lochlann. *Those eyes...* "Your name... Lochlann, right?" He waited for Lochlann to nod. "Look. I don't know what you called me. But whatever it was, forget about it. Forget you ever met

27

me." He scrambled to his feet and stood looking down at Lochlann, totally ignoring the leather-jacketed blond who was apparently his boss. "You have no idea how sorry I am." The whisper was so soft, no doubt the human was sure Lochlann couldn't hear it.

Which he almost couldn't, not over the roaring of his heartbeat in his ears. The aura. The blood. The panic. *Shit.*

Before Lochlann could manage a word, or even collect his thoughts, Garrett turned on his bare heel and pushed his way through the crowd, And as quickly as that he was lost, even to the keen sight of a Fae.

"Come on, pretty boy. On your feet and off my dance floor." Tiernan's words were directed at Lochlann, but he never took his eyes off the place where the dancer had disappeared.

As Lochlann slowly stood, Tiernan unwound a flexible microphone from around his ear, touched an earpiece, and murmured instructions to someone to do a 'full sanitary' on the dance floor, then replaced the mic before turning back to Lochlann. "I said, show's over—"

Tiernan stopped dead, staring, and Lochlann knew what he was seeing. Fae eyes, a shade closer to aquamarine than blue topaz, but unmistakably non-human, to one who knew how to look. "Oh, fuck me."

"Thanks, I'll pass." Lochlann could feel a pull, almost as if a cord bound him to the young dancer; he wanted to follow him, wanted to so badly he could almost feel his feet doing it. *Forget you ever met me, my ass.*

"Care to step into my office?" Without waiting for an answer, Tiernan turned and walked off the dance floor; Lochlann shrugged and followed. He wasn't looking forward to an inquisition, but if he could find out anything that might let him stay close enough to Garrett not to lose him entirely while he figured out what the hell was going on, he could put up with a bit of interrogation.

Tiernan skirted the edge of a sunken maze of black leather sofas, chairs, and loveseats, each occupied by at least two men. The pounding music provided all the privacy any of them had, and it was very obvious none of them cared. Lochlann didn't care either. He was busy doing his best to keep Tiernan in sight as the blond pushed his way through the ring of onlookers. He'd stopped counting lovers after the first couple of centuries, and had only become very choosy about taking them after the first thousand years or so; there was little he hadn't done, and less he hadn't seen. Nothing in the pit particularly surprised him.

And at the moment, the only body that interested him had disappeared into a crowd of club-goers without a backward look.

He caught up with Tiernan as the other Fae was unlocking a door set into an inner wall of the club; plain fluorescent light came spilling out, cutting through the darkness shot with neon firelight that filled this end of the room. He entered ahead of Tiernan, and looked around as the door clicked shut behind him. A spare room, mostly filled by a desk, with a chair before and a chair behind, and a couple of computer monitors.

"Sit down." Tiernan motioned toward the chair in front of the desk as he dropped into his own.

"Thanks, I prefer to stand." Lochlann arched a brow, looking pointedly down at the other Fae.

"I am sprung from the loins of an entire race of assholes." Tiernan rolled his eyes, turning in his chair to check out the monitors before swinging back to look narrowly up at Lochlann. "Although without the attitude, I have to admit, I'd have a hard time believing you're Fae."

"*Sus do thón*," Lochlann offered pleasantly.

"Yeah, up yours, too, and may you have much joy of it." Tiernan leaned back in his chair, put his bare feet up on the desk, and crossed his arms behind his head. "Speaking of which, what did you say that spooked Garrett like that? I don't take kindly to my dancers being treated badly. Unless they want to be, in which case it's none of my fucking business."

Lochlann's lip curled in a snarl. "It was nothing I said. It was..." His voice trailed off, as he remembered the way the ash-grey aura had curled up out of the human's body, wisps of smoke from a fire nearly dead, weaving themselves into a shroud. "He has AIDS."

Tiernan shook his head. "No. He's HIV-positive. There's a big difference."

"Don't condescend to me." Lochlann bent forward, knuckles resting on the desk, looming over the other Fae. "I know what I saw. My Demesne is Water, my gifts are healing and empathy. I saw his aura. He's dying."

The words caught at his throat, clawed, as they left him. *My* scair-anam *is dying, and there's not a fucking thing I can do about it. A healer who can't heal.*

Tiernan lifted his feet from the desk, swung his legs down, and stood, leaning forward, consciously or unconsciously mirroring Lochlann. This close, the male's eyes were disconcerting, a shade of blue that made Lochlann think of glacier ice. "Tell me how you saw this, *lasihoir*." The word *healer* was heavy with sarcasm. "Tell me how you saw this, when there's a river of the raw stuff of magick flowing right under the floor of this room and sending up eddies that even a Noble like me can see, and you're not so much as twitching. Tell me how you saw this, when I've been watching you with every sense I have and I would swear on my brother's corpse if he'd left one that there's absolutely nothing of magick about you."

"Do you think I don't know that?" Lochlann, voice was low, cold, even. "I spent the last of my magick in London, in 1348. During the Black Death. Unable to Fade, unable to die, and trapped in a city and a country of the dead. And I can see Garrett's aura, my empathy works with him, because he's my SoulShare. After more than two thousand years, I have found my *scair-anam*." Lochlann's gaze flickered to the monitors, wishing one would show him what had happened to Garrett. "And he is dying, and I am six hundred fucking years too late to do anything about it."

"Spent the last of your magick?" Lochlann suspected the Fae before him would have to be dead for at least three days before he'd stop sounding arrogant, but it seemed he was making an effort. "That's not possible. I've been here for a hundred and fifty years, and I'd only spent a fraction of mine before I could replenish it."

"It took me sixteen centuries to lose mine—did you say replenish?" Lochlann straightened, trying to keep the sudden hope from his face. How quickly the old habits returned, even after millennia. Never, ever let another Fae think he has something you need, knows something you don't. But this... *Maybe it's not too late.*

"I did, but that's not an option for you, at least not until after you Share." The blond still looked unconvinced as to Lochlann's true nature. "There's too much power there for us to tap into without getting fried, unless we have a human buffer."

"That's all a SoulShare is? A tool? A means to an end?" None of that sounded anything like what he'd felt when he first saw Garrett. Or touched him. One didn't want to get lost in a tool, or hear it screaming one's name in ecstasy as one pushed it up against the wall and found its pleasure spot, over and over.

"My *husband* is not a fucking tool. And if Conall Dary thought you were saying that about his Josh, he'd have your balls for breakfast, trust me." Tiernan looked Lochlann up and down, one pierced eyebrow arched. "Did I hear you say sixteen centuries?"

"You did." *So others found their* scair-anaim. *In considerably less than twenty-three centuries.* "I was the first one through the portal."

For the first time in their brief acquaintance, Tiernan looked impressed, whistling softly. "What did *you* do to piss somebody off?"

"Nothing. They needed a volunteer, I was it."

"You poor stupid bastard."

Lochlann smothered a laugh. "For once, I'm inclined to agree with you."

"So you've lived, what? At least twice a normal lifespan." Tiernan shook his head. "I guess all the old stories about Pattern immortality were actually true."

"That was what I was told to expect." The words issued through clenched teeth. There were a lot of things he'd been told to expect. Far more that he hadn't. Such as losing his magick. That would have been a useful piece of information to have, before he'd spent it all. Though once he'd passed through the portal, to be fair, there had been no way to tell him.

"What if it all catches up with you, when you Share?"

"Congratulations. I think you just set a new Fae record for lack of tact. Considering the competition, even the way it was back in my era, that's quite an accomplishment." Under the snide commentary, though, his mind was racing. And reeling. *If I were to Share with Garrett—however that's done—I could tap into this source, whatever it is. I could heal him. But if two lifetimes catch up with me at once...* The mental image refused to go away, his body crumbling to less than dust in the space of a heartbeat. *Thanks ever so fucking much, Noble.*

"Shit. Maybe you could ask Cuinn."

Racing mind came to screeching halt. "Would that be Cuinn an Dearmad?" *If that's the name the bastard kept.*

The pierced brow went even higher. "It would. Do you know him?"

"I did." One human archetype he'd come to understand very well was the notion of the sacrificial lamb. Not that he had any idea why the Loremasters had needed one, but it would have been infinitely kinder to kill him outright than to exile him to the human world with nothing except a slender hope. A hope that had arrived 600 years too late. And Cuinn

33

had been the one to draw him into their scheme. *I know just the one*, he could imagine the bastard saying to his fellows. *He calls me 'friend,' he'll never think to question what we ask of him.*

Tiernan cocked his head, his expression carefully neutral. "I recognize that tone of voice. Just so you know, *a'gár'doltas* isn't a good idea, this side of the Pattern. There aren't enough of us here that we can afford to waste any."

Smiling-murder. Vendetta. Not a bad idea. "Not all Fae are natural resources. Some are natural liabilities."

The other Fae snorted. "Not that I'm disagreeing with you at all. The male is a bigger pain in the ass than an enema with a live porcupine, but Cuinn would kick your ass even if you had magick left. He may not be able to tap into the ley energy to restore his reserves, but he doesn't have to, he can pass to and from the Realm whenever he wants."

"...whenever he wants." The words echoed in the sudden dead silence in Lochlann's head. *The son of a bitch can come and go as he pleases. Which means that there were at least sixteen fucking hundred years in which my friend could have told me I wasn't alone in the world. Could have told me what I was doing to myself. Just a hint, and Garrett might have had a chance to live.*

"Was it something I said?"

Lochlann blinked, willing the room to come back into focus. "Give Cuinn an Dearmad a message from Lochlann Doran, the next time you see him."

Maybe it was something in his voice that was making the other Fae sweat. "What would the message be?"

"D'súil do na prachán, d'croí do na gaoirn, d'anam do n-oí gan derea."

Lochlann turned and let himself back out into the din of the club, leaving behind him a stunned Tiernan, and an ancient challenge hanging in the still air, the words nearly tangible and with edges sharp enough to draw blood.

Your eyes for the crows, your heart for the wolves, your soul for the eternal night.

35

Chapter Three

Cuinn looked the delectable drag queen up and down. The bar stool showed off long, long legs to perfect advantage, and the thigh-high slit in the skirt certainly helped. Silk dress clinging in all the right places and loose enough in others to let one's imagination run wild. Stiletto heels he could easily imagine in the small of his back, at least until he did something to reassert a more appropriate relational dynamic. A fall of gleaming black hair, and long slender fingers wrapped around the stem of a martini glass. And no escort. *Score.* Now if he could just figure out whether he was looking at an actual drag queen or a Victor/Victoria. Just a whiff of pheromones would give it away, of course, but that would be cheating. And it wasn't like he really gave a damn, he was good either way.

His phone buzzed in his pocket, and he cursed under his breath. Cursed *as'Faein,* because the pulsation of the buzz told him that it was one of his own. Tiernan Guaire, in fact. He rolled his eyes, and it seemed to him the stuffed zebra head over the bar commiserated with him as he pulled out his phone. Fuck if he could figure out what the thing was doing in Easternbloc, it certainly didn't fit with the pseudo-Soviet decor. "This had better be important, your Grace, there's a luscious young man/woman/other whose appointment with paradise you're delaying."

"You'll have to tell me how important it is."

For once, the Noble wasn't rising to the bait—which was kind of like the sun deciding not to rise—and Cuinn frowned. "Go on."

"Someone left here just now. He seems to be Fae—has the eyes, knows the language, but claims to have lost his magick."

"Lost his—" Something with cold sharp talons clutched at Cuinn's gut. *Oh, shit.*

"Yeah. And he's either telling the truth or he's a complete fraud, because I didn't see so much as a trace of magick on or in him and he couldn't see the ley energy."

And I had no choice but to let it happen. A muscle twitched in Cuinn's jaw as he ground his teeth. *The Pattern's good and faithful servant. Observing and reporting. Serving the greater design. All the way to the bitter end.*

"You still there? He claims to know you, gave me a message for you."

Cuinn's grip on the phone tightened. The drag queen was eyeing him with improbably violet-eyed interest. *Sorry, gorgeous, my buzz has been officially killed.* "It's possible. Who is he, and what did he say?"

"Name's Lochlann."

Fuck.

"And he said to tell you, *d'súil do na pracháin, d'croí do na gaoirn, d'anam do n-oí gan derea.*" A pause. "I don't think he likes you."

"Brilliant diagnosis, Dr. House." The wisecrack was pure reflex; Cuinn's conscious thoughts had stopped having any input by the time Guaire was halfway through reciting the ancient curse. The only more vehement vow of vengeance was to go oathbound, to swear on your own life not to eat or drink or sleep until you saw your revenge acted out on the body of your enemy, the way Guaire's sister had done to him after he murdered their brother. He'd watched that play out, too, only not quite the way Moriath Guaire had planned. *Son of a BITCH.*

"Oh, diagnosis. Right. The male's a healer, or he was until he lost his magick—"

"I knew that."

Guaire didn't so much as pause. "He's found his *scair-anam.* One of my dancers. And he claims he can see Garrett's aura, even though his magick is gone, and that his HIV has somehow developed into full-blown AIDS. Didn't think that was supposed to happen these days, or at least not that fast."

The cold talons in his gut were back. He'd had twenty-three centuries to learn what a mistake it was to assume anything that happened where the Pattern was concerned was a coincidence. *No fucking way am I interfering with this one. They can't make me. Lochlann would feed me my balls with shaved truffles for garnish.*

And he'd be in the right.

"Look, Goldilocks, it's been sweet, but I have to dash."

"You can take your Goldilocks, and you can—"

"I love you too." Cuinn touched off the phone, worked his fingers into the tight back pocket of his jeans in search of the cash to pay his bar tab. Time to subject his colleagues' plans to a spot of peer review.

***

Cuinn Faded into his darkened apartment, grimacing as always at the expenditure of magick. Fae on this side of the Pattern could Fade, but it was a neater trick than in the Realm, where there was free magick to be had, magick to touch at one's destination; here in the human world, a Fae had to have been there before, or at least have a good enough idea of where he was trying to go to project some of his own magick on ahead of him.

It had to be done this way, though, at least when there was a chance the ground floor tenant might be home and might spot a Fae walking through the small lobby. Bryce Newhouse wasn't a complete tool of the *Marfach*, the way the more or less late Janek O'Halloran was, but it was a safe bet he served as its eyes and ears in the building that housed the only known ley nexus other than the great nexus under Purgatory in D.C. Tiernan and his human partner, Kevin Almstead, hadn't been thrilled about giving up their Greenwich Village retreat, but when reminded that it was going to be the job of whoever occupied that apartment to keep an eye on both the quiescent nexus and the unmitigated asshole parked directly over it, Tiernan had tossed him the keys without hesitation.

He switched on the lights, shielding his eyes from the light until they adjusted, glancing around the little space under cover of his hand. Sometimes enhanced senses were a pain in the ass, at least in the human world, and at least when the Fae in question had just maybe recently been partying to what less hardy souls might consider excess. The darkened bar at Easternbloc had been just about perfect, as far as he was concerned. *Where the hell did I leave the book?—oh, there.* Under his pillow. As if he could somehow smother anything his fellow Loremasters might have to say to him.

Leaving that happy thought for another time, Cuinn stretched and slid the leather-bound book out from under the pillow, falling onto his stomach on the bed as he did so and propping himself up on his elbows. Quickly he leafed through the thick, luxurious pages. He could use any kind of paper he wanted for this, even toilet paper, although several of his colleagues had been unamused by that, to say the least, but he enjoyed the feel of the expensive stuff.

All enjoyment fled, though, when he reached the last of the filled pages, and was greeted by the stylized image of two incomplete circles, joined loosely as if by chains, the joining not to be wrapped tight until the Fae and human had completed their SoulShare bond. *Fucking Noble, why did he have to be right?* And there underneath it, a unique shaping of knotwork and spikes, identification and indictment. *LOCHLANN DORAN. THE HEALER.*

No shit. Cuinn plowed a hand through his hair, unclipped the stylus, and started shaping. *FUCK ME IF I'M BABYSITTING THIS ONE.*

The reply took a few seconds. *They weren't sitting there waiting for me to show up. Maybe I should be hurt.*

WHY ARE YOU RELUCTANT? LOCHLANN WAS YOUR FRIEND.

40

Growling, Cuinn dug his stylus into the shaping of "was", nearly gouging through the page. *MY FRIEND UNTIL YOU MADE ME STAND AND WATCH AS HE SPENT HIS MAGICK.*

WE NEEDED YOUR OBSERVATIONS.

Shit. Twenty-three hundred years in the Pattern was obviously ossifying whatever passed for the brain cells of his fellow Loremasters. *AND LOCHLANN NEEDED HELP. ADVICE. WHICH YOU WOULDN'T LET ME GIVE HIM.* He'd watched other Fae, the few who survived the Pattern, enter the human world, find a place in it, or not—the exiled Water Royal couple who had finally realized they weren't going to be each other's SoulShares and had given up on the whole idea, shapeshifted, and started a family in Loch Ness had been amusing—but he'd never given enough of a damn to want to step in and try to make things right, for any of them except Lochlann.

YOU MAY NEED TO INTERVENE. This shaping was almost apologetic. *LOCHLANN AND HIS HUMAN HAVE TO SHARE.*

Cuinn snorted. *YOU MEAN, YOU NEED THEM TO SHARE.* He added a shape of his own, a little curlicue shaped almost exactly like a flipped bird.

He could almost swear the paper sighed. *OF COURSE. BUT SO DO YOU.*

THANKS FOR THE REMINDER. Yeah, he needed to know what happened when a Fae who had lived twice a normal lifespan lost the immortality the Pattern gave him. And he was sure his colleagues were keenly curious on the subject as well. *ME GETTING INVOLVED ISN'T LIKELY TO HELP. That whole 'eyes for the crows, heart for the wolves' thing.*

41

YOU MUST MAKE IT HELP. Cuinn recognized Aine from the gentler curving of her shaping; she was one of the few Loremasters who bothered to try to understand what life was like for the only one of their number who hadn't joined in the grand self-immolation. *LOCHLANN'S* SCAIR-ANAM *NEEDS HIS MAGICK AS MUCH AS HE NEEDS LOCHLANN HIMSELF.*

Cuinn's eyes narrowed to slits. There was only one way any of his Pattern-bonded fellows could know that particular detail about life here in the human world. *YOU PLANNED FOR THIS. YOU GAVE THAT POOR BASTARD AIDS.*

SINCE WHEN HAS A HUMAN LIFE MATTERED TO YOU? Aine's shaping was genuinely puzzled.

Cuinn had to stop to think about it. *IT MATTERS TO LOCHLANN*, he shaped at last.

THEN YOU HAVE TO MAKE SURE THEY JOIN. The shaping flowed across the page, as gentle and unstoppable as water. *DO WHAT YOU MUST, SPEND WHAT YOU MUST. BUT MAKE CERTAIN THEY SHARE.*

Cuinn an Dearmad, last of the Loremasters, pimp for the Pattern. Cuinn pinched the bridge of his nose, hard. *FUCK. I'LL BE ON A TRAIN FIRST THING IN THE MORNING.* Conserving magick was a habit, after twenty-three hundred years—a habit he should have been allowed to pass on to Lochlann, damn it, instead of watching him spend his own magick to nothingness—and trains, while slower than planes, were marginally less claustrophobic.

BE WATCHFUL. The shaping was slow, pensive. *THE GREATEST RISK TO THE HUMAN IS NOT OUR DOING.*

Cryptic much? Cuinn rolled his eyes as the intricate weaving knotted itself off, signifying that his audience was at an end. He tossed the leather volume aside with a groan. *So much for getting laid tonight.*

And tomorrow? Tomorrow he was well and truly fucked.

Chapter Four

Garrett hefted his bag to hang more comfortably from his shoulder, and used his other hand to hold his wool coat closed at the throat. It wasn't really all that cold, but he'd worked up a sweat tonight. He could almost hear his mother's voice. *Garrett, child, close your coat, you'll catch your death.*

Yeah, right. Should have listened to Mom.

Listen to me, shit, I've turned into a drama queen overnight. Not that he didn't have at least some justification, what with his magic pharmaceutical bullets inexplicably losing their mojo and all, but it wasn't an attitude he cared to cultivate. He hadn't done it when he was turning tricks for a living, and he sure as hell wasn't going to start now.

He was surprised at how many people were out at this hour. He usually didn't finish at the club until two or three in the morning, which meant by the time he started home, the streets were more or less deserted, but he'd begged off tired just after midnight, and there were plenty of people around.

A few were coming up from the Metro, off to his right, their nights apparently just starting. One guy caught Garrett's attention; quickly, he looked away and pulled his coat even closer, shivering. Big man, wearing a dirty gray hoodie, filthy jeans, boots the size of boats. It was the ink on the backs of his hands, though, that made Garrett shudder. He'd known one man with hands like that; he'd been a bouncer at Purgatory, back in the bad old days. The way the fucker used to look at him made Garrett want to go take an hour-long shower and scrub himself raw. But he was dead now, that's what everyone said. Some even said he'd been killed at the club, but no body had ever been found on the premises.

He trudged on, not really noticing as blocks went past, and the more affluent neighborhood immediately south of the club gave way to small storefronts and offices, crowded together and topped with apartments. Not nearly as much foot traffic here, nothing to attract anyone outside of working hours. Or maybe stepping-out-to-the-deli hours. He had just spotted the recessed doorway that would take him up to his own apartment, directly over Luigi's Italian Ristorante with the missing "n" where a rock or a bullet had taken out the neon tubing two or three years ago, when he first heard the footsteps behind him. Not quite running, but coming up fast.

Shit. His grip tightened on the strap of his bag, ready to swing it—or ditch it, if it looked like that would help him escape. And for one sick, sweaty, gut-wrenching moment, he was ten years old again, hearing the kids closing in behind him, knowing there was no way in hell he was going to get away without another split lip, ruined shirt, blackened eye. Almost hearing his mother's voice again. *Garrett Lee Templar, I swear, you find more trouble than any ten other boys ever dreamed of. Do you think I can just make new clothes appear out of thin air?*

"Garrett?"

He recognized that voice from somewhere. Slowly, he turned. And stared up into eyes that gleamed blue even in the crappy light from the streetlight on the corner.

"Lochlann?" He hadn't had to rent his ass out for a while now, but the idea of a john following him home from the club still made his skin crawl. Yet there was something about those eyes, something different.

No. Fuck that shit. *You get hurt the worst when you let yourself hope.*

"Yes." The guy looked almost as uncomfortable as Garrett felt, shifting from one foot to the other, hands plunged deep into the pockets of his heavy wool coat. "Look, I'm not stalking you, and I don't mean to frighten you. I just wanted to see how you're doing. And maybe talk for a few minutes."

The john's smile flashed briefly, transforming the beard-shadowed face above him into unexpected, breathtaking beauty. For a second, all Garrett could do was stare and hope his mouth wasn't hanging open. *Oh, Jesus. Ask me to do anything. Anything at all. Just smile when you do it.*

Then the smile faded, and Garrett shook his head, trying to clear it. "I, uh, yeah. Sure." He looked up, almost afraid to look in those eyes again. Way up. Guy had to be six-four at least, putting his five-nine at a decided disadvantage if things got rough. *Here's hoping they don't.* "You want to come in? It's kind of cold out here."

"Thanks, I'd like that."

Garrett fumbled in his pocket for his keys, somehow managed to get the street level door open, looked back in startlement as the john held it for him—a gentleman, then, at least some of the time— and preceded him up the narrow stairs. Which gave him plenty of time to think. Not that there was much going on in his head besides *why the HELL am I doing this?* and *the guy's fucking gorgeous.* And then the kicker. *Nothing's going to happen anyway. Nothing can. Unless I want to kill him.*

He stopped on the stairs, just short of the landing, stopped short enough that the guy nearly ran into him. "Is something wrong?"

"Yeah. *This* is wrong." Garrett turned. *Don't look him in the eyes. Just don't.* So he kept his eyes down. Which was a mistake, because Mr. Blue Eyes was a couple of steps below him, and *wham!*—he was lost again. "I... you ought to go." Fuck, he was stammering. As if the john was one of those schoolyard Neanderthals, waiting for the right moment to pound him. "This is a mistake."

"No, it isn't." Somehow, without his noticing it, the guy had taken his hand. "You're afraid. You don't have to be afraid of me. I would never harm you." He shook his head, slightly, laughing softly. "You have no idea." The grip on his hand tightened, then relaxed. "And I'm not afraid of you, either. Even though you think I should be."

"How the fuck do you know that?" Damn restaurant must have cranked the thermostat again, he was starting to sweat.

"You're not hard to read." One dark brow swept up. "Look, can we go inside? I'm not used to looking up at people."

There was that smile again. Damn. "All right. Just as long as you know, nothing's going to happen. Whatever you were expecting, I'm sorry."

Without another word, he unlocked the door, dropped his bag in the hall closet, and flipped on the lights, before standing aside to let Lochlann in. "My apologies, it's the houseboy's day off."

"I've seen worse."

"You make a habit out of chasing tornadoes?" Garrett stopped off in the tiny kitchen to grab a couple of bottles of water from the fridge.

A laugh was the only answer. He came out of the kitchen, a bottle in each hand, and tossed one to the man perched on the edge of his sofa, who had shed his heavy coat. He flung himself into the armchair opposite instead of taking the space on the sofa that had very obviously been left vacant for him.

"Disappointed?" He wrenched the cap off his bottle and took a good long pull, wiped his mouth with the back of his hand, and only then looked over at the john.

"Not really. You don't have to mistrust me, but I can understand why you do."

"I can't think why I should trust you. You or anyone, don't take it personally."

"Lochlann." He spoke quietly, but firmly. "It would be a good start if you would at least use my name, Garrett."

Garrett shivered, both at the john's name and at the way the soft voice made music out of his own. "A good start at what? Lochlann."

"You not being afraid of me, for one thing." Lochlann glanced at the bottle in his hand, set it on the sofa. Or, rather, on the sweat-stained shirt he'd tossed on the sofa a couple of days ago.

"I'm not afraid of you." Garrett drained the rest of the little bottle, and pitched it in the general direction

48

of the open kitchen door. "I'm just not sure why I asked you up here. I don't know what they told you at the club, but I stopped turning tricks a long time ago."

"I'm not a trick." Christ, those eyes were blue. "I just want to talk."

"Bullshit. I've seen that look before." Well, no, he hadn't, not really. What he'd seen, over and over, was hunger. Lust. From men who had seen what his body could do, and wanted that body to do it just for them. The look in Lochlann's eyes wasn't that. But that was as close as he could come to describing it without getting suckered into imagining this smoking hot total stranger actually gave a damn about him.

"I doubt it." One corner of the other man's mouth curved up in a half-smile that somehow managed to be twice as devastating as the full-power version. "I don't think anyone else has ever seen what I see, when I look at you."

That voice. Shit. "I'm not showing you anything a few thousand sweaty guys haven't seen already." He willed his voice to steadiness. "You're getting a lot less, in fact."

"You're trying to push me away. But you don't want to succeed." Lochlann leaned forward, gently took Garrett's hand again. "And I *do* want you to succeed. Even though it's going to feel like an amputation when you do."

"Wait a minute." Garrett blinked, sat up straighter. "You want me to push you away? Then what the hell are you doing here?"

"I'm not sure." Lochlann's hand tightened around his; gentle fingertips stroked his palm, almost unconsciously. "I have a very good reason not to get involved with you. And no, it has nothing to do with

49

your illness. But I also need to be close to you. I have ever since I first saw you at Purgatory."

"How did you know about my—oh." The way he'd freaked out when he'd waked up bleeding all over Lochlann's lap, and what he'd told Tiernan after, yeah, that made it pretty fucking obvious. And thinking about that made it easier to ignore the intent expression of the man opposite him. Johns who wanted to 'get close' were even worse than the brutal ones. They made you think maybe something was going to be different. Maybe the hell was over. Until they weren't there any more, and the whole world was laughing at you for being such a fucking moron again.

Lochlann's pained expression startled him. Mostly because it looked like it belonged there. *What does a guy that beautiful know about hurt?*

"How do I convince you I'm not trying to use you? That I'm not here to buy you, or rent you?"

Rewrite my life? "I don't know. That's what I'm used to." Behind the indifference, he could feel anger rising. Not at Lochlann, but at himself. At the small, still voice he could never quite silence no matter how hard he tried. Hope. Fucker just wouldn't shut up.

"That needs to change, *lanan*."

Before Garrett could react, ask him what the hell *lanan* meant, Lochlann had risen from his chair, just enough to close with him. His kiss was warm, tender, almost chaste, and probably the last thing Garrett would have expected from a guy who looked as ferally hot as he did. Yet Garrett felt a shiver race through his whole body, a tingle of pure delight. He parted his lips, asking for more, and groaned softly when Lochlann pulled away instead, and knelt beside the chair.

"Did you feel that?"

Lochlann's voice sounded like his kiss felt, and all Garrett could do was nod.

The dark-haired man studied him intently, then slowly smiled. "Want to try it again?"

"Hells to the yes."

He closed his eyes, this time, not wanting to risk meeting those baby blues again. Lochlann brushed first one unshaven cheek and then the other against his lips, before covering his mouth and breathing in his answering sigh with his kiss.

Damn. This one was better. Garrett's arms went around Lochlann as a hungry, questing tongue entered his mouth, teased at the rounded stud in his tongue. There were hard muscles under his hands, and when Lochlann shifted to kneel between his knees instead of off to the side, he started to think he'd died and gone to heaven. There were arms around him, too, Lochlann working his arms around him and drawing him closer. His erection was pressing painfully against his zipper, but it was the good kind of pain. And the delight, the joy rippled through his body in waves that deepened along with the kiss.

But then it stopped. Lochlann tore away from him, with a soft cry that sounded like a curse. "I have to stop. *Damn* it."

"Why? *"This is what you get for hoping. Asshole.*

Instead of pulling away, as Garrett expected, Lochlann took his hand again, this time in both of his. "Because if I don't leave now, you're never going to believe another word I say. I told you I just wanted to talk."

Garrett felt dizzy, going from bliss to *asshole* to that other four-letter h-word so quickly. "I think I

51

could forgive you if you change your mind."

"I do, too." Lochlann's smile was damn close to a lethal weapon. "But I want to start this off right." His tongue flickered out, the tip tracing around Garrett's lips as a prelude to one last scorching kiss.

One that ended much too soon, when Lochlann got gracefully to his feet. "No, stay where you are." The other man motioned Garrett back, throwing in a flicker of a wink. "You're sexy as hell all sprawled out the way you were." He snagged his coat with two fingers, picked it up and tossed it over his arm. Then he watched, an eyebrow arched, until Garrett took the hint and leaned back in his chair. "Perfect." Once again that intense gaze raked him from head to feet, pausing at his groin on the way up.

"I'll see you again." The murmur was barely above a whisper. "Don't be afraid next time, *lanan*."

Garrett jerked, feeling like he was waking from a dream of falling, at the sound of the door closing behind Lochlann. *Fuck.* He looked around himself, trying to get his bearings. *Did that really just happen?*

Then he looked down his body, moved the T-shirt away from his washboard abs, and glared at the swollen red eye peering up at him from the waist of his jeans. *Well,* some*body thinks it happened.*

He tilted his head back and closed his eyes, sighing. And was immediately caught up again in that motherfucking amazing kiss. Johns didn't kiss. None of them did. But he could still feel Lochlann's mouth on his, taking it, as if it was the most natural, normal, and at the same time red-hot sexual thing in the world.

When Garrett opened his eyes again, he was not entirely surprised to discover he'd unzipped his jeans and taken his commando self firmly in hand. Sighs turned to groans as his palm whispered against veined flesh already proud, hard, and hungry, caressed the small heavy ring piercing the skin just under the flare; he caught his lower lip between his teeth and leaned back as the first clear drops appeared.

Imagining it was Lochlann's hand. As if that would ever happen. But the fantasy was sweet. More than sweet. Hotter than hell. Garrett's hand worked faster, gripped tighter; his moans filled the little apartment, and the sound inflamed him even more. He could see Lochlann's eyes, taste his kiss, feel his hand. His back arched up off the chair, as a familiar heat raced down his spine, pooled in his balls, hung poised and ready for release. "Yes. Fuck, yes. *Yes.*"

Garrett's free hand gripped the chair arm, white-knuckled. He shouted something, it might have been Lochlann's name, as the first white jets of his release shot from him to splash on his abs and paint his t-shirt. His cock throbbed in his hand, hot fluid poured down over his hand and pooled in his sparse blond curls. Each pulse sent a ripple through his body, pure pleasure. It went on longer than he could ever remember an orgasm going on, until he was short of breath and his legs trembled up and down their length.

The whole time, he saw eyes. Blue eyes.

Eyes that weren't there when he opened his own.

You didn't seriously expect them to be, did you? Moron. He was playing with you, and you fell for it. And that orgasm was as good as it's ever going to get for you again.

Hope? Hope was for suckers.

Chapter Five

"Would you for fuck's sake wait until I stop puking?" Actually, Janek O'Halloran wasn't puking any more, he was long past the point where there was anything left to come up, but he didn't appreciate being prodded out of hiding before he was done with whatever it was he was doing now.

If a creature that lived in solid living crystal could sigh, the *Marfach* probably would have. ***Your tender stomach is beginning to be an issue***. This was its female voice, being the fastidious bitch she usually was. Except when she was enjoying the blood from a fresh kill, then she wasn't happy until Janek looked like something out of one of the *Saw* movies.

Janek choked back the *Bite me* that would normally have been his response. The female would do exactly that, if invited. Mentally, at least. One experience with serrated fangs had been more than enough. *Fuck you* was out of the question, too, for basically the same reason. "You can thank Conall Dary for my tender stomach," he snarled. One more fucking Fae for him to cut up. He wouldn't have thought his condition could get much worse—more or less dead, except for the brain Tiernan Guaire had shot away half of and replaced with the living Stone, originally crystal clear but now more often than not a stomach-churning blood red, that harbored the monster he now carried around with him—but it had. The magickal super-charge the goddamned mage had given him when he showed up to kill Guaire turned every time the *Marfach* tried to piggyback on his senses into a very special living hell.

Not to mention it strengthened the monster. In a way, that wasn't such a bad thing, because the more juice it had, the more willing it was to keep his brain functioning. The only times he went completely switch-off since last October were when he slept. He had no idea what the *Marfach* did with itself, or itselves, while he wasn't there, and he didn't want to have one.

You can thank Conall Dary for a great many things.

It sounds smug. Not good. That thought went carefully in the box of thoughts Janek kept to himself. He had no desire to be bitch-slapped. "Only if I can deliver my thanks in person."

I would think you would wish to keep as far from him as possible.

Definitely smug. Preening, even. The thing's tone made him want to gag. Which was a very bad idea right now. Janek leaned over, his head as close as he could get to between his knees, retched again, spat, and decided to change the subject. "Who were we following? The dancer's nobody, he's just one of the whores left over from before Guaire took over the club."

Some time, you will have to explain to me why

you worked there, if you despised the club and everyone in it so much. Smugness gave way to cool amusement, which was the bitch-thing's other favorite way to express itself. *And you were not following the dancer, you were following the one who followed him.*

"Yeah, well, I didn't recognize him either." Janek took a deep breath, waited for his gut to heave, and sighed with relief when it didn't. "And it was you using your fucking magickal sense to look at him with my eye that set my delicate stomach off."

Poor baby. The mocking voice was suddenly male, and Janek groaned as his cock twitched. The male voice had a permanent hard-on, and the combination of horny and just barely not throwing up sucked balls. *Learn to recognize him. He's going to be the answer to almost all of our problems.*

"Why?" Janek pushed away from the wall, carefully, and was happy to be able to stand without assistance. "Some dick who followed the dancer home for a quickie? What's so special about him?"

That dick is a Fae. One I recognize.

Janek gritted his teeth and managed to stop the male from using his hand to stroke his cock. "Maybe you're losing it. Even I could see that he didn't have any magick."

That makes perfect sense, since he's over two thousand years old. I last saw him just after I was imprisoned here, when he came over. And I'm guessing the little whore is his SoulShare. Somehow, even without seeing it, Janek knew the male was leering. *The game may be changing, very soon, once those two finally figure out they're supposed to fuck.*

"How do you know they didn't?"

SoulSharing changes a Fae. And he was the same when he came out as he was when he went in.

Janek was compelled to start off down the street, and to turn for one last look at the window over the restaurant. The window went dark as he watched, the curly-haired whore outlined for an instant before darkness. He wanted to ask how the game was going to be changing, but the question would give away the fact he had more going on in his brain than he was supposed to have. Between the shot Dary gave him when he fried the nexus in Greenwich Village and the supercharge that had fucking near killed him, something had jolted his brain into a level of activity he hadn't experienced since... well. Since he'd been alive.

"Jesus Christ!" Janek lurched backward, just in time to not be run over by a speeding taxi. "Where the fuck did you learn to drive?" This earned him a few curious looks, which he returned with glares; the assholes probably figured he was talking to the cabbie.

Penny for your thoughts. The female was back, and Janek instantly tensed. She was the brains of the unholy threesome in his head, and the most likely to figure out his secret. The male was the driving force of the three. And the abomination... He shuddered. The abomination was pure evil. More evil than a formerly petty thug like Janek had ever been able to imagine. ***They must be deep, for you to be so distracted.***

"Fuck off."

Janek braced himself, but as usual, the bitch-slap was more than he was ready for, and he rocked with it before trudging across the street. It was worth it, though. He could almost feel the *Marfach* getting bored with him. Bored was a hell of a lot better than curious.

Over there.

Janek's head was turned for him, his one-bloodshot-eyed gaze drawn across the street and up the next block, just in time for him to stumble over the curb on the far side of the street he was crossing. "Son of a *bitch*. What do you want with that?" He was being forced to stare at a small boarded-over storefront, almost hidden between two larger ones.

A trap.

Oh, shit. The monstrosity. Best to just shut up, lie low, and wait for it to turn its attention somewhere else.

A trap for a Water Fae.

Janek was steered, almost dragged, up the street, to peer around the boards over the storefront windows. The windows behind the boards were covered with steel shutters. *So why the fuck did they want boards too?* The door next; locked, but not so securely that a few stomps from an iron-soled boot wouldn't take care of it. A side door, likewise secured, and a barred and padlocked corrugated metal cover over what was probably a ladder or set of stairs going straight to a basement.

Perfect. The only time the abomination's voice made Janek's balls shrivel up smaller than they did when it was angry was when it was gloating. And right at the moment, he wouldn't have been able to find the little fuckers if his life depended on it. ***And soon, you will bring me the bait for this trap.***

Chapter Six

"Excuse me, is this seat taken?"

Lochlann started, turned away from his single-minded perusal of the dance floor. A dark-haired man in a conservative, expensive suit was looking questioningly at him, one hand resting on the bar stool next to him, pretty much the last empty one at the bar. Purgatory was crowded, for a Monday night. And this man fit in with the pierced, tattooed, leather-clad crowd every bit as well as a long-haired cat in a basket of eels. He shrugged. "Suit yourself."

Oddly enough, the Armani didn't seem perturbed by Lochlann's gruffness. He slid onto the bar stool, and out of the corner of his eye Lochlann saw him take off his silk tie and stuff it into a pocket, then unbutton the collar of his stiff white dress shirt. "Thanks. It's been a long day."

Well, if he'd come straight from work, that would explain the suit. And, at this hour, it would also explain the need for a good stiff drink.

Drink. Right. Lochlann turned around and picked up the shot the bartender refilled for him while he'd been watching the dance floor, waiting for the night's show to start. He drained the heavy shot glass and set it back on the bar, turning it around a few times, watching the light shift and bend under it. He'd been fascinated with the bar at Purgatory from the first, drawn down the stairs and through the thick black glass doors. To a human, no doubt, the darkness upon entering the club was nearly total. The only bright lights anywhere were further in, playing over the dance floor or strobing to catch a couple or a trio or an orgy in a moment of passion in the maze of leather furniture that filled the club's lower level. But the bar, now that caught the attention from the moment the door opened. The top of the bar was glass, and light flickered under it in all the colors and patterns of sullen flame and smoldering embers, playing over the faces of the lustful and the jaded and the curious alike. Mesmerizing.

"You're new here." The guy in the suit had to raise his voice to be heard over the pounding of the music on the dance floor, and over the men trying to be heard over the music. Humans might like the effect, but to a Fae's enhanced senses, it was a constant distraction.

Maybe a conversation would ease the headache he could feel creeping into the spot between and behind his eyes. "I suppose I am. And you must not be, if you know that."

The man grinned, teeth flashing white in an unshaven face; his easy laughter would probably have been utterly fucking charming, if Lochlann had been at all interested. "True. I met my husband here, almost a year ago."

"Does he know you still hang out in a place like this?" The jerk of Lochlann's head managed to take in most of the club, and most of its denizens, in all their metal and ink and finery—or, in the case of the finery at least, their lack thereof.

"You might say. I'm just waiting for him to get off work." The man accepted a Jack and coke from the bartender, took a sip, set it down, and held out a hand. "Name's Kevin, by the way."

Lochlann hesitated a fraction of a second before taking the offered hand. It had taken him several centuries to stop interpreting the human gesture as an attempt to disarm him. "Lochlann."

Kevin's dark gaze went from amused to curious. "Lochlann. Now, where have I heard that name before?"

Any reply Lochlann might have made was cut off by the music. It didn't seem possible that it was getting louder than it had been, but it was. *How the hell does Garrett stand it?* The driving beat and the clamor of the crowd on the dance floor drew his gaze like the scent of a stag drew a hunter's hounds, to stare until a head of curly blond hair emerged over the heads of the watching men, a hard-muscled body twisted its way up the pole. Kevin, and his question, were forgotten, as completely as if neither had ever existed.

Two nights ago, he could have taken the body that spiraled down the center pole. Garrett would have let him. Probably. They'd both wanted it, he was as sure of that as he'd ever been of anything. But something had told him it was wrong to push so soon. Oh, he'd long ago lost count of the number of men, and women, and before them Fae males and females, he'd bedded with no more than a look and a few words. He had few if any qualms in that respect. No Fae ever had. But Garrett was different. Not only hadn't he pushed, he hadn't even gone back to the dancer's tiny apartment. He'd come here, instead, and watched his *scair-anam* lose himself in music and movement. Last night, and again tonight.

Lochlann couldn't look away, even though Garrett was so beautiful it made his eyes hurt to look at him. He'd thought at first that this was an effect of the SoulShare, the fact that this male held a part of him he'd gone without for over two thousand years. But it was more. It had to be. Their SoulShare bond wasn't complete—hell, it was barely started. They'd had no more time together, no more contact than those few moments on the dance floor after the human's fall, and the kisses they'd shared, and there had to be more to Sharing than that. *Love*, Cuinn had said, in explaining the Loremasters' plan, before the last battle with the Marfach. *Find the other half of your soul, and love will do the rest. Or it should. We're really not sure at this point.*

Lochlann only realized he was snarling when Kevin cleared his throat beside him and edged away. *Oh, for fuck's sake. I need to get a grip.* He turned back to face the bar and slid his empty glass toward the bartender, tapping the bar top with a finger, nodding as the heavily pierced Scandinavian hefted the bottle of Metaxa he'd been pouring from. *Maybe I should say something tonight. When Garrett's done dancing.*

But what? *"Excuse me, but I'd like to fall in love with you, and then find out what happens when the channeling that's been keeping me alive for a couple of thousand years collapses. Would that be all right with you?"* Damn, he sounded insane even to himself.

Accepting a fresh brandy, he shook his head as he turned back to the dance floor, toward the pounding music and the exquisitely writhing human who gave it a body.

His glass slipped through suddenly nerveless fingers and crashed to the floor. On the edge of the crowd ogling Garrett stood a sandy-haired male in tight black leathers and a harness hung with steel chains, rising slightly on his toes to watch the dancer invert himself and spiral down the pole.

As if he felt Lochlann's gaze on him, the other male turned.

Cuinn an Dearmad. Dead Fae walking.

Cuinn's lips moved. *"Oh, fuck me backwards."*

"Christ on a crutch." This was Kevin, his murmur barely audible over the bass throbbing that shook the floor and seemed to make the air vibrate. "You're *that* Lochlann."

Lochlann hardly noticed the words. But the hand clamping around his bicep as he tried to dismount from the bar stool, *that* he noticed. "You can move that hand, or I can break your arm. Your choice." His eyes never left the other Fae.

"Neither one's going to happen." The human's grip tightened. "I run interference with the cops for pretty much all the shit that goes on around here, because my husband is about as diplomatic as a rhino with a rash. But I am *not* going to try to explain a fight between two Fae to D.C.'s finest. Whatever issues you two have, you can take them off the premises. Am I clear?"

Lochlann continued to glare slow murder at the apparently stunned Fae, but gradually, the human's words started to fit themselves together in a way that made sense. "You're Tiernan's husband?—his *scair-anam*?"

"I am. And—"

"Son of a *bitch*." Cuinn had turned, and was working his way into the crowd watching Garrett. Toward Garrett. "Fuck that, *bodlag*. You're not touching him." He wrenched out of Kevin's grip and charged toward the dance floor, pushing between oblivious onlookers almost without noticing them.

The chains dangling from Cuinn's harness wrapped cold around Lochlann's wrist; he yanked hard, and unbalanced the other Fae, turning him away from Garrett. *Fuck*. Those eyes. Pale green, looking right through him. Just exactly the way they had when Cuinn had called down the winds, and hammered him through a sieve of knives. Agony beyond comprehension. And that had only been the beginning of it. More than two thousand years of it.

"About fucking time." Cuinn's hand clamped around Lochlann's wrist. "I thought I was going to have to send you an engraved invitation."

Before Lochlann could reply, everything vanished.

***

Lochlann staggered as he became corporeal again, fetching up against a cold white marble surface. Every nerve in his body sizzled in the aftermath of the forced Fade, his first taste of magick in six and a half centuries, the tingling half-pain-half pleasure of life returning to a sleeping limb, multiplied a thousand times over.

His fist was still tangled in the chains hanging

from Cuinn's harness, and the other Fae fell against him with a soft curse *as'Faein*. Snarling, Lochlann shoved him away and struggled upright. Damned if he was going to let the bastard think he was weak.

"Shit." Cuinn hit another wall of the same white marble, hard enough to jar the breath from him, chains jingling softly. "Can we at least talk before you beat me senseless?"

"I don't know, the thought of making you swallow your lying tongue is very tempting."

"Be careful, someone might notice. At least, I hope so."

"What?" For the first time, it occurred to Lochlann to wonder where Cuinn had Faded the two of them. He was leaning against a curved, fluted marble column in a dimly lit alcove; Cuinn was straightening after being knocked into one of the walls of the same alcove. It was cold, but warm air blew gently through the enclosed space. And there was writing, chiseled into the wall opposite.

...that we here highly resolve that these dead shall not have died in vain...

"Son of a bitch," Lochlann murmured, peering around the pillar he leaned against and looking up at the sad, thoughtful face of Abraham Lincoln.

Cuinn shrugged. "Private enough that I figured I could get us here without anyone noticing, public enough that hopefully someone will see if you try to kill me. Or feed me my tongue, as you so creatively suggested." He settled the leather harness more comfortably on his broad shoulders, glanced around, and stepped out into the open area in front of Mr. Lincoln's statue.

Lochlann growled and followed. No one was standing in the lighted area, though a few people sat on the steps outside, looking out over the public face of nighttime Washington, D.C. Probably too public for a murder, at that. "You didn't worry about us being noticed when you yanked me out of Purgatory."

He was going to get sick of Cuinn's shrug very quickly. "No one was paying any attention to us, they were all ogling your *scair-anam*. Who is, I might add, magnificently hung."

"Are you betting I can't kill you before those humans out there turn around? Not smart."

"Just an observation." Cuinn hooked his thumbs into the straps of the harness, and turned to look up at the statue that towered over them. "And it's interesting how jealous a SoulShared Fae can be over someone he hasn't even known yet, in the Biblical sense."

Lochlann made an effort to relax the fists his hands had curled into. Choking the bastard would be much more satisfying than punching him. "You say that like you've seen it happen before."

Cuinn turned back, and for the first time Lochlann saw what looked like genuine regret in his pale-green gaze. "I've seen a hell of a lot happen in the last couple of thousand years. And I haven't been able to do a damned thing about any of it."

"Don't even try to make me laugh." Lochlann's lip curled in a sneer. "You're forgetting, I know you. I know your power." He made a sharp chopping gesture as Cuinn opened his mouth to protest. "And even without power, you could have told me sometime in my first sixteen hundred centuries I was going to run out of magick." His voice caught in his throat. "You

66

could have spared me six hundred years of hell. And I could have kept enough magick to save Garrett's life."

Cuinn shook his head. "No, I couldn't." Regret gave way to bitterness, even anger. "I'm nothing but the Pattern's agent. Tool. The Loremasters still don't know how everything they did is going to play out. There are things they need to see. And I'm the only one who can do the seeing for them."

"Pathetic." Lochlann bit off the word. "You used our friendship to deceive me into throwing away my life for your friends' experiment, you watched me for them for two thousand years without so much as a word to me, and then for an excuse you try to make me believe they're using you too?"

"It's the truth. I probably shouldn't even be telling you this much, except that they apparently worry less about secrecy once a Fae has found his *scair-anam.* Then they let me take my fucking muzzle off." Yes, that was definitely anger, and if Lochlann were even a little less pissed off, he might almost muster some sympathy. Use a Fae, manipulate him, cage him, and invite the whirlwind.

Which image struck just a little too close to home. The memory of the male before him calling up the winds to force him through the portal's sieve was twenty-three centuries old, but it had lost none of its clarity. "Were they using you when you used the wind to hammer me through the Pattern, too?"

Not waiting for an answer, he turned his back on Cuinn. A deliberate gesture of contempt, in this context, a total lack of concern that the other might attack. As good as calling the mage impotent. Now he was face to face with the writing on the opposite wall.

With malice toward none, with charity for all... Lochlann barely managed to keep from laughing out loud. *Abraham Lincoln was no Fae, that's for damned sure.*

"No." Cuinn spoke softly, so softly that for a moment Lochlann wasn't sure he'd said anything. "That was my fault. I panicked. And I paid for it."

"Paid? You?" Furious, Lochlann turned back to the leather-clad Fae, his exclamation still echoing off the walls.

"Yes." The voice was still quiet, and Cuinn's unsettling eyes were closed, his expression twisted with some emotion or memory he obviously fought to repress. "After you went through, I had to construct an enclosure for the portal, and figure out some way to make it work without me having to intervene. So I built a stone cell, triggered the protections the rest of the Loremasters set up to ward it, and made it so the moon shining full through a window in the wall triggered a latent channeling, opening the portal." Cuinn took a deep breath. "And then I went through it myself. To be sure that what happened to you wouldn't happen again."

Shock drained away Lochlann's anger. Sympathy was the last thing one Fae ever expected from another. Or nearly the last. Love was last. "Did it?"

"I didn't get stuck." Cuinn's eyes opened, giving Lochlann a glimpse into a memory of hell. "But I think the rest of it was just as bad as what you went through. And that's been one more thing I've had to sit back and watch for the last two thousand years. Over and over again. Transition, and its aftermath. Remembering how it was, every fucking time."

For a moment, Lochlann felt a small flicker of compassion. But only a moment. Was he supposed to forgive betrayal simply because his betrayer had also tasted its fruits? "*Lámagh tú an batagar; 'se seo torq a'gur fola d'fach.*" He smiled, coldly, as Cuinn winced. *You shot the arrow; this wounded boar is yours.* With all the joy of tracking a wounded and maddened animal.

"Lochlann—"

"I have nothing more to say to you. Other than stay the hell away from my *scair-anam*, or I won't let Kevin hold me back next time."

"Your *scair-anam*." Strangely, Cuinn wasn't rising to the bait, didn't even seem to notice Lochlann's veiled threat. "Are you going to bond with him?"

"Were you planning on telling me how?"

"I already have. Although I shouldn't have." Cuinn made as if to shove his hands into his pockets, only to discover that his tight leathers didn't have any. "You need to get there on your own. And if you don't do it, your Garrett's going to die."

Lochlann stalked back to where Cuinn stood, at Mr. Lincoln's feet. He would have grabbed him by the shirt or jacket collar, if the other Fae had been wearing either; instead, he contented himself with looming over the shorter male, and letting a little of the murder he was feeling show in his eyes. "How do you know that?"

"I have my sources." Cuinn's face was blank, unreadable. "And does it really matter? It doesn't change anything."

"So many things you can't tell me. Poor little puppet." Lochlann watched Cuinn's hands ball into fists. *Oh, yes, please, hit me. Try to. Give me a reason to beat you bloody, damn you.* "Can you tell me if *I'll* survive the attempt? After two lifetimes of immortality?"

"No." If Cuinn's face had been unreadable before, now it was carved from marble as cold and hard as the President who towered over them both. "I can't tell you that, either."

"Then damn you to hell." Lochlann spat on the floor at Cuinn's feet. "And yes, I know it's a human concept. I thoroughly enjoy the thought of you spending eternity there."

Lochlann turned and strode toward the entrance to the Memorial, white pillars lit against the darkness. He would be damned if he'd let Cuinn Fade him back to Purgatory, when a taxi would do just as well; he'd had centuries to fight his innate claustrophobia to a standstill, most of the time.

One more thought, though, pulled him up short. "You never said what you were watching me to learn." He spoke without turning, knowing a Fae would hear him regardless. "Another secret, I suppose?"

Cuinn sighed. "It should be, but fuck that. They need to know what happens when magick returns, after it's gone."

"Why the hell do the Loremasters need to know that?"

The silence stretched out. "Because cut off from the ley energy, the Realm is going to die. And they need to know if it can be saved."

Lochlann stared out into the darkness. "*Lámagh sádh an batagar,*" he whispered at last, and left without looking back.

Chapter Seven

Garrett slumped into the chair in the tiny cinderblock dressing room, nearly boneless with exhaustion. He hadn't wanted to get off the pole tonight. Any other time, this would have been a good feeling, totally and blissfully spent after three hours of working the pole. Now, of course, there was a fucking specter looking over his shoulder, whispering that maybe there was another reason he was so tired.

Fuck that shit. He drew himself up in the chair, glaring at himself in the mirror. There was no way he was symptomatic yet. His mind was playing tricks on him, nothing more. *I'm as healthy as I was the day before I got the diagnosis. Nothing's changed.*

Nothing, except everything.

Sighing, he reached into his duffle bag and took out the ratty old sweatshirt he'd stuffed into it before going on stage. He'd have to stand up to don his jeans, and that was too much work right now. He pulled the shirt over his head—

And, of course, right on cue, there was a knock at the door.

Garrett grumbled as he tugged the shirt into place. Tiernan had let it be known it wasn't open season on the dancers any more, the way it had been when Fabian ran the place, though he didn't mind if a guy made his own arrangements. But Garrett hadn't asked for company, didn't particularly want any, and probably shouldn't even be entertaining the thought of having any. *I'm a fucking plague carrier, that's what I am.*

"Garrett?"

Lochlann's voice. Damn. The one man he shouldn't be seeing ever again. Because if Lochlann gave him what he couldn't help wanting, what he'd dreamed about the last two nights in a row, the other man would probably also be sentencing himself to death. "Maybe you ought to just give up and go away."

"Not a chance in hell."

Son of a bitch. "Come in, I guess."

Garrett made himself look away as the door opened. It didn't help, though; he saw Lochlann in the mirror over the dressing table. Saw the way the other man's eyes went straight to him, how he kicked the door closed without so much as a glance at it. His coat was buttoned, his collar turned up as if he'd just come in from outside, his unruly dark hair falling over the collar. His cheeks were unshaven, and Garrett shivered, remembering how that stubble had felt against his lips, right before Lochlann had kissed him.

You asshole. Next thing you know, you're going to be buying him candy and flowers. And trust me, they don't make a Hallmark card to cover this situation. "You're the fucking hottest man I've ever seen, and under any other circumstances I'd beg you to pin me to the wall, but unfortunately that would kill you." Maybe with a nice picture of Fire Island at sunset in the background. Shit.

"I told you before, you don't have to be afraid. Of me, or of yourself." Lochlann's hands rested on his shoulders, and amazingly blue eyes met Garrett's in the mirror. "You can't hurt me."

"What, are you invincible?" Garrett's laugh was bitter. "Show me the red 'S' on your chest, and maybe I'll think about it.

"No 'S,' sorry." Yet Lochlann unbuttoned his coat, pulled his shirt out of the waistband of his jeans, and unbuttoned that as well. Garrett caught his breath, as the widening 'V' revealed both chiseled pecs and a beautiful tattoo, an intricate pattern of silver-blue knotwork that went almost from his neck down to a perfectly straight line across the bottom of his ribcage, stopping just short of a six-pack that made Garrett's fingers twitch.

He turned, reaching for the beautiful, vivid ink, seized with a sudden need to touch it. Just to run his fingertips across it. But he stopped, his hand clenching into a fist before his fingers found the warmth of flesh. "That's amazing." Even to him, the words sounded awkward. "Where did you get it?" Maybe upstairs, at Raging Art-On, the complex design looked like something Josh LaFontaine could pull off.

"I got it—" Lochlann paused, his gaze turned inward; then shook himself, and looked down, his hand closing gently around Garrett's still-raised fist. "I can't tell you where I got it. Not yet."

"Yet?" The abs so close to Garrett's face were distracting the hell out of him. *Fucking perfect.* "What has to happen before you can tell me?"

"I'm not sure." The deep, soft voice drew Garrett's gaze to Lochlann's face. "But I think this has

73

something to do with it." He caught Garrett's upper arm and drew him clumsily to his feet, and into a kiss hot enough to melt steel.

Garrett's attempt to protest only lasted until Lochlann's tongue entered his mouth. *I shouldn't be letting him do this, either*, was his last coherent thought for quite some time. Lochlann's hands moved down his back, slowly and methodically fitting him to the taller man's body; Garrett had to tiptoe to keep kissing him, and doing that only guaranteed that the rigid bar of heat barely contained in Lochlann's tight jeans would grind against his abs. He moaned faintly into the kiss, his hips swaying into Lochlann's as his own cock swiftly rose and hardened.

And it was just like the first time, back at his apartment. As if he weren't already dizzy and breathless and half out of his mind with arousal, there was a strange, intoxicating joy sweeping through him hot on arousal's heels. He wanted to laugh, wanted to hold Lochlann tighter just for the sheer delight of it.

Which was, in its way, even more frightening than the thought of what this kiss could be doing to the other man. Garrett wrenched his head away, tried to pull away, but the promise of strength in Lochlann's beautifully muscled chest was a true one, and he didn't stand a chance. All he could do was look up into blue eyes gone dark with passion, and shake his head. "No," he mouthed, his voice fled. "No."

"Why the hell not?" The dark music of Lochlann's voice was strained, hoarse. "I told you, you can't hurt me. I mean it."

"That's not it. Not all of it, anyway." Garrett bit down hard on his lower lip, looking away. *I can't let myself feel like that. Can't believe a promise of happiness. Not from a john. Because that kind of promise is always a lie. And it hurts a thousand times worse to have hope taken away than it does to refuse it in the first place.*

Except that he'd already felt the joy, and now he was just going to have to learn to live without it.

"*Tá dócas le scian inas fonn, nach milat g'matann an garta dí g'meidh tú folath.*" Lochlann nodded, almost imperceptibly; Garrett felt fingers working into his hair, burying themselves in the thick curls, tilting his head up and making him meet Lochlann's gaze. Something about his eyes... something strange. Their color.

"What language is that?" *Talk about something else. Anything else, anything but those eyes. That kiss.* "What does it mean?"

"It's my native language, though I haven't spoken it in a while." Lochlann's open palm caressed the small of Garrett's back, and even through the sweatshirt he felt scorched. "It's a proverb, I guess you'd call it. 'Hope is a knife so keen, you don't feel the cut until you bleed.'" Soft lips brushed Garrett's forehead, his temple, his cheekbone. "We're both bleeding, *lanan*. Too late to stop it."

Stunned, Garrett closed his eyes as lips, and then a tongue-tip, caressed the lids. "How did you know?—oh, Jesus, don't, *damn* it, Lochlann!" The sweetness welled up again, along with the kisses; Garrett tried to toss his head, but Lochlann held him firmly.

"If I tell you, you might have to hope." Lochlann whispered into his ear, sealing the words there with the tip of his tongue.

"*Damn* you!" And damn himself. He knew what he was inviting. Begging for. Again. His life had been like this ever since those schoolyard days, when the beatings would stop and one of his tormentors would offer him shelter. Kindness. Friendship. Every time he was sucker enough to believe the offer, trust it, the laughter would begin. The pointing fingers, the taunts. Because he was too stupid to recognize the joke that was being played on him. Other human beings could be cruel, sure. But hope was even crueler. His hopes were the only things that knew his dreams well enough to destroy them.

"Garrett, *lanan*, please, don't fight me." A rough cheek brushed against his own. "What do you feel, when I kiss you? When I touch you?"

"Nothing." He barely managed to get the word out through clenched teeth. "Not a fucking thing."

"Really?"

Lochlann's grip on Garrett's hair loosened, just enough to allow him to stroke the pad of his thumb along his cheekbone. The gently possessive gesture sent an ecstatic tingle racing through his body, straight to his groin, which was *so* not obeying orders at the moment. But he sucked in a breath, and kept his face impassive. "Really."

"Not true." Lochlann shook his head, tousled dark hair falling over his forehead, nearly into his eyes. "I know exactly what you're feeling. I can see it. And I feel it too. The joy, all out of proportion to what it's supposed to feel like when you touch someone. Even someone you want as much as I want you."

"What do you mean, you can see it?" Better to talk about that than about the other. About joy, about being wanted. "Let me guess, you're psychic." The impulse to push, push back hard, put this danger at a safe distance, was overwhelming. "You never did say what you do for a living—do you sit around your house and answer calls on one of those bullshit four-dollar-a-minute hotlines?"

"Psychic?" Lochlann arched a brow, his gaze capturing Garrett's with abrupt impossible intensity. "Not in the sense you mean." The hand on the small of Garrett's back slid under his sweatshirt, and he shivered with the delicious heat of it. "But I'm not human. And if you'll stop fighting me, I might be able to heal you. If I don't die trying."

Chapter Eight

Lochlann was prepared for any reaction from the male in his arms. Almost any. He hadn't anticipated Garrett's bitter laughter. Or his sudden attempt to twist away. An attempt that nearly succeeded, and would have, if Lochlann hadn't found a reserve of strength he hadn't needed to call on in centuries, and held him close.

The harsh laughter continued, though, sharp enough to cut. And it did; the sound tore at Lochlann, as did the pain underneath it. "Oh, fuck. And here I was worried you were nothing but a clinger. You're a full-blown nutjob."

"You don't believe that." Lochlann's voice caught in his throat. There was no laughter in Garrett's aura, no scorn. Only fear, imperfectly masked by anger turned inward, and the terrible ash-grey pall of death over all of it. "You're afraid. But not of me." He couldn't help himself, he brushed his lips over the shorter male's forehead. "What are you afraid of?"

Garrett went silent as abruptly as if Lochlann had choked him. "How the hell do you *know*?" The whisper was as intense as a shout. "What are you?"

"I'm a Fae. And an empath. I can see your emotions. Sense them directly, when I'm close

78

enough, and when I choose to." Emotions still almost too painful to look at. "And yours is the first fear in more than two thousand years I've given enough of a damn about to want to put an end to it." No more than the truth; even in the early days of his sojourn in the human world, when auras were as plain to him as the light of noonday, no fear, no sorrow, no pain had moved him past empathy to compassion. "Tell me how I can, *grafain*."

Garrett shook his head, eyes wide, white showing all the way around the golden-brown irises. "What does *that* mean?"

"It means love. Untamed. Wild." Lochlann could feel Garrett's heart pounding, he held him so close.

"You're just a crazy john." The human's hands balled into fists at his sides. "Look, it's okay, just tell me what you want."

"I thought you said you don't turn tricks any more."

"Yeah, well, you didn't take 'no' for an answer, did you?" Garrett was slowly calming, but the resignation replacing the panic in his eyes made Lochlann ache to lash out at every male who had helped to put it there. "Do what you want. Let's get it over with. Before..." His voice trailed off.

"Before what?"

Garrett looked away. "Before I start believing you."

"Why would that be so terrible?"

"Because... oh, fuck." Garrett's nostrils flared with a deep, quick breath. "You don't look like any mythological creature I've ever heard of. But Fae means magic, right?"

"Sometimes, but—"

"And I won't let myself fall for that shit."

Garrett shivered in Lochlann's arms. With fear, his aura said, not with cold. And suddenly Lochlann understood why. "Because you'd hope."

The human nodded tightly. "I'd want to. And I gave that up a long time ago. There's too much to hope for, and it will hurt entirely too fucking much when it all turns out to be a lie."

"It's not a lie." *I may die before I can give you what you'd hope for if you let yourself, but that doesn't make it a lie.* At least he knew he was willing to try, regardless of what might happen to him personally. He'd come away from the encounter with Cuinn resolved to blow up the Loremasters' plans for Garrett, no matter the cost to himself. And if the bitches and the sons of bitches had actually contrived for Garrett to contract AIDS, instead of manipulating a personal tragedy, Lochlann hoped fervently for an afterlife. Something like the Norse Valhalla, so he could kill them anew, every morning. "Though I don't think you believe me."

"I don't dare believe you. I'd ask for too much."

"Too much?" Lochlann's hand moved slowly over the smooth skin of Garrett's lower back; he felt the human jump, then settle under the insistent, sensual stroking. "I doubt that." He was abruptly aware of Garrett's scent, sweat and musk and the leather of the fingerless gloves he still wore after his stint on the pole. "What do you want, *grafain*? Tell me."

Garrett shuddered. "How about a magic bullet that actually fucking works, the way the drugs are supposed to?" His gaze flashed to Lochlann's eyes, then away, and when he spoke again there was a tightness in his voice, almost despairing. "Or if I'm asking for miracles, how about you truly giving a damn?"

The anger in Garrett's aura spiked so brightly it made Lochlann's eyes water. That was what caused the sudden tears, surely. "You have no idea how much of a damn I give."

The silence stretched out to the point of pain, with Lochlann acutely aware of the way Garrett's lean, hard dancer's body pressed against his, and the way the human's anger was gradually giving way to something else. Something just as strong, with edges just as sharp. Something that would devour them both, if they let it.

Lochlann was more than ready to let it.

Finally Garrett spoke, his sweet tenor hoarsened to a dark whisper. "The last time you held me like this, you left me. Because you only wanted to talk."

"I was a fucking idiot."

"I agree."

Garrett's kiss was raw, and hungry. All need, blindly searching. There was nothing blind or inexperienced about his body, though; he fitted himself to the Fae with all the practiced ease that had no doubt brought hundreds of men to quick and intense release, and left Garrett himself free to make a quick escape. This time, though, there was no escape in sight or contemplation; both males fought to breathe without breaking the kiss, both groaned as the other's hands explored and gripped and teased.

Lochlann sucked in a breath as Garrett found his open shirt front, pushed shirt and coat over his shoulders to fall to the floor, ran his hands over his chest and shoulders and abs. The human's mouth followed his hands, hot and needy, tongue tracing the loops and spikes and whorls that patterned Lochlann's chest, the piercing the Fae had felt during their first kiss stroking over his nipples.

Fingertips brushed over the tip of Lochlann's cock, where it emerged from the waistband of his jeans; he gasped, his hips jerking forward, and a groan came from low in his throat as Garrett worked at the button. "*Grafain...*"

"I know. I shouldn't." Teeth teased at Lochlann's pebbled-hard nipple. "But I need to." The zipper gave way to Garrett's insistent tugging, and the Fae's cock fell hard and heavy into a waiting, leather-clad hand. "I can't explain it... can't describe it... but I need to."

"I'm sure as hell not telling you to stop."

But stop the human did, and Lochlann groaned as his erection fell free. Only long enough, though, to let Garrett quickly strip off the gloves he needed for the pole and toss them aside. Then the dancer took him back in hand—both hands, the Fae's thick cock standing up proudly in a firm two-handed grip. The sight alone nearly brought him off, his cock swelled visibly, throbbed, curved. Then the hands began to stroke, and Lochlann's head fell back, his lips moving in silent pleas. It couldn't get better, but it did. Hand over hand glided up, thumb sweeping over his sensitive tip before returning to stroke him again from balls to head.

"Jesus, I wish I dared to blow you."

Lochlann's head jerked upright and his eyes snapped open. A low, trembling moan escaped him as he looked down at Garrett. Sweaty blond curls tumbled around the human's face, not quite hiding the intense brown gaze fixed on the erection that made the hands stroking it look small. "You can."

Garrett looked up, at the choked words that were all the Fae could manage. "No." His tongue swept over Lochlann's nipple, and Lochlann bit his lip hard at the sensation of the piercing teasing at the puckered flesh. "Too dangerous. I'm drug resistant now, for some reason, no fucking way am I getting my mouth anywhere near your cock." The human's hands never stopped, never slowed. "But this, this is good, too. It's almost like I can feel it, myself, when I touch you."

This is what the soul-share does. It had to be. It all made sense; the immediate intensity of his need for Garrett, from the first sight of him, Cuinn's cryptic two-thousand-year-old advice that the cure for a sundered soul was love, his wiseass remark about SoulShare jealousy earlier tonight. And the joy cascading down every nerve in Lochlann's body, like the bright spray of a waterfall. It all fit.

Just for a moment, Lochlann froze. If this was what it took to complete the bond, if his pleasure finished it, these might be his last few moments of existence. Because Garrett was very, very good at what he did off the dance floor as well as on it.

Even that moment of hesitation was enough to catch Garrett's attention; the human looked questioningly up at him, his hands slowing, uncertainty plain in his aura. "You sure you don't want me to stop?"

If I have to die, is there a better way than this? Lochlann reached down and closed one of his hands around Garrett's, using the human's hand to stimulate himself. "I'm sure."

"Oh, fuck." Garrett's eyes went wide. "I do feel

it. You. Something." Sweat shone on the human's forehead, and his groans were perfectly timed with the grunts Lochlann couldn't help. "So good..."

Wave after wave of delight, of joy surged through the Fae. Each more intense than the one before, cresting higher than the last, every time Garrett gripped and stroked and wrung. His own hands rode lightly atop the human's, now, for the pleasure of feeling the skill with which he was worked. His voice all but gone, he whispered, again and again. "Garrett. Garrett, oh *damn*, Garrett."

Tiny, impossible pinpricks of light responded to Lochlann's hoarse whispers. For the first time, he saw clear, untainted light in Garrett's aura, brilliant traces of silver-blue, sparks flaring through the gray of death. The human's own joy, breaking through the pall that shrouded him. "Garrett, *grafain, lanan...*" His hips bucked hard, clear fluid streamed from his tip and bathed the human's hands.

Garrett, too, was whispering, brokenly. "Yes. *Yes.* Please, Lochlann. Come for me. You're almost there, I can feel it. *Please.*"

Yes. He was almost there. White heat flowing down his spine, pooling at the base. Shaft curving, going hard as steel. Warm hands gripping it, coaxing. A soft voice, pleading wordlessly now, begging for his pleasure. He couldn't breathe, didn't want to; everything in him was focused on the next moment, on what he could feel building.

If this kills me—

Lochlann's knees nearly buckled as the first spasms of pleasure seized him. His cock pulsed in Garrett's hands, and thick hot clear fluid jetted from him with enough force to soak Garrett's shirt before flowing back down over the human's hands, slicking his grip and kicking the sensations up several notches past mind-blowing. He was silent, because he had no breath to cry out, but low, keening moans still filled the tiny room—Garrett's, interspersed with gasps and soft cries.

The pleasure wasn't what whited out his vision and dropped him to his knees, though. No, that was the joy. More than two thousand years of solitary exile were over. Even if he never opened his eyes again, in this moment he was not alone. And he never would be again. *I never knew how lonely I was, until I wasn't any more.*

"Oh, Jesus, Lochlann." Garrett's awed whisper came to him from what sounded like a great distance. "What happened? What the hell *was* that?"

I must still be alive, was Lochlann's first, dizzy thought. Followed closely by *did it work?* and *oh, shit, how do I explain this?* He opened his eyes to discover that Garrett had followed him down to the floor, and was steadying him with one hand on his shoulder even as he continued to stroke his softening erection with the other. And brilliant silver-blue delight was still swirling through the human's aura, a sight that gave him nearly as much joy as Garrett's ministrations had.

First things first. Lochlann's fingers sought Garrett's thick blond curls and drew him in close, close enough that their lips brushed as he whispered. "*G'ra ma agadh.*" As if thanks could ever be enough, but they were a beginning. So was the kiss they shared, long and lingering. Then, while Garrett's eyes were still closed, Lochlann took a deep breath, reached within himself and sought the magick he needed in order to Fade.

Nothing happened.

No, not quite nothing. Lochlann still knelt on the cold concrete floor, his knees starting to throb in time with his heartbeat; Garrett still knelt in front of him, close enough that the heat of his body chased away the chill. The Fade hadn't worked. Yet there was a tingle, all through Lochlann's body. As if all of him at once had waked from lying on an arm, or having one leg crossed too long over the other.

For good or ill, life or death, magick was waking.

Chapter Nine

"Lochlann?" Garrett shook the taller man gently, hoping the movement disguised how his hand was trembling. It wasn't like he'd never seen that dazed expression on a john's face before—though it was getting harder to remember what Lochlann was, what he had to be, and after the last few minutes it was setting up to be fucking impossible. *What the hell happened to me, just now?*

"I... uh, yeah." Lochlann shook his head. "I'm here." He stared at his hands for a few moments, his fingers curling and uncurling, watching them like he'd never seen anything quite like them before. Then those blue eyes met his again, and he was more certain than ever there was something strange about them. Beautiful, but strange. "You said something happened to you?"

Garrett started to reply, but the faint sound of applause drifting through the closed door cut him off. "Oh, sweet bleeding fuck—Leandro and Antonio are going to be in here any minute."

Lochlann cursed, or at least that's what Garrett assumed he was doing. He didn't recognize any of the words, but they sounded sort of like the things Lochlann had been saying earlier. The dark-haired man got to his feet, somehow managing to look graceful even after falling hard to his knees on concrete covered only with carpet tiles, and started putting himself to rights.

And I want to help him. Shit. There was at least one way the fucking virus was his friend, at least he probably didn't have much longer left to be an idiot. But who wouldn't want it back, what he'd just felt? How long had it been, since sex made him want to laugh, and cry with the laughing because it was so goddamned good?

Lochlann reached down, offering him a hand. He didn't need the help, but he took it. *I want him touching me. Dammit.* He bent and fished his jeans out of his duffle bag, shook them out and stepped into them.

Only then did he turn and look at the dark-haired man, and stopped short at his stricken expression. "Look, let's go out into the cock pit, okay? We can talk there."

"Talk?" Lochlann's laugh was short. "The sound level out there is somewhere between earsplitting and assault and battery. You'll never hear a word I say."

"It's not that bad everywhere." Garrett forced himself into his jeans, not sure whether he was surprised he was still hard enough to need to use force. "The pit's set up acoustically so there are a few places where you can still hear, no matter what. Some guys like that."

Lochlann arched a brow, and Garrett shrugged. Lochlann knew what he was. Had been. Whatever. "We can talk there. And it'll be a hell of a lot more private than this is going to be in a minute."

Lochlann nodded, just as the door swung open to admit two sweaty Brazilians.

"Oh. Hey. Sorry, Garrett."

"*Merda*, sorry."

"It's okay, we're just leaving." Antonio and Leandro were new enough to Purgatory they'd never walked in on him turning a trick, they were two of Tiernan's new hires, but they still didn't seem all that surprised. It was part of the life, after all.

But it was strange that Lochlann didn't seem bothered at all by the intrusion. He nodded to the two men, squeezed between them, and stood waiting for Garrett in the narrow hallway. *Does he do this that often?* Garrett grimaced at the thought, and again as he realized the answer mattered to him. *I truly will never learn.* He snatched up his duffle bag and slung it over his shoulder. The Brazilians made way for him, and he heard the door close softly behind him as he joined Lochlann.

"Lead on." There was still a strange, faraway look in Lochlann's eyes, but at least he was smiling.

Ignoring the pounding music, Garrett made his way around the edge of the crowd that still packed the dance floor, past the bar and down to the sunken, irregularly-shaped, dimly-lit area filled with black leather furniture at the far end of the club. Everyone called it the cock pit, for reasons obvious even to the most casual onlooker. He felt Lochlann come up behind him as he surveyed the possibilities; most of the sofas and loveseats were occupied by men in various states of undress who looked like they wouldn't welcome interruptions. One of the quiet seats was empty, though. He reached behind himself, grabbed Lochlann's hand, and pulled him down the stairs and through the maze, nearly tripping over the platform heels of a drag queen kneeling to administer an intense BJ to a heavy-set man in an expensive-looking suit.

He pitched his bag ahead of himself to land beside the empty loveseat, claiming it, earning him dirty looks from a couple of bears headed in the same direction. Paying no attention, he sank down into the soft black leather with a sigh of relief, drawing Lochlann with him. "There. See, I told you it would be better here."

"You're sure you can hear me?" Lochlann settled onto the loveseat, turning to Garrett and wrapping an arm around him.

"Clear as a bell." Garrett shivered as the strong arm went around him; the casual possessiveness in the gesture was almost as unnerving as the warmth of it. "You can probably even lower your voice."

"I'll do that." Lochlann's deep voice dropped to a murmur as he bent his head so his lips brushed Garrett's ear. "I don't have any real way to know how acute human hearing is. But I'd hate to be overheard."

Garrett stiffened. *Human hearing.* The chances were excellent the soft-spoken, hotter-than-fucking-hell man who held him was completely insane. "So what is it you think you are, exactly? 'Fae' doesn't tell me much. Most of the fairy stories I know involve tiny people with wings. And whatever you are, you sure as hell aren't tiny."

He felt Lochlann's laughter as well as heard it, and the sound brought him right back to the one thing that let him think maybe he *wasn't* dealing with a head case. The sensation that gripped him when Lochlann came. He could have sworn he heard laughter, except that Lochlann had been totally silent and he himself had been fighting to keep back moans like he only gave up when he was the one being brought off. Laughter. Pure, delighted, full-throated laughter. And for an instant, he'd felt a joy so intense his mind couldn't hold on to it. He was sure in that moment, he'd been happier than he'd ever been in his life, but he couldn't remember what it had felt like.

"Thank you for the testimonial." Lochlann was still chuckling, a rich dark sound. "And I know you still doubt, and that's all right, I would too, in your position." He sobered, and pulled back just far enough to let him look into Garrett's eyes, their foreheads nearly touching, the club around them already forgotten. "I'm not a fairy, I'm a Fae. Our world split off from yours over two thousand years ago. You still have some stories about us that are fairly accurate, but Tinkerbell isn't one of them." The corner of Lochlann's mouth quirked up in another little smile. "I'm not sure where the tales of little winged people came from. Although I've always suspected that some of the birds in the human world still harbor a touch of magick, even after all this time, so maybe that's it."

"You sound like you really believe what you're saying." Garrett had winced at the other man's use of the word 'magick.' It was too closely related to 'hope' for his comfort, they both promised what could never be delivered.

"I do. It's because I'm a Fae that it's safe for you to do anything you want with me." Now Lochlann was wrapping a leg around Garrett, freeing up his arm to let him stroke Garrett's face with gentle fingertips. "In the Realm—our world—Fae live a thousand years or more, are never sick, and heal quickly from any injury that isn't immediately mortal. And the same is true when we come to your world, except that here even a mortal injury can't kill us. At least, not until we find our SoulShares."

The touch of Lochlann's fingers was soothing, so much so that Garrett's eyes were starting to drift closed. Something about that last word, though, brought them wide open again. Not so much the word, as the way the other man said it. "What the hell is a SoulShare? Assuming I believe you."

Lochlann sighed. "I'm not sure I can tell you exactly. I was the first, and there was a lot nobody knew about SoulShares two thousand years ago. Especially me." For a moment, the dark-stubbled face so close to Garrett's own went cold, hard, expressionless. But the moment passed, and Lochlann sighed. "In order for a Fae to come from the Realm to here, he has to go through a portal that guards the Realm. And when he does, his soul is torn in half. Half he keeps, and half gets thrown out into the human world where it's reborn into a human."

"Is this where you tell me we're soul-mates?" Garrett tried to keep the bitterness from his voice, but he didn't try hard enough, and Lochlann flinched. "That pretty story didn't get you anywhere with me, I don't believe in fairy tales no matter who they come from." *And I almost forgot that. He makes me want to forget. Which makes him fucking dangerous.*

"Garrett. Please. Listen to me." Lochlann took Garrett's chin between two strong fingers. "I don't know who hurt you to the point where you can't even hear what I'm saying. If I did, I would kill them."

"You would *what*?"

Lochlann shrugged, as if what he'd just said was no big deal. "It would be a pleasure. But it wouldn't help right now, because I need you to believe me. We're more than soul-mates, Garrett. We're two halves of the same soul. Neither one of us is complete without the other."

Garrett tried to look away, but Lochlann wouldn't let him. The fingers of one hand tunneled into his curls, caught tightly. But it was the other man's eyes that really held him. Beautiful blue, clear and compelling and gemlike even in the dim light.

He gasped, staring. Not gem*like*. This close, he could see facets in the aquamarine irises. "You *aren't* human." His stunned whisper was barely audible.

Lochlann heard, though. He shook his head, almost imperceptibly. "I'm glad you believe me, *grafain*. Because there's more you need to believe."

"Let me just work on this one for a minute, all right?" The words were flippant, but Garrett spoke past a lump in his throat and was just glad they didn't catch on it. If Lochlann was telling the truth about not being human—which he was—then he was probably telling the truth about the shared soul thing. Which made a strange kind of sense, actually. How long had he felt empty? Hollow, filled up only when he was dancing? Or when Lochlann looked at him. Touched him. Allowed him to pleasure him. With Lochlann, he didn't feel empty. Which, frankly, scared the shit out of him. "What else is there?"

All the answer he got for a few moments was

more of that incredibly intense gaze. Then a surprise, as Lochlann slowly took his mouth, gently and thoroughly, the same unexpected gentleness he'd showed back in Garrett's apartment.

Garrett didn't usually close his eyes when he kissed, he never let go that much, but he did this time. Everything narrowed down to just this kiss. The taste, the scents, the sensation of Lochlann's surprisingly soft mouth on his, and then stubble rasping against his own lips as Lochlann went exploring.

God, I'll make you a deal. Don't take this away from me, just this once in my life, and I'll even forgive you for the damned virus. He was hardening again, the ring of his Prince Albert somehow caught on the zipper of his jeans, but even the pain was sweet.

"Damn." Lochlann laughed softly, and the sound was an echo of what he thought he'd heard as the other man came. Another kiss wandered over Garrett's cheekbone. "What else? Well, for starters, I think I need you. Need to be with you."

An hour ago, those words would have made Garrett laugh, and not pleasantly; the cruelest bullies had always been the ones who held out hope, respite, comfort, and then snatched it back laughing when he dared to trust. Now? "If you're fucking with my head, I swear to God I am going to grow a set and make you pay." He swallowed hard, but the lump in his throat refused to budge. "But I feel the same way."

Lochlann's amazing smile flared again, and Garrett sagged back against the cushions with relief even as his heart punched into overdrive. "I don't think you have to worry about growing a set, *grafain*, the set you have is quite impressive."

94

Garrett couldn't help rolling his eyes. "Spare me. Please." Yet he was smiling, genuinely smiling. "You going to tell me the rest of your secrets?"

"All at once?" One corner of Lochlann's mouth quirked up. "All right. The Fae are magickal beings. I suppose you could say that in a way, we're made of magick. But I've been waiting for you to come along for over two thousand years, and during that time, I've lost my magick. I spent it all." All hints of laughter were gone, now. "I've been feeling something, though, ever since you brought me off. And I suspect that if I do the same for you, if we finish the SoulShare bond, I'll get my magick back." Lochlann's hand folded around Garrett's. "Before I spent all my magick, I was a healer. A damned good one. And if the SoulShare works the way I hope it will, once I have the magick back..." The grip on Garrett's hand tightened. "I think I can cure you."

"If you don't die trying." The words came out without any conscious thought on Garrett's part; his brain was far too busy being stunned to have remembered the declaration that had started this conversation. When Lochlann had first said those words, first held out hope for an impossible cure and then tacked on that casual P.S., he, Garrett, had still been operating under the assumption that Lochlann had a sleeper car all to himself on the crazy train. But now...

Lochlann—the Fae—had meant every other word he'd said. So he must have meant those.

"Garrett—"

"Why would it kill you to heal me?" Garrett kept his voice low with an effort; the last thing he wanted now was for someone to overhear. "Do you have to take the virus into yourself or something?"

"No. No." Lochlann drew him closer. "Shit. I shouldn't have said that."

"If it was true, you fucking well should have. What could kill you?"

He felt Lochlann sigh. "Curing you wouldn't put me at any risk at all. Healing is the gift of my Demesne. My element, I guess you'd say. I'm a Water Fae, we're the only ones who can use magick to heal without causing pain."

"You're trying to distract me." Garrett's eyes narrowed. "I'm not buying it."

"Damn." Lochlann bowed his head, resting his forehead on Garrett's shoulder, enclosing Garrett within a protective wall formed of his own body. When he finally spoke again, his voice was muffled, indistinct. "Fae live a thousand years. I've lived more than twice that. Until I found my SoulShare, my *scair-anam*, nothing could harm me. Period. And that apparently includes the aging process."

"Christ." Garrett shuddered convulsively. "If I let you finish the bond, two lifetimes of aging catch up with you in the amount of time it takes me to shoot my wad."

"I don't *know* that." Garrett could hear the pain in Lochlann's voice, like dark silk catching on briars. "It makes as much sense to think I'll just start aging again where I left off."

"You think I'm going to take that chance?" A pure, cold rage swept through Garrett, and he let it take him. Better that than heartbreak. Hopefully he could get home before that hit. Not rage at the man, the Fae, who held him. No. Rage at a sadistic God, a merciless Fate, who had once again dangled hope in front of him. Only this time it wasn't going to be snatched away from him. Oh, no.

This time he was going to throw it away.

"The chance is mine to take, g*rafain*—"

"Like fuck it is." Garrett wrenched away from Lochlann's embrace, moved as far away as the loveseat would let him. "We only finish this when you do for me what I did for you, right? You are fucking *never* touching me again. Are we clear?"

"*Garrett*—"

The pain in Lochlann's eyes was more than Garrett could stand. So he didn't stand it. He stood, barely evading Lochlann's grasping hand, and snatched up his duffle bag. "Stay away from me." His words were broken, ragged; even to him, it sounded as if a sadistic cat toyed with his throat, claws out. "You aren't getting back in here. Your name is going on the bouncers' Do Not Admit list." Jesus, it really did feel like something was ripping his heart out.

"Don't do this, *m'lanan.*"

Everything in Garrett wanted to turn, to fall back onto the loveseat and let Lochlann take him into his arms and make the pain stop.

Everything except the part that loved Lochlann. "It's done."

Garrett refused to look back.

And the night was entirely too fucking cold.

Chapter Ten

"Would you like me to call you a taxi, Mr. Doran?"

The mellifluous, cultured, oh-so-veddy-English tones of the concierge followed Lochlann toward the lobby door. He could almost feel them digging fingers under the collar of his coat, grabbing, trying to pull him back in to be fussed over and catered to. Another reminder of why he only rarely lived the way his trust fund allowed. "No, that's all right, Gerald. I'm not going far."

"But the weather's dreadful." He heard footsteps behind him. No one else would have been able to hear them, surely, the boutique hotel's thick carpet swallowed feet nearly to the ankles. "And it's nearly dark already. I *do* hate winter."

Sighing, Lochlann turned, forcing a smile at the silver-haired, impeccably dressed human who was trying to shadow him. Fae hated small talk, as a rule, and him more so than most, but he had a long-term residential contract at the Colchester, and the longer he could keep from alienating the help, the more tolerable it would be for everyone. Not that he'd be able to put the alienation off forever, he'd never managed that particular trick yet in twenty-three hundred years. "So do I. But I've been closed up all day, and I can't take it any more. And the *last* thing I need is to be shut up in a box." He'd had something like four centuries to get over a Fae's innate terror of enclosed conveyances—he still blushed when he remembered what had happened the first time he was invited to ride in an enclosed sedan chair with a young English lord—but that didn't mean he had any desire to subject himself to a cab ride.

"Very good, Mr. Doran." From the expression on Gerald's face, it wasn't very good at all, but Lochlann knew how willing he was to accommodate the eccentricities of the handsome lad in Room 302.

All the accommodation I need is to be let the fuck alone. Lochlann nodded, and ducked out into the lowering dusk before the concierge could change his mind.

The Fae shivered as the wind flung icy needles into his face. Of course, as fate would have it, his route took him straight into the wind; he grimaced and set off, collar turned up, head down, one hand holding his coat closed at the neck. It wasn't the cold so much that bothered him. More the combination of the cold, the wind, the sleet, and oh yeah, not sleeping a fucking wink since getting reamed out in the small dark hours of the morning by the male who held the missing half of his soul.

He had to get through to Garrett somehow. Had to. If he got to Purgatory before the human did, he'd be able to get past the bouncer. Then he would wait. Wait, and use the time to try to figure out what the hell he was going to say.

Lochlann barely saw blocks passing by, hardly

noticed the pedestrians he wove his way between. His sleep-deprived mind was still in Purgatory's cock pit, trying to figure out a way to bring Garrett back. Which was bizarre beyond belief, to a Fae.

Twenty-three hundred years of one-night stands. Not quite three hundred years before that, in the Realm, staying with one lover for a week, another for a month, once in all those decades managing to stay with the same partner for almost a year. And that had been pure stubbornness on his part. Well, that and laziness. Never in his life had he known anything like this sense of connection. Hell, he'd never even known how to imagine it.

It wasn't a *sense* of connection, either. He wanted to give Garrett what Garrett had given him, yes. But not because that would complete the SoulShare bond. He still had some work to do to convince himself he wasn't scared shitless about that prospect. No, he wanted to do it because he wanted Garrett to feel the overwhelming sense of joy he had felt when it was Garrett doing the giving. Wanted to hear him laugh, see his amber eyes light with his smile. The human looked as if he hadn't done nearly enough of either in a very long time. And Lochlann wanted—no, he *needed*—to be the one who gave that to him.

Fae don't love. It was a truth as old as the race. No love could last a thousand years, so no Fae ever loved.

Fuck that.

He stumbled over a curb and looked up, bemused to discover that he'd already come three blocks since the last time he was aware of his surroundings. There was a Summoning at work here, he was sure of that now. Even though he hadn't felt one since just before leaving the Realm, there was no mistaking it, especially not this close to the source. *It figures, I can still have my leash yanked, even with all my magick gone.* A Summoning didn't call to magick, it called to a Fae. So he'd felt a vague but persistent urge to take an extended vacation in Washington, D.C., and had chosen a hotel on what felt like a whim. A fucking expensive whim, but who cared? Three weeks ago, just after the new year, he'd moved into the Colchester. It hadn't quite taken him a week to stumble across Purgatory, where he quickly became a regular.

Now that he'd found Garrett? It was as if someone had harpooned him and was reeling him in.

Reeling him nearly to the front door, in fact. He stopped a couple of storefronts down from the entrance to the club, trying to chafe some feeling into the hand that had been holding his jacket closed, watching warm light spill out from the window of the tattoo and piercing parlor that shared the recessed entryway with the matte black glass rectangle that gave onto the stairs leading down to Purgatory. Odd to see that door closed, but then he generally wasn't here this time of day.

The window outside which Lochlann stood was even less inviting than the blank glass, a dark, curtained window, underneath a battered but neatly-lettered sign that read *Big Boy Massage*. Someone had used paint that didn't quite match the rest of the sign to cross out "Big" and add "Bad".

Lochlann shrugged and walked into the entryway, pulled the door open, and followed the damned harpoon down the stairs.

Another black glass door at the bottom of the

narrow stairs swung open at his touch, and he caught his first glimpse of the after-work rush at Purgatory. Judging from the sparse assemblage at the bar, it ran mostly to men in suits, probably downing quick drinks before heading home. And the music was at a tolerable level for Fae ears.

"Sorry, sir, I'm going to have to ask you to leave."

Startled, Lochlann turned toward the gravelly voice. If a bulldog could have a love child with his favorite fire hydrant, that child would probably look a lot like Lucien; short, bald, stocky, lumpy, and exuding 'don't fuck with me' in every language spoken by human or Fae. Yet he was sweet on the amputee bartender who usually worked the early evening shift, who obviously returned his affections. Lochlann had never seen him be other than polite, and he counted on that politeness now, thinking quickly even as his heart began to sink. "I just need to see the owner for a minute, Lucien."

The bouncer wasn't buying. "We've had a request that you not be admitted, sir. And you should know, management doesn't tolerate harassment of the dancers."

Sweet bleeding fuck. "I didn't harass anyone. I just need to talk to Tiernan." Lochlann craned his neck, wishing that Fae had gods to pray to so he could pray that Guaire walked out of his office sometime in the next thirty seconds.

"That's not what I've been told, sir. And I need to ask you to leave. Now."

"*Tam g'fuil aon-arc desúcan an lanhuil damast i d'asal. G'mall.*"

"I beg your pardon?" The bouncer obviously wasn't begging for anything; his arms uncrossed, he advanced a step toward Lochlann, his expression all business to the extent it was readable at all.

May a unicorn repair your hemorrhoids. Slowly. Lochlann backed up, hands out. There were still options, still ways he could talk to Garrett without making a scene here. Some way to make the hollow feeling stop. "It doesn't matter. I'm going. Just tell Tiernan I was here."

He turned and pushed his way through the door, making his way blindly up the stairs. Blindly, because he was cursing *as'Faein* and oblivious to the world around him. Garrett must have called ahead instead of waiting until he came to work. *Son of a bitch,* grafain, *why do you have to make this so hard for both of us?*

Traffic into Purgatory was light, this early, and even as preoccupied as he was, Lochlann didn't actually collide with anyone until he emerged from the doors at the top of the stairs. A man staggered back, fetching up against the wall next to the door opening onto the tattoo parlor. Slight, red-haired, green-eyed, he glared at Lochlann as if he expected his gaze to do damage.

His gaze. Faceted.

The very last thing in this world or any other that Lochlann needed in this moment was to deal with yet another Fae. "Leave me the fuck alone," he snarled, and ducked out of the shelter of the entryway into the welcoming sting of the sleet-swept night.

Chapter Eleven

"This is harder than I thought it was going to be."

Josh laughed softly, setting the tattoo machine down on the steel tray beside his elbow and stroking Conall's erect cock, inspecting the tattoo that presently ran halfway around the base of it. "I think that's supposed to be my line."

Conall's answering laughter was more than a little breathless. "If you think it's easy to stay just aroused enough to let you channel, while you're fondling me with one hand and using the other to drill needles into my—what did you call it the other day? Mancrank?—I suggest you try it."

"Faecrank, in your case." Josh was apparently trying very hard to keep a straight face, and not succeeding very well. "And I wasn't referring to yours, anyway. That was the customer who wanted an anteater on his groin. God knows why, it's like proclaiming to the world 'I *never* have a hard-on.'"

"Just be sure you get the buckle and the holes right." Conall studied the cock ring his *scair-anam* was so painstakingly rendering. "If this little experiment actually works, I want to be able to get the damned thing off."

"Assuming I let you." The gleam in Josh's dark eyes was pure wickedness; tattoos he inked while near a source of magick, such as the ley lines under Purgatory, had a way of becoming real in the presence of powerful channeling. The human picked up the pen again, dipped the needles in the brown ink, gave Conall one more skillful stroke, and bent back to work.

Conall cursed under his breath, even as he smiled. "I thought that was a given—"

The front door of Raging Art-On opened, closed. Conall caught Josh's frown, and one red-blond brow arched. "Not expecting anyone?" Just in case, he reached out, sensing the presence of the power flowing through the great nexus that lay two stories below them, under the floor of Purgatory's basement where the four ley lines intersected, familiar enough with it by now that he could feel the comforting flow even at this distance. Of course, he would still need to touch it to channel from it. With his SoulShare at his side, Josh's human nature was his shield against the staggering power.

"No, no appointments, I cleared out my book to do you."

Conall would have replied, but the door to Josh's studio opened, and what came out instead of what he'd intended was "Oh, shit."

"And a pleasant good evening to you, too, Twinklebritches." Cuinn smirked. "Just the Fae I wanted to see."

"If it was mutual, you'd be the first to know."

Josh shook his head, setting the tattoo machine aside again. "*D'orant*, you promised me you were going to behave the next time you two were together."

"This *is* behaving."

"You want to put that weapon away?" Cuinn nodded toward Conall's midsection. "I actually need to have a serious conversation with you, and that's kind of distracting."

Now it was Conall's turn to smirk. He took his time about putting himself to rights, pausing to ruffle his fingers through his *scair-anam*'s thick dark hair before finally buttoning his jeans. Which ruffling he would have done anyway, he had yet to exhaust the sheer delight touching Josh still brought him, but he took a little longer about the touching than he might have otherwise, just on principle.

"If I may interrupt." Cuinn leaned back against the wall of the little studio, hands plunged deep into the pockets of his leather jacket. "We have an issue. There's a new Fae in town, and he's met his SoulShare."

Conall edged onto the table and sat. "Sounds more like your issue than mine. You're the one who keeps calling yourself our babysitter."

"Yeah, well, the babysitter needs the design specs on the channeling you did to ward this place. Guaire had me downstairs looking at security footage from last night; the human is one of his dancers, and last night he got in a fight with his Fae and walked out on him. And called in this afternoon to have him put on the DNA list."

"Shit." Josh spoke up before Conall could say anything. "Which of the dancers is it?" He returned Conall's quizzical look with a shrug. "I've inked or pierced most of the guys who work there. Maybe I know him."

Cuinn nodded thoughtfully. Apparently his brief to be the most irritating son of a bitch since the first bitch whelped only extended to other Fae. "You might, he's been around a while. Garrett Templar."

Josh whistled under his breath. "Yeah, I know him. Prince Albert, maybe four years ago." He looked from Conall to Cuinn, a frown line appearing between his brows. "He's HIV-positive, he made damn sure I was extra careful when I pierced him. Is that going to be an issue for a Fae?"

"Shouldn't be, and this particular Fae might be able to heal him. Once they start speaking to one another again." Cuinn grimaced, turning his attention back to Conall. "My worry at the moment is about what might happen before then. I've seen Garrett since he met Lochlann, and he's not glowing in all magickal frequencies like Josh here did before you two finally finished deflowering one another. But the *Marfach* may be able to pick up on the human half of a pair even without that. It found Kevin Almstead and nearly killed him, thanks to the flaw in that bond, and that was *after* he and Guaire fully bonded."

"You almost look worried, Loremaster." Conall reached for Josh's hand, needing the comfort of a touch despite his glib retort. His pairing with Josh had been flawed as well, and the flaw had nearly killed them both, Conall from something like suffocation, resulting from his inability to channel the magick that was his life force, and Josh from being a human forced to channel the magick that should have been flowing through Conall. His thumb caressed Josh's palm in gentle circles. "Do you know what their flaw is?"

Cuinn shook his head, and if Conall didn't know it was impossible, he would have sworn that the sandy-haired Fae was blushing. "I have a guess, nothing more. But I didn't come here to talk Pattern metaphysics."

You don't want to talk about their bonding. Interesting. "Don't tell me you actually came for the peep show."

Cuinn snorted. "Please. I have other ways of dealing with homesickness."

Josh turned a facepalm into a finger rake through his already unruly hair. "Any chance of you getting to the point, Cuinn? I'd like to finish Conall's ink."

Conall smothered a grin. His *scair-anam* was learning how to deal with Fae.

"I love you, too." Cuinn shaped a kiss at Josh, who ignored it, then turned back to Conall. "What I want to know is, if the *Marfach* can figure out what Garrett is before he and his Fae stop fighting and get snogging, does Garrett get any protection from that ward you put up around this building?"

"You mean, does the ward follow people who walk through it?" Conall was intrigued despite his reflexive irritation with Cuinn. "No, I didn't think of that before I put it up. I was more interested in protecting the nexus, the immediate emergency." The nexus had to be protected, together with the building under which the ley lines intersected. The *Marfach* preferred to reside in living magick, such as a Fae, but it had made shift for more than two thousand years in the non-living magickal force in the ley lines that ran under the surface of the human world, and it wasn't smart to take the chance it wouldn't go back there again if it could. "I might be able to modify the ward, though. I'd have to give it some thought."

"You do that, Twinklebritches." Cuinn grinned,

which was almost as irritating as the nickname he'd hung on Conall. "Garrett's not dancing tonight anyway, so the earliest he'll be passing through the ward is tomorrow night."

"What about the other Fae?" Josh put in, with a quick glance at Conall.

Conall himself was indifferent to the prospect of encountering another of his race; he'd only left the Realm a little over six months ago, and frankly he was rather enjoying this brief vacation from having too many other Fae around. Although Cuinn occasionally managed to be "too many" all by himself. Even the Noble Tiernan Guaire didn't manage to be as insufferable as the ancient, eternally delinquent Loremaster.

But Cuinn was definitely blushing. Which, as far as Conall was concerned, made this other Fae suddenly fascinating. "He can take care of himself. He's been doing just fine at that for two thousand years."

You know him. Conall wasn't sure how he knew, but he knew. *And you don't want to talk about him. I wonder why.* "Well, then, why don't you get the hell out of here and let me think? And let Josh finish his work."

"As if you're going to be thinking while he does that. How's the whole making up for three centuries of celibacy working out for you?"

"Quite nicely, thank you." Josh, Conall noticed, was turning red; well, he'd make it up to him later. Sooner, actually. "Much better once I see your overachieving ass headed out that door."

"You're a fucking sex maniac even for a Fae, you know that?"

That's more than enough out of you. Conall

whispered a word *as'Faein*, air to shape Air, and Cuinn choked as a gag formed from Air appeared in his mouth. "You have no idea what it feels like to touch your SoulShare." He spoke softly, tightly controlled, smiling slightly as Cuinn's lips moved in an unsuccessful attempt to channel away the gag. "And you might remember, before you piss me off again, that you might be a Loremaster, but I'm a freak of nature, and I can take you." He waited the space of one more of Cuinn's labored breaths before releasing the gag. Purely for emphasis.

"Far be it from me to come between a freak and his human." The Loremaster's cockiness appeared undiminished. Not that Conall had expected anything else. "Knock yourself out, Twinklebritches. Just try to spare a couple of minutes before tomorrow night for that little issue with the wards, hm?" He disappeared out the studio door, blowing Conall an elaborate kiss as he went.

Just to be sure, Conall waited until he heard the outer door close before turning back to Josh, his hand already going to the button of his jeans. Yes, he'd think about the pretty theoretical problem Cuinn had set him.

But not right now.

Chapter Twelve

You're almost too thorough, Meat. The male voice in Janek's head chuckled, a thick, gloating sound.

Janek ignored it and continued his inventory. Razor wire, check. A coil of it leaned against the oil drum he'd stolen from a construction site a few blocks over, along with a pile of wood to feed the fire flickering in it. He grabbed a few boards and tossed them into the drum. Not that he particularly gave a shit about the cold, in his condition, but he did need some light, and the fire got the business ends of the iron rods he'd stood up in the barrel tolerably hot. Not as hot as he'd like, but he could improvise. He was good at improvising.

You do realize, you have to leave him recognizable? The female voice dripped distaste.

"Shut the fuck up and let me do this my way." He looked over the set of knives in the bucket next to the battered but sturdy chair that was the only real furniture in the boarded-up storefront. No using Guaire's fancy super-sharp blade. That was too good for what he had in mind. The knives he had were as sharp as he could get them, but a few were rusty. *Boo fucking hoo*. The little fucker was going to have a lot more to worry about than tetanus, and not much time to spend worrying about anything. Though it was going to feel like forever to his guest. "He'll still work as bait, whether it's live bait or chum. And don't try to tell me you've suddenly lost your taste for blood. You're the one who wallows in it every time I kill someone, and you showed me what you threatened to do to Almstead. You're going to be watching and loving every minute."

Janek heard a distinct sniff. *He needs to remain alive. If we learn he has no mental link with his SoulShare, he will need to persuade the Fae to rescue him.*

"You've thought of everything, haven't you?" Janek tested the chair, one more time. Little shit didn't look that strong, but dancers could surprise you that way, and once he started playing in earnest, there was going to be a lot of jerking and thrashing happening in that chair. That was why he was going to use razor wire instead of rope, but it didn't pay to be careless. His brain might be mostly dead rotting mush, but this sort of thing still came easily to him. Maybe he got that from his passenger.

Just about. The male voice made Janek want to put his forehead through a wall, it was so full of good cheer and bullshit. *Right down to that phone in your pocket and the Fae's number.*

"Do me a fucking favor and don't do me any more fucking favors, all right?" The monster had made him haul ass all the way across D.C. to find someone to kill for the phone, and then he hadn't even been able to finish the kill because of the goddamned parking lot attendant showing up when he wasn't supposed to.

Then he'd tried using the phone to order the razor wire over the Internet. Fucking touchscreens. *There should be a Web site. WhyZombiesShouldntText.com.* "And you're forgetting how you got that phone number in the first place."

I suppose you want a parade, Meat?

Janek rolled his eye. He knew better than to expect gratitude, but just once it would have been nice to hear the monster recognize that he contributed something to this unholy partnership besides his mostly dead carcass. He'd been the one to wonder what the hell a Fae without magic was living on, after all. And when the bitch had reminded him that this *particular* Fae had had about two thousand years to make and save money, he'd been the one to remember the *Marfach*'s porn-star-mustache tool in New York was some kind of banker. Then he'd been the one to puke for two hours after the monster did its mojo shit with the piece of itself that was in Bryce Newhouse's gut to make the asshole look up Lochlann Doran and call the motherfucking cellphone with the phone number and ten minutes of bitching about the inconvenience. Ten minutes that the monster had made him listen to, because it thought the rant was funny. *Dickhead.*

I heard that. A jolt of hot, electric pain like gangrene shot down Janek's spine. And if any human being had ever actually managed to have gangrene in his spine, it would have to be the mostly late Janek O'Halloran. *Keep a civil tongue in your head. Although you can have the dancer's tongue, if you want, once he's made his call for help. You look like you could use a few spare parts.*

Carefully, Janek segregated the sweet mental image of one of his hot iron rods going repeatedly up the *Marfach*'s ass, in the corner of his mind that was his own. Yeah, he was rotting faster. The motherfucker was sucking what life he had left out of him rather than draw on its own charge of mojo, leaving him only enough to haul it around. "You'd love to watch me eat some brains, wouldn't you?"

It might be amusing. The bitch was back, sounding anything but amused. *Time for you to get back to your surveillance, Meat. We can worry about your menu later.*

Janek would have argued, but there was no point; the monster had taken over the driving, and herded him toward the door leading into the alley. The front door was still chained shut, boarded over, and undisturbed, but he'd kicked down the back door days ago. Now it was held shut from the inside by an improvised bar, and nothing secured it from the outside. That was all right, he'd be back soon. He yanked the door mostly closed behind him, slamming his fingers in it in the process and not really giving a damn. It had been a very long time since he gave a damn about anything that didn't involve making someone bleed.

Janek cursed as he walked down the dark and deserted street. The freezing rain from earlier had turned to snow like tiny pellets of ice. His balance had sucked to start with, and snow over ice coupled with feet he could barely feel and his usual no depth perception at all made the couple of blocks' walk back to the dancer's apartment a very special kind of hell.

If you take him tonight, make sure he's

unconscious before you try to bring him back. The male was sniggering, and his god-damned never-ending erection was chafing Janek's cock against the very cold zipper of his jeans. *I'd imagine he's delicious when he wriggles, but just the same, I'd hate to see you ending up on your ass*.

"Would you for fuck's sake quit playing with yourself?" It was a relief to sit down, on the crate in the alley opposite Luigi's, and turn his attention to the door leading to the apartment over it, and the darkened apartment window.

Quiet, Meat, someone might hear you.

"There's no one to—"

Janek's head was jerked around toward the far end of the block. A man made his way down the treacherous sidewalk, clutching the collar of his coat closed around his throat, dark hair slicked down by melted snow. He drew even with the doorway across the street and stopped, looking up at the window over the restaurant; shivered once, sharply, and let himself in.

We're just in time. For once, Janek wasn't sure if the voices were actually talking to him; he could hear echoes of three voices in his head at once. The male's sniggering and the female's gloating he could stand, but the sound of the monstrosity's laughter sent a stab of blinding pain from one temple to where the other temple used to be.

Patience, Meat. It's almost playtime.

Chapter Thirteen

Garrett woke from a fitful doze to the sound of feet pounding on the staircase outside. Rolling, he propped himself on an elbow and blinked owlishly at the clock on the stack of plastic crates beside the bed. 4:21 a.m. *Really?*

The pounding of feet was followed by the pounding of a fist on his door. "Garrett?"

Oh, shit. Garrett sat bolt upright in bed, staring into darkness at the wall opposite his bed, hands clenched into fists. *Nobody's home. Go the hell away.*

"Damn it, *grafain*, don't make me knock the door down. Because I will."

Somehow, Garrett had no doubt Lochlann would do exactly that. With a groan, he rolled out of bed, snatched up the boxers he'd shed before going to bed, stepped into them, and padded out into the living room, switching the light on as he went. *I am* not *meeting this man... Fae... whatever... naked in the middle of the night.* The wood of the entry hall was freezing on his bare feet; quickly he slid the chain free, opened the deadbolt, and turned and headed back toward the living room. "It's open," he called back over his shoulder.

He heard the door click open, and closed, but he ignored it, instead scooping an armful of shirts out of the armchair in the living room and tossing them on the floor to make a place from himself to sit. Turning on one heel, he dropped into the chair.

Mistake. The turning, anyway. Now he could see Lochlann, framed in the doorway leading from the little entry hall, black hair dripping with melting snow, coat hanging open to reveal a tight-fitting white tee that perfectly accented his six-pack and jeans that were wet through and clung like denim skin. And his eyes. Jesus, those eyes.

"No, I'm still not going to let you risk your life for me." Garrett meant the words to sound harsh, but they came out hoarse and unsteady. *Fuck, I might as well have said 'do me now.'*

Because that was what he wanted. That was the problem. He'd wanted it ever since he'd opened his eyes on the dance floor, with his head cradled in Lochlann's lap. He'd been fighting the idea there was a bond between them, not because he didn't want it to be true, but because he was afraid it *was* true. Because if it was true, if the bond was real, then it would be taken away from him, the same way every other hope of goodness he'd ever known had been.

The worst part was, he was right. It was true.

"I don't need your permission." Slowly, Lochlann stripped off his coat and let it fall to the floor, revealing the wife-beater, and the impossibly well-muscled arms, beneath it. "It's my life." He took one slow, deliberate step toward Garrett. "And my life isn't complete without you." Another step. "*Grafain.* Let me—"

"You do need my permission. Because you're not touching me without it." It was hard to breathe, and Garrett felt his pulse pounding, at throat and temples, the way it did every time he danced, right before he lost himself in the pounding beat and the movement. But he wasn't going to lose himself now. No fucking way. "And you're not getting it."

"I'm not asking."

"You—"

Lochlann was standing in front of him. Gripping his arm. Hauling him to his feet. Holding him. One hand around his arm, the other gripping his ass. Bending over him. Looming, even. Garrett felt the cold water dripping from the Fae's hair, rolling down his own cheeks like tears, like sweat. The heat radiating from the hard body against his.

"You want this." Lochlann's lips brushed his. "I know you do."

"Fuck, yes." Two or three days' worth of dark stubble shadowed Lochlann's cheeks. Garrett wanted to feel his own lips swollen and tender, burned by that darkness. Ached for it.

"Then why are you fighting me?"

A tight band around Garrett's chest made it hard for him to breathe. "Because if I don't fight you, if I let you do what you want to do to me, it could kill you." He closed his eyes; the drops sliding down his cheeks were hot, now, and all his own. "And if I have to choose between having you once and losing you, and never having you, but you walking away whole..." He shook his head, eyes still closed. "It's no choice at all."

Lips searched his cheeks, taking up his tears. "It's

too late, *grafain*. You already have me." Lochlann's grip slackened just enough to let him run his hands roughly over Garrett's arm, his thigh. His hands were cold—Jesus, how long had he been walking around in the sleet and the snow?—and yet, somehow, they burned. "The only question is, will you let me take you where you took me?" A flat hand slid into the small of his back, possessive. "Will you let me give you that?"

I shouldn't have opened my eyes. He couldn't escape that hot blue gaze, eyes wide and dark and God *damn* Garrett knew what need looked like, and it was looking at him through those gemlike eyes. *I can't tell him no.*

"No."

He took advantage of Lochlann's moment of shock and pushed, hard. *Nobody dies for me, damn it. Especially not you.* He twisted away with a soul-deep groan.

And gasped, as he was drawn back in, as eyes blazed into his own. As whatever choice he thought he had vanished in a punishing kiss.

The hand on Garrett's back slid down, into his boxers, gripping, grinding him against the taller man's thighs. Pinned between their bodies, his cock stirred, rose; his hips swayed, and he moaned into the kiss as the ring below the head was pressed deep into hardened flesh. Lochlann's tongue swept his mouth, fought to possess it. But Garrett was every bit as insistent. His need already betrayed him, along with his hope; it was time for his body to follow suit.

Lochlann kissed a hot trail back to Garrett's ear, his unshaven cheek rasping roughly against Garrett's softer blond stubble. His tongue probed, tested, tasted, played until Garrett's cock ached and wept. Johns never kissed, never teased, never played, and he was starved for what Lochlann was so determined to give him.

"You're ready, aren't you?" Lochlann's whisper went straight into the depths of his ear. "I can tell. My senses are keener than yours." The Fae inhaled through his nose, long and slow, and let the breath out again on a shuddering sigh. "Damn. You smell incredible. I suppose I'll have to settle for filling myself with you that way first. Just your scent." His tongue teased Garrett's earlobe into his mouth; his teeth toyed briefly with the stud there before he suckled.

"First?"

Lochlann pulled back, at this, just enough to look Garrett in the eyes. And his smile, Garrett had never seen a curve of lips so full of wicked promises in his life. "I can think of so many ways I want to be full of you, *grafain*. After the first time."

The hand that cupped Garrett's ass slid over his hard flank and curled around his rigid shaft, and Lochlann murmured approvingly as Garrett's back arched. "That's it, lover. Let go. Let me do this for you." A hot mouth traveled down Garrett's throat, pausing for gentle bites; Lochlann's hand slid up and down Garrett's cock, his thumb tweaking the stainless steel ring in his Prince Albert on each insistent upstroke.

"Oh, fuck." The fervency of Garrett's moan made it sound almost like a prayer. He couldn't help it, his hips bucked hard into Lochlann's grip, and when he was rewarded with a tighter grasp, a gentle wringing, his knees damn near buckled.

"Maybe you should sit down." Soft laughter

sounded in his ear, and then Lochlann guided him back to the armchair, following him down to kneel between his spread thighs, keeping firm hold of his cock all the while, easing the loose boxers down to let it stand up proudly.

Garrett clutched at the arms of the chair, his knuckles going white as he looked down his body, over his hard and heaving abs to the incredible sight of Lochlann eyeing his weeping erection with a lover's rapt intensity. The Fae leaned forward, tongued the ring on the underside of Garrett's cock into his mouth, tugged it with his teeth.

"Shit—no, Lochlann, don't." He struggled to sit up, caught the dark-stubbled chin in the palm of his hand, and groaned as he moved the soft lips and questing tongue away from his piercing. "If you're wrong, if this doesn't finish the bond..."

Lochlann nodded. "It will. But I can wait. Whatever makes it good for you." One hand continued to play up and down Garrett's length, pale against brick-red flesh traced with dark veins. The other disappeared from view, but Garrett was left with only a moment to wonder where it went before two fingers probed his entrance and he started to swear again.

The fingers slipped deeper, then paused; the hand that stroked his cock stilled, gripping him gently.

"Is something wrong?" Garrett bit his lip.

And then Lochlann laughed. It was like no laughter Garrett had ever heard, possibly the least human sound he could imagine, and the most beautiful. "Can't you feel it, *grafain*? I can feel it, in you."

Garrett started to shake his head. But then a

shiver ran down his spine, and he caught his breath. Another. And yet another. Pure joy. He could actually feel it, something physical, tangible, spreading through him, running along every nerve, riding every breath. It didn't lessen his arousal; it made it sweeter, in fact. The pleasure Lochlann was giving him had already been more intense than any he could remember. It still was, the Fae was working him in earnest now, and his hips were responding with tight little jerks and a familiar heaviness in his sac signaled that he wasn't going to be able to hold off much longer. But the new sensation made it all so much more.

It was happiness. It was arousal. It was need. It was hope. "Lochlann?"

No more than a whisper, but the Fae heard; he half-rose from where he knelt and worked an arm around behind Garrett's back, holding him close. "I'm here."

"Why was I so stupid? Why did I fight this my whole life?" He groaned under the sweet torture of Lochlann's thumb, playing with his piercing.

"Maybe so I could be the one to give it to you." Lochlann kissed him. "I'm sorry you had to wait so long."

"It's worth the wait. All of it." Garrett laughed breathlessly, a sound that caught on a groan, as Lochlann grasped him more tightly, ran his thumb over the head of his cock, spread hot fluid over the smooth hard flesh. "*Lochlann...*"

"I'm here, *grafain.*"

Garrett stared into the faceted aquamarine of Lochlann's eyes, entranced, even as his body tensed and trembled, his pleasure about to crest.

122

Lochlann kissed him once more, long and slow, delicious contrast to the short frantic pumping of hips and hand, and then broke away just far enough to murmur against his lips. "No matter what happens to me, your laughter was worth it."

No matter what happens to—

Garrett slammed up against Lochlann's body, twisting, arching, his cock pulsing in the Fae's relentless grip. Thick white ropes shot from him, one after another streaking his abs and trickling down to slick Lochlann's hand. He had no breath to cry out with, so it was easy to hear the wet intimate sounds of that hand sliding up and down his length, and Lochlann's choked moans into his shoulder.

He couldn't hear the joy. But it was there. It was everything.

Finally, Garrett opened eyes he'd forgotten he closed, and tried to remember how to breathe again. He blinked, trying to get Lochlann's hair out of his eyes. "Shit." He laughed softly. "Is that what it felt like for you, back at the club?"

The tense trembling of the body in his arms was the only answer he received.

"*Lochlann—*" From paradise to panic in five seconds flat. No answer.

Chapter Fourteen

Fae are made of magick.

Lochlann stared at Garrett's bare shoulder, onto which he'd fallen forward, overcome, at Garrett's choked pleasure-cry, and wished that Cuinn would shut the fuck up. Of all the voices he didn't want to be hearing in his head right now, Cuinn's headed the list. In fact, it was the only one *on* the list.

On the other hand, if he was able to remember his former friend's last lecture before the great battle of the Sundering, it meant he probably wasn't dead. Unless he was in hell. Listening to Cuinn drone on about the way the world was going to be different after the Fae and human realms were walled off from each other fit most of the descriptions of hell he'd ever read. But hell was for humans, so chances were he was alive.

But he couldn't move. Not a muscle, not to save his life. Which was pretty fucking awkward, considering his arousal was exquisitely painful. The tingle he'd felt when he and Garrett had started their bonding was back, too, and building quickly in intensity, in a way that would probably have made him hold his breath in anticipation, if he were breathing.

Here in the world we know, we channel magick from the world itself, through ourselves. Out there, you'll channel your own magick.

Would you for fuck's sake tell me something useful? Lochlann tried to close his eyes, couldn't, and started to think about panicking. *No, bad idea. Think about something else.*

Completing the SoulShare bond hadn't killed him. That was a positive. And it hadn't aged him. Some of his hair fell over his eyes, and it was still the same coarse black; out of the corner of one eye, he could see his hand, where he'd wrapped his arm behind Garrett's neck to brace them both, and the skin was still smooth, the fingers graceful. But he knew what it felt like to have magick stirring inside him. It didn't matter that it had been six centuries since he'd last felt it, he knew its touch. He wasn't feeling it now, only that strange prickling.

We aren't solid magick, of course. His inner Cuinn was laughing, and totally ignoring his attempts to distract himself. *But the magick is what keeps the physical part alive.*

That much, he knew now, was bullshit. If it had been true, he would have died six hundred years ago. Or, alternative theory, he would have died a couple of minutes ago, when the channeling that had given him his immortality collapsed. So there was more to what kept a Fae alive than magick.

The difference between the generalization and the truth might just be a matter of semantics, though. Because it was true, without magick, he was empty. Hollow. He'd known that for a very long time. Garrett eased the emptiness, but there was some space within him that could be filled by nothing but the flow, the presence, of the magickal force he'd known since he came into his birthright of power.

Garrett. Oh, shit. Lochlann strained again to move, even enough to turn his head. Just to whisper, to tell his *scair-anam* that he was alive. He couldn't. And he couldn't snarl with frustration because he couldn't.

But Garrett wasn't moving either. Not at all. He should be able to feel his SoulShare's heartbeat, as he lay atop the human's bare and sweat-slicked chest. His empathy should at least be letting him sense what Garrett was feeling. But there was nothing.

Find the other half of your soul, and love will do the rest. Or it should. Cuinn's remembered voice in his head sounded mocking. Maybe it always had been. But, then, the Loremaster never said his task in the human world was going to be easy. Or even possible. Or that Lochlann would be able to keep his SoulShare, once he found him.

He searched, frantically, for Garrett's aura. The shifting colors had always faded to nothing when Lochlann chose not to see them, but he'd been able to see them on his SoulShare when he wished, the moment he thought to look for them.

What the ever-loving fuck? Yes, Garrett's aura was there. But instead of the shifting patterns that were the hallmark of a living awareness, what little he could see of his human was limned with a frozen, feathery tracing, like frost the exact color of mind-blowing orgasmic bliss. Lochlann was half afraid he would break it, if he could brush against it.

And with an abrupt lurch that left his stomach protesting, he was seeing right through Garrett, with

126

his magickal sense. A sense that had been as dead as his magick, until now. He saw through Garrett, and the chair, and the floor; through everything, in fact, until he saw a line, almost too bright in magickal light to look at directly, probably below the ground. A blue-white line of fire.

What was it Tiernan had said? *...there's a river of the raw stuff of magick flowing right under the floor of this room and sending up eddies that even a Noble like me can see.*

Lochlann watched, fascinated, as a curl of light wound slowly upward from the river of fire. Turning, spiraling. Like a falling leaf in its unpredictable path, only the brilliance was rising.

It took him a few moments to realize that the light was reaching for him.

Oh, fuck. He knew what had happened to him, now. What was happening. The act of *scair'ain'e* was complete, the SoulShare bond was formed, and his sense of time had stopped. Not time itself, but his perception of it, to let him try to brace himself. Because it was coming, like a rising tide. A tsunami. Two acts of love had opened floodgates closed for six hundred years, and the magick of the lines was coming to reclaim him.

He waited, watching, yearning, terrified. Closer.

Garrett, grafain, *don't let go. Don't let me go.*

Something grazed his ankle, mindless power barely leashed, setting him trembling. It was like a great beast on the hunt, nosing at him, as if undecided about this strange morsel.

Garrett stirred under him, softly laughing; wonder and contentment washed over him, bathed him. Warm fluid trickled over his hand, which still encircled his human's semi-erect cock. "Shit. Is that what it felt like for you, back at the club?"

Before Lochlann could reply, or even move, a coil wrapped around his ankle, burning cold. The chill shot through his body. He was light, magickal light, barely contained by skin.

And then he was darkness.

Chapter Fifteen

"Lochlann!" Garrett shook the unconscious man in his arms, his heart hammering. "God *damn* it, Lochlann!"

Lochlann responded to being shaken by starting to slide out of Garrett's arms, toward the floor. Garrett cursed and held on tighter; no fucking way was he going to let Lochlann sprawl out over the floor. Holding on that way, he could feel the Fae shaking, and in a bizarre way that was a relief. Dead people didn't shake. And he could feel a pulse at his throat. Thank God. Hopefully that was a pulse, and not just his hand trembling.

What the *fuck* was going on? Lochlann had been afraid he would age, and die, after the two of them bonded. At least *that* hadn't happened. Garrett's own fears had run more to passing on his viral curse, but even if that *had* happened, it wouldn't have caused this. Whatever this was.

Garrett's teeth clenched so hard he thought he felt one of them crack. He buried his face in Lochlann's hair and breathed deep, trying to let the soft touch calm him, clear his head.

Somewhere in the little apartment, a cell phone went off. Not Garrett's, though the ringtone was a song he vaguely remembered from the emo side of the Purgatory playlist. *Shit!* It wasn't coming from anywhere on Lochlann, either, from what he could tell.

I was ready to dive, ready to go deep
Sense of wonder
You freed me to wonder
Wonder what's waiting...

Garrett eased himself out from under Lochlann's inert form and looked around frantically. The Fae's coat was where he'd let it fall to the floor, and Garrett dove for it, feeling for pockets. If someone knew Lochlann well enough to be calling him, maybe he knew him well enough to be able to help. Which was the closest thing Garrett had to a plan.

But one stolen kiss and you threw me away
Dragging me under
Current's dragging me under—

Garrett's fingers closed around the small rectangle of Lochlann's phone, pulled it out of an inner pocket of the coat, slid the toggle. "What?"

There was a long silence, so long that Garrett began to wonder if there was anyone on the other end. *Hell of a time to be ass-dialed.* Then he heard a deep, hoarse breath being drawn. "Lochlann Doran?" The voice was heavy, thick, almost a monotone, and Garrett was instantly wary.

"He's indisposed. Can I take a message?" Garrett hoped he didn't sound as desperate as he felt. "Or are you a friend of his?"

This pause was even longer, and Garrett wasn't sure, but he thought he heard the speaker talking to someone else in the background. "No. Not a friend. No message." The phone went dead in his hand.

Snarling, Garrett put the phone back in the coat pocket he'd taken it from, and turned back to Lochlann, who was starting to slowly slide out of the chair he'd been left in. *Damn.* He lunged, awkwardly, and caught the Fae, easing him down to lie on the floor.

At least now he could see Lochlann was breathing. That calmed him down a little. Lochlann's eyes were closed, and if it weren't for the shaking, and the occasional twitch, he'd almost look asleep. Asleep would be good. Except that nothing seemed to be waking him up.

I've never felt so goddamned helpless in my life. Garrett sat back on his heels and gathered Lochlann up as best he could, cradling the taller man in his lap. The way Lochlann had held him, that first night at Purgatory. *If I hadn't let him in, if I'd been stronger...*

"No, God damn it. *No.*" The sound of his own voice, overloud in the still apartment, startled him. But he squared his shoulders, took a deep breath, and drew Lochlann closer. I *don't know why this is happening, but it isn't fucking karma smacking me down for taking a stupid chance. And it isn't punishment for daring to hope that someone this smoking hot might want me.* His fingers combed through Lochlann's dark, unruly hair. *This is my... what did he call it?* Scairanam. *My SoulShare. Not my punishment.*

The floor shook under him. A heavy tread was coming up the stairs. The stairs that led only to Garrett's apartment. *What the hairy fuck?*

Garrett curled protectively around Lochlann's upper body as the door to his apartment crashed in and slammed into the wall. A figure loomed in the doorway, nearly filling it. At least six foot six, a filthy gray hoodie pulled up over his face, torn and stained jeans that were probably blue once, shitkickers with inch-thick soles. And a smell that would, as his late Grandpa Earl would have put it, knock a buzzard off a shit-wagon.

The figure laughed, a sound that made Garrett want to hurl. "Indisposed, is he?" It was the voice from the phone. "Looks like an O.D. to me."

Then he pulled back the hood, and all Garrett could do was stare. He recognized that face. Well, no, not really. He recognized the ink on half of the shaved head over part of the face. The faded gray and dull red patterns were all that told him that the man in front of him was the homophobic former bouncer from Purgatory. Fabian had hired him because of his size, and kept him because he considered it useful for a gay club to have a bouncer who didn't mind smashing a faggot's face in, should the need to do so arise. The guy had always made Garrett's skin crawl. And that had been when he looked kind of human.

Those days were over. Most of the right side of the hulk's head was gone, replaced with something that looked like glass glowing a sick shade of red, except where there was a hole bored all the way through. His one remaining eye was totally bloodshot, and in fact it was actually bleeding, brownish streaks running down his face like tears. His rictus smile revealed rotting gums and teeth that looked like badly-kept-up gravestones.

All of which made a bizarre kind of sense, since everyone at Purgatory knew the guy was dead. *Not dead enough. Not nearly dead enough.*

Garrett was suddenly acutely aware of the man trembling in his arms. Getting away from this thing wasn't an option. Even if he himself could get around the lumbering nightmare—which actually looked possible, the guy didn't look like he could move all that fast—no way was he leaving Lochlann behind. His arms tightened around the Fae. "You're not taking him."

To Garrett's surprise, his voice didn't break, or even tremble. The words came out low, controlled, and edgy. He didn't feel like a mouse staring up at a lion. He felt dangerous. Shit, let this motherfucker lay a hand on Lochlann, and he would *be* dangerous. *So this is what love does to you.*

"Why am I not taking him?"

The question, in that thick, clotted voice, threw Garrett, until he realized the thing wasn't talking to him. Wasn't even looking at him, at the moment. And the glass or crystal or whatever it was in the hulk's head was bending light in a way that made Garrett wonder if *his* eyes were bleeding.

"You've been jones'ing for a Fae from the start. Here's one right in front of you." The thing—the name 'Janek' popped into Garrett's head from somewhere, probably overheard at the club—sounded confused, maybe even angry, though in that near-monotone, it was hard to tell.

Dead, rotting, and completely bugfuck crazy. Garrett glanced down at Lochlann. *God damn it, wake up, will you?*

When Garrett looked back up, Janek was apparently done with whatever freakish internal conversation he was having. The death's-head grin was back, and the former bouncer, former human

133

being, was laughing silently. "You're so fucking precious." Garrett could feel the floor shake with each step as Janek closed the distance between them. "You'd better hope this asshole thinks you are, too, or you're going to die tonight. And I'm going to be the only one who enjoys it."

The behemoth moved faster than Garrett expected. Before he could react, Janek was on him, grabbing him by the throat and hauling him to his feet. Lochlann slid off Garrett's lap to sprawl on the floor as Garrett clawed at the hand around his throat. No good. He could feel his bare toes just barely brushing the floor as Janek held him; his pulse was like thunder in his ears, and the more he struggled, the more his lungs burned with the need to breathe.

Janek's laughter wasn't silent any more. "Fuck, it's like drowning a kitten. Except you squeak better, Princess."

If he takes me away from here, Lochlann will be safe when he wakes up. It was an unbelievably slender hope, but it was the only one he had.

I picked a hell of a time to start hoping, was his last thought before something came down hard on his head and blackness closed over him like a sack.

***

He was cold. And hot. And he couldn't move.

Warily, Garrett opened his eyes, the barest slit possible. He was looking down his own body, which was still wearing nothing but the boxers he'd had on when he answered Lochlann's pounding on his door. Something was wound around his legs, and his arms

134

were bound together behind his back from wrists to elbows, wrenching his shoulders. There was light, but it flickered. Firelight, probably. He could sense something hot off to his right, but whatever it was, it was only warming what was right next to it, which was his side. Which had the tight stretched feeling of a really bad sunburn. Or just a burn.

This is not fucking happening. He closed his eyes again and tried to slow his breathing, to look as unconscious as he'd been moments before. Closing his eyes, though, only made it easier for him to remember his last sight of Lochlann before Janek had knocked him cold. Lying on the floor where he'd fallen, curled on his side, trembling. *If he's been hurt, I am going to finish that bastard. I don't care what it takes.*

"Good morning, Sleeping Beauty."

The hoarse, flat voice made Garrett start. And then he cried out, as knives sliced into his thighs and calves and forearms and hot trickles started to crawl over his flesh. Looking down, he could see a knot of small blades embedded in his right thigh, shining red in the firelight, and another knot over his left knee that was for now lying flat against his skin. *Jesus fucking Christ, razor wire!*

Laughter snapped his attention to the shadows at the edge of the firelight; Janek was standing back from the fire, not much more of him visible in the unsteady light than the glowing red glass of his head and his rotted smile. With his head turned that way, Garrett could see things that seemed to be fireplace pokers stuck into what turned out to be a metal barrel with a fire built in it, and a bucket on the floor beside it full of, apparently, butcher knives.

It was a measure of how truly loathsome Janek looked that Garrett felt calmer when studying the torture implements.

Torture. Four days ago, the only thing in his life that made no sense was a stratospheric viral load. Now, he had a lover, a soul-mate, who wasn't human, and a putrefying homophobe with a glass head who had spirited him off somewhere to play pain games.

"Is this where I'm supposed to start whimpering and begging for my life?" Attitude had gotten him through beat-downs and stompings too numerous to count. Why give up on a winning formula? "I'd hate to miss my cue."

"You can save the crying for when we call your Fae fuck-buddy." The snarl did not improve Janek's appearance. "I owe him. Watching that magick surge damn near cost me my eye."

"No idea what you're talking about."

"Doesn't matter." Janek stepped out of the gloom, revealed in all his decaying glory as he reached for one of the iron rods sticking out of the barrel. The flesh of his hand sizzled as he pulled one free, but he didn't seem to notice or care. "I'll enjoy this whether you get it or not. Maybe more if you don't."

The hot iron tip moved closer to Garrett's face, and despite himself he flinched away. He nearly bit through his lip to keep from crying out again as the razors sunk deeper into the skin and muscle of his arms and legs.

Then, abruptly, Janek plunged the iron back into the barrel. "No, Meat."

What the ever-living fuck?

For an instant, Janek's face was contorted with

fury; then it smoothed, and when the former bouncer spoke to him again, his voice had an eerie, almost feminine quality. "The human wishes to be melodramatic, and welcome you to hell. I prefer not to waste time on politeness."

The voice cut deeper than the razors, and Garrett shuddered.

Janek laughed, softly, as he bent and withdrew a rusty butcher knife from the bucket.

"I also prefer blood to fire."

Chapter Sixteen

Lochlann moaned without sound. How long had this been going on? No way to know; his time sense was as numb as every other sense he possessed, hammered flat by the torrent trying to force its way into his body. Part of him was caught up in a raging river of magickal power. Part of him *was* the river, pure energy, trembling with the force of the surge. And part of him was exhausted and battered and so fucking sick of trying to hold on to any sense of who and what he was, he was nearly ready to just let go and let the river carry him wherever the hell it wanted.

Nearly ready. But Garrett needed him. Needed healing. Needed to be rid of the virus that cast such an ugly pall over what should be a vibrant and healthy and passionate aura. And for that, Lochlann needed his magick back. So he held on, struggling to breathe.

Shit. Is this what it feels like when I heal someone?

It couldn't be like this for another Fae. The magick hammering at him wasn't living, it had no sense of what a Fae's body could bear. It was pure mindless force, needing a Fae to shape it, to channel it. That was his function, as a healer of the Demesne of

Water. He poured living magick into the body that required healing, and shaped that magick into a healed form, whether Fae or human. Living magick, not this raw energy. And no one he had ever healed had mentioned anything like this assault.

Which was lucky, because a cure like this would probably kill Garrett.

The feeling of helplessness was almost worse than the battering. He couldn't move, except to shake, couldn't so much as open his eyes. He'd only gotten a glimpse of his *scair-anam*'s face, after the time-stop ended and before the ley energy hammered him literally senseless, and the shock and the fear he'd seen there had magnified his sense of powerlessness almost more than he could bear. Not even enough time to show Garrett a sign of life, let alone reassure him.

And he was blind. Trapped in a body with closed eyes, and his inner sight was no good either, since he couldn't see the energy, or see by it. He'd lost the sense that let him see by magickal light at the first touch of the power, his virtual retinas fried by a glare as brilliant as the sun. If there had been anyone who could see by that sense within a couple of city blocks when that first contact had been made, that unfortunate Fae was probably several degrees beyond stone blind.

Hold on to me, Garrett. More than anything, he wanted to be able to wrap his arms around Garrett's neck, let his SoulShare anchor him against the torrent. But he could hold on to nothing, and no one. *Don't let go...*

Then, in the space between one thought and the next, the energy released him. He could feel the floor under his back, or he thought he could. He could sense light through his closed eyelids. And he could smell—

Holy fuck. Lochlann opened his eyes, gagging even before he could see. The stench of rotting meat in Garrett's apartment was unbearable. *"Grafain?"* Nothing came out; he coughed, cleared his throat, tried again. "Garrett?"

There was no answer, and he struggled up onto his elbows.

What the hell? Garrett's chair was overturned, and Lochlann's acute senses picked up the scent of blood in the air. He scrambled to his feet and stood swaying, dizzy, his heartbeat roaring in his ears. *"Garrett!"*

No answer, only the odor of putrefaction and the blood scent. Lochlann staggered, leaned against the wall, and stared in horror at the front door, wide open with a crack running down the middle of it, the jamb splintered.

Something has him. There wasn't a chance in hell it was a some*one*, not with the stench left behind. Without a thought, he bent and snatched up his coat and raced through the open door and down the stairs, settling the heavy coat over his shoulders as he ran. The street outside was dark, deserted; the sleet and snow had given way to a cold rain, and the thin coating of ice and snow that had been on the street was gone.

"Magarl lobadh!" Lochlann snarled as he ducked back into the entry hall and let the door to the street swing closed again. An apt curse, because no doubt the testicles of whatever had Garrett were as rotten as the rest of it. *What the hell do I do now?* The only place he could imagine going for help was Purgatory, mostly because that was the only place other than his hotel

140

where he knew anyone at all, and as much as it would grate on him to ask for Tiernan's help, his pride didn't matter a damn next to Garrett's safety.

But was Purgatory open? He knew that it had been around 4:30 in the morning when he had finally given up on wandering the streets of D.C. in the abysmal weather and headed for Garrett's apartment, but he didn't wear a watch and hadn't thought to look for a clock upstairs. It had been long enough for the snow and ice on the walk to melt, anyway. And by the time he could find a cab...

No. Wait.

Lochlann leaned against the wall and closed his eyes. Being without magick had left him dependent on human conveyances, despite his terror of them, for over six hundred years. Time to break that dependency. Taking a deep breath, he reached within himself, to that place that had been so empty for so long.

He would have wept as the magick sprang to exuberant life under his touch, but there was no time for that. He conjured his memory of Tiernan's inner sanctum, the tiny office behind Purgatory's cock pit; with one last despairing look up the stairs—as if Garrett might somehow, against all hope, materialize there—he Faded and vanished.

***

Lochlann took form in near-total darkness. The only light came from the computer monitors, the telltales and the exit and emergency lights that showed on the screens. This was enough light for the Fae, but just barely, his senses were still numb from the battering they'd taken. The darkness still drew a curse from him, though, since it meant that whatever time it was, Tiernan had gone home for the night.

What the fuck do I do now? There was a phone on the desk, but a quick check told him it had no speed dial programmed, so he was shit-out-of-luck there. Opening the office door, he looked out into the darkened club, not sure what he was hoping for. But there was nothing and no one out there.

One of Lochlann's hands plowed through his hair as he tried to focus; the other, fisted, beat a frustrated rhythm on the doorframe. *I do not have time to waste on this shit.* None of the channeling a Water Fae could do would be of any help at all in finding a missing human. Now, if he had a Loremaster's gifts…

Jaw muscles rippled as he clenched his teeth. Call Cuinn? Even if he knew how—which he didn't—

"What the particular fuck are you doing in here?"

Lochlann spun to see an obviously pissed-off Tiernan, wearing only jeans, and those unfastened and not quite hiding a raging erection. The other Fae was also straightening from what had apparently started out as a kick-ass knife-fighter's crouch, and was wielding the kick-ass knife to go along with it. And even with his aural sense and his empathy nearly burned out in the aftermath of his recent magickal overload, he was half blinded by Tiernan's frustrated lust.

"I didn't know where else to go." He raised his hands, palms open and empty in the ancient gesture that said *I come unarmed*, hoping it hadn't come to mean something else in the last couple of thousand years. "Garrett's been kidnapped."

"Holy shit." Tiernan straightened, pissed-off

slowly giving way to oh-fuck. "Have you two finished bonding?"

"Hello? Locked office, locked club, middle of the fucking night, if I couldn't Fade I wouldn't be here. Hence, SoulShared."

"You have a point. I did think it was strange when my ward told me my office door was being opened from the inside."

"I should have guessed you'd have the place warded." Lochlann shaded his eyes as Tiernan brought up the lights. "I don't suppose you know how to channel a Finding?"

Tiernan shook his head, and Lochlann suddenly realized how disheveled the other Fae's long blond hair was. And how open his jeans were, and what scents he was carrying with him. His intrusion had apparently come at an incredibly awkward moment. Not that he cared.

"A Finding? Not in the slightest. I'm Demesne of Earth, remember? And Noble into the bargain, which means I really can't do shit with pure magick, other than party tricks."

"Well, that worked the way they planned it, at least." Tiernan's raised brow earned him one of Lochlann's, right back. "When the Loremasters created Royals and Nobles and commoners, they hoped you elemental types would breed true and stop using up the pure magick everyone else needed."

"The Loremasters *created*..." Tiernan's voice trailed off as his jaw set. "I thought humans were the only ones who did the eugenics bullshit."

"Take it up with Cuinn. The bastard was in on it."

"I keep forgetting how old you two are." Tiernan

shook his head, looked at the knife in his hand like he'd completely forgotten about its existence, and set it on the edge of his desk. "And that's a good idea." Pulling the leather chair out from behind the desk, he sank into it and reached for the phone.

"Fuck, no, I don't want you to—" Lochlann cut himself off, even before the other Fae gave him a warning glare and started to enter a number. No, he didn't want Cuinn there. The duplicitous son of a bitch was the last person in two worlds he wanted to see. But the duplicitous son of a bitch might also be the only one who could help him find Garrett.

Anything. I'll do anything. Even be civil to a Fae I'd rather see dead.

"Cuinn? It's Tiernan." Tiernan grimaced, as if he were being interrupted. "I don't care what you're—" Another grimace. "I don't care who you're—" He slammed his open hand onto the desk. "I don't care how *many* you're doing, damn it, you need to get your ass into my office and make it useful." He listened a few moments more, with an air only slightly less irritated, then nodded and hung up the phone. "He'll be along." This to Lochlann, with a deep breath and a 'what-can-you-do?' shrug.

"He'd better fucking hurry."

If the clocks in the corners of the surveillance monitors hadn't been blinking off the seconds, Lochlann would have been willing to swear that the ley energy had stopped time again. Until, finally, the air in one corner of the room wavered, went translucent and then opaque, and became Cuinn, in a pair of black silk boxers and a smirk aimed at Tiernan. "Fear not, fair maiden, I'll save you!"

Lochlann growled, and at the sound the sandy-haired Fae paled.

"Oh, fuck me," Cuinn groaned.

"Not even if I didn't have to take a number."

Tiernan delicately slid his knife away from the edge of the desk, where it rested near Lochlann's hand, and made it disappear. "If I'm the one reminding everyone to focus, things are very bad. Don't make me do it."

Lochlann took a long, slow, deep breath, and made himself look at Cuinn. *Get it over with, damn it.* "I'm the one who needs help." He gritted the words out through clenched teeth. "Garrett and I finished the SoulShare. And he's been taken."

"Taken? As in scorching-hot-Irish-leading-man-I-would-do-in-a-heartbeat taken?"

Lochlann's lips curled back from his teeth in a snarl, and he started for the Loremaster, gathering magick as he went; he hadn't gone more than a step, though, when Tiernan's knife flashed through the air in front of his nose and stuck quivering in the nearby wall.

Lochlann and Cuinn both turned to Tiernan, who hadn't risen from his chair. "I fucking meant it," the blond Fae said simply.

Lochlann opened his mouth, realized he had no idea what he was going to say, and shut it again.

His phone went off.

"What the hell?" He fumbled in his coat pocket, toggled the phone on. "What?"

"Lochlann? Is that you?" The voice was low, and thick, yet somehow Lochlann got the impression that the speaker was a woman. And in the background, there were sounds. Moans. Gasps for breath. Barely recognizable.

But recognized. Lochlann set the phone on Tiernan's desk and switched it to speaker. Motioning the other Fae to silence, he clenched his shaking hands into fists and took a deep breath. "You know it is." No point to 'If you hurt him...' It was obviously too late for that. "Whoever or whatever you are, you are dead."

The voice on the other end of the phone laughed, a sound that reminded Lochlann of blood flowing out of a wound. "Not exactly. But your pretty toy will be, unless you come to me. Alone."

Cuinn stepped forward and held his hand out, palm down and open, over the phone. Lochlann's battered senses barely detected a trickle of magickal energy leaving the Loremaster's hand and entering the phone. With his other hand, Cuinn motioned for Lochlann to keep talking; Tiernan, for his part, looked on with a faint, thoughtful frown.

"If you want me that badly, why didn't you just take me instead of him? It's not like I could have stopped you." Lochlann wasn't sure how he managed to keep his voice so even. Hell, he wasn't sure how he managed to speak at all.

"I have my reasons. And you will learn them soon." Again the hideous laughter. "Here, Fae, greet your pet."

The cold that gripped Lochlann's heart turned it to ice at the sound of Garrett's faint moan. "I'm coming for you, *grafain*."

"...you don't listen..." Garrett's voice was barely audible, and his breath whistled, as if something had struck him in the throat. "...told you to stay the fuck away."

"Don't bother, *m'anam*. It knows what I am, it

146

knows what we are. It knows I'm coming for you. And it knows I'm going to kill it."

"Save your breath, Fae." Shit, it was the creature's voice again. "And come alone. If you don't, I promise you, the little *fracun* will be dead before you lay eyes on him."

Cuinn swore loudly as the connection was cut off. "Motherfucking son of a *bitch*, I needed ten more seconds."

"Was that a Finding?"

Lochlann was barely aware of Tiernan's question; he was too busy wondering how Garrett's captor had known the word *as'Faein* for *whore*. And contemplating what he was going to do when he found the two of them.

"Yeah, I picked up on the phone on the other end of the call. And I have its location narrowed down to an area maybe a couple of blocks on a side. Can you call up a city map on either of these?" Cuinn gestured at the monitors.

Tiernan shook his head. "Those are dedicated to the security system. Here." Reaching into a drawer, he pulled out a tablet computer, and the screen came alight at his touch. "I don't have the fucking patience for a keyboard," he muttered as his fingers danced over the little screen.

Lochlann didn't really see the city map that sprang up. He was seeing tears sliding down Garrett's cheeks, hearing his soft voice. "*...if I have to choose between having you once and losing you, and never having you, but you walking away whole...*"

It's not going to have you, grafain. *I refuse to lose you.* There was no Fae equivalent of the Hippocratic

147

Oath, with its human healers' promise to 'do no harm,' and not only because Fae had no gods to swear by. *It will feel every wound it's given you, a hundred times over, before it dies.*

"There." Cuinn straightened, letting Lochlann see the marks he'd made on the map, tracing around an area two long city blocks or three short ones on a side. "They're somewhere in there. That's the best I can do."

Lochlann snarled as he read the street names. One edge of the demarcated area was only a few blocks from Garrett's apartment. *So close. Shit.* "I'll find them."

Before he could start to Fade, Cuinn grabbed his arm. "Don't go alone. We have no idea what you're walking into."

Lochlann glared at Cuinn's hand until Cuinn loosened his grip. "Who's going to come with me? You?" All the considerable scorn of which a Fae was capable rode that one word. "Even if your masters would let you off the leash long enough, what you call help is the last thing Garrett needs."

Cuinn blanched, but when he answered, his voice was steady. "Then let Tiernan. You've seen what he can do with a knife."

The blond Fae didn't look happy about being volunteered, but he nodded. "I probably can't do much damage magickally, not away from the ley lines. But I'll fight for your *scair-anam*."

Lochlann considered the Noble's offer, but slowly shook his head. "No. I believe what it said. If I don't come alone, Garrett's dead. And even I can't heal death." He yanked his arm out of Cuinn's grasp.

"I'm leaving. And if either of you tries to follow me, and Garrett dies because of it, you'll be apologizing to him yourself. Assuming humans and Fae share an afterlife."

Cuinn grimaced. Then his nose wrinkled; he leaned forward and sniffed at Lochlann's coat, and then at the hand he'd been using to hold on to him. "Why do you smell like rotten meat?"

Tiernan looked startled, for some reason. "I don't smell anything."

"That's because you're over there, and we're over here—"

Lochlann stepped back from Cuinn. "Garrett's apartment reeked of it, when I woke up and found him gone." He closed his eyes and visualized the ground floor entry hall in Garrett's apartment building; too far away from the area on the map, but out of sight, and the only place he knew well enough to Fade to. Touching the magick within him, he started to lose form.

The last words he heard before he vanished came from Tiernan. Words to strike terror into the heart of any Fae, but especially the heart of a Fae who had witnessed the devastation of the Sundering.

"Shit, it's the *Marfach!*"

Chapter Seventeen

"Tell me that was just for dramatic effect." Cuinn's gaze snapped around, from where Lochlann had just vanished to where Tiernan had half-risen from the chair behind his desk.

"There's only one drama queen in this room, and it isn't me." For all the wise-ass that always seemed to roll off Tiernan in waves, the Noble was pale. "I thought I recognized its voice, Kevin and I have heard it more than you or Josh or Conall. But the female quality threw me off. There wasn't much of Janek there."

Cuinn leaned back against the office wall, rubbed his eyes with the heels of his hands, and willed himself alert. He'd been nearly exhausted when Tiernan's call had come in—in all fairness, though, so had the triplets—but he needed to think.

I am NOT letting Lochlann down again. It didn't matter that the Loremasters had had his balls in a knot in the centuries immediately following the Sundering, blocking him from using magick outside the Realm, or that even after they'd unblocked him, they'd threatened him with nothing less than the failure of the Pattern and the death of two worlds if he contacted any

Fae before SoulSharing started to happen. Or that they were still being pricks when it came to giving him information. Maybe he couldn't have helped his friend. But that didn't change the fact that he should have.

"It's a safe bet the *Marfach* isn't after Garrett. It needs a Fae."

"Yeah, and the part of it that's human wants one Fae in particular." Tiernan shook his head. The Noble had had a while to come to terms with the fact he'd accidentally created a zombie that wanted him slowly and messily dead, but that probably didn't mean he was comfortable with the situation. "But it's not above using a human as bait. Like it did with Kevin." Even the passing reference brought obvious pain to the other Fae

"I remember. But it can't get into Lochlann, now that they've Shared." This was another part of the Loremasters' plan; since human nature was for the most part incompatible with magick, the human essence in the SoulShared pair protected the pair from magickal attack. "Or the human, either."

"That doesn't mean it can't kill the human," Tiernan pointed out reasonably.

"True enough, but if it does, Lochlann's going to—"

The tablet computer on which Cuinn had indicated where the *Marfach* had gone to ground flashed and lit up a brilliant white. "What the fuck?" Tiernan smacked the tablet, sending it sliding across the desk.

"And that helped how?" Cuinn couldn't keep back a smirk.

151

"It works on idiot humans, and every once in a while it works on idiot electronics."

Lines started to trace their way across the whiteness, slowly at first but then with increasing speed, silver-blue against the white. *"Lanh bodlag onfatath,"* Cuinn whispered under his breath. *"Now you learn to use a computer?"*

"Which particular offspring of a limp infected dick are we talking about?" Tiernan eyed the screen with a lively curiosity.

Cuinn snatched up the tablet, pointedly shielding it from Tiernan's gaze. "Do you mind, fair maiden? This is a personal call." He was reasonably certain there were no Fae left but him—and Lochlann—who could read *d'aos'Faein* script, the ancient form of the language, or even knew it for what it was, but the way his luck was running lately, he didn't feel like taking a chance.

YOU NEED TO FIND THEM.

Cuinn grunted. *NO SHIT.* His fingers slashed through the elegant curls, creating new patterns that were no less beautiful for being spiky and jagged and generally pissed off. *AND WHAT AM I SUPPOSED TO DO AGAINST THE MARFACH, ONCE I DO?*

NOTHING.

Cuinn felt all the blood drain from his face. *WHAT THE FUCK DO YOU MEAN, NOTHING? IT'S GOING TO TRY FOR LOCHLANN.* Fingers beat a staccato pattern on the screen as the computer, or the Pattern, made beauty out of his scrawls.

LOCHLANN DORAN HAS FENDED FOR HIMSELF THIS LONG, HE WILL MANAGE NOW. WHAT WE NEED FROM YOU ARE YOUR OBSERVATIONS.

152

What we need from you.

For more than two thousand years, that had been his function. To give the Loremasters of the Pattern what they needed and wanted.

The *other* Loremasters.

Fuck this shit.

The shaping glowed serenely, oblivious to Cuinn's cold rage. Tiernan wasn't quite as oblivious; his chair rolled slowly back, away from the desk. Cuinn had no idea what the other Fae's expression was. His attention was all for the slow, careful tracing of his own fingers.

I AM NOT YOUR SERVANT.

I AM THE EQUAL OF ANY OF YOU.

I WILL NOT BETRAY LOCHLANN AGAIN.

The pause after he drew the last furious curves went on so long he started to wonder if the computer had somehow been overloaded. Then the shaping on the screen dissolved, to be replaced by a new one, with gentler and more intricate curves. Cuinn recognized the shaping, and even before it was finished, he reached out and reshaped it. *GIVE IT UP, AINE. I WON'T BE CONDESCENDED TO AGAIN.* The one Loremaster who seemed to have some kind of memory of what it was like to be alive and walking in the world, who seemed to think of more than just the endless game of manipulation the rest of them lived to play. To the extent that what the Loremasters in the Pattern did could be called living, anyway. But having her pat him on the head wasn't going to work any more. *I FINALLY REMEMBERED THAT I'M ONE OF YOU.*

WE HAVE NOT FORGOTTEN, CUINN. The

curves of Aine's shaping were graceful, almost warm. *BUT SOME OF US HAVE FORGOTTEN THE THINGS THAT CONCERN THE LIVING. YOU ARE THE ONLY MEMORY SOME OF US HAVE OF THOSE THINGS.*

"Fuck," he whispered. "Don't do it."

"Don't do what?" Tiernan had apparently used up his daily quota of not being a wiseass, and was trying to crane his neck around to see the tablet's screen.

"Shut up." Cuinn turned his back on Tiernan entirely, as much as that went against pretty much every instinct a Fae had, but he wasn't going to be able to keep the screen entirely hidden if Tiernan continued to be an asshole about horning in. Which was a given, really. At least he probably wouldn't be able to read it.

YOU KNEW LOCHLANN WAS MY FRIEND, AINE. The word in the Fae language was *chara*, and Cuinn had to stop and think about how to shape it in *d'aos'Faein.* Not a concept that had seen a hell of a lot of use, back before the Sundering. Or after it, either. *AND IT ONLY MATTERED BECAUSE IT WAS SOMETHING YOU COULD USE TO GET HIM TO SACRIFICE HIMSELF FOR THE SAKE OF YOUR KNOWLEDGE BASE.*

HE IS NOT A SACRIFICE. The curves flowed like water across the screen. *AND WHAT YOU OBSERVE THIS TIME IS NOT FOR US.*

"What the hell?"

"Are you at least going to tell me who you're talking to?" Tiernan had given up trying to see the screen, but now he was watching Cuinn with an intensity that made a liar out of his casual tone.

"Just getting my choke chain yanked." The words

154

didn't come out quite as caustically as he wanted, and he was leaning forward and shaping even as he spoke.

I'M NOT OBSERVING AT ALL. I'M GOING TO HELP HIM.

IF YOU TRY, YOU WILL DESTROY HIM. AND OUR ANCIENT ENEMY WILL HAVE YOU. It seemed the shaping was quieter, like ripples on water. *YOU NEED TO SEE WHAT LOCHLANN DOES. HOW MUCH HE CAN CHANNEL, NOW THAT HIS MAGICK IS RESTORED. WHAT HIS LIMITS ARE.*

Cuinn ground his teeth in mostly silent frustration. *WHY THE HELL DO YOU NEED TO KNOW THAT?*

It seemed that the flow of the shaping hesitated. *WE DO NOT. YOU DO.*

Abruptly, the image shattered, dissolved. Now it was Cuinn's turn to smack the little screen.

"Quit beating on my electronics," Tiernan drawled. "I'm not going to be able to get my technician in here at six in the morning." The blond Fae was slouched back in his chair; he gestured, and his dagger flew from the wall in which it was stuck, back to his hand.

The gesture with which Cuinn answered him was an ancient one common to human and Fae. "If it bothers you that much, your Grace, I—oh, shit." The image was re-forming, but Aine's graceful lines were gone, replaced by someone else's more formal shaping.

YOU HAVE NO DEFENSE AGAINST THE MARFACH. *AND IF YOU EXPOSE YOURSELF TO THE ABOMINATION, IT WILL KILL THE HUMAN BEFORE TAKING YOU.*

Being lectured was bad enough, but being lectured by the smug revenant of a soul sealed in black glass for eternity was more than Cuinn could stand. Especially when that soul was right.

REMIND ME AGAIN WHY I'M HERE LISTENING TO YOU WHEN OUR ANCIENT ENEMY IS GETTING ITS ROCKS OFF TORTURING A FAE'S SCAIR-ANAM *AND PLANNING ITS HAPPY HOMECOMING TO THE REALM?*

The screen flared. *DO NOT INTERFERE.*

YOU'RE NOT EXACTLY IN A POSITION TO GIVE ORDERS.

THIS IS NOT AN ORDER. THIS IS A FORESEEING. The background dimmed, but the lines themselves blazed so brightly that Cuinn had to raise a hand to shield his eyes. *IF YOU INTERVENE BEFORE IT IS OVER, THE* MARFACH *WILL WIN. AND THE REALM WILL DIE, ONE WAY OR ANOTHER.*

The tablet went a dull, flat black.

Cuinn leaned on the desk, palms flat on the teak surface, head bowed. *Son of a bitch.* His fellow Loremasters couldn't see everything. They couldn't pick and choose what they wanted to see. Several of them, he suspected, were incapable of seeing, because their heads were shoved too firmly up their own asses for the light to get in.

But when they Foresaw, they were always right.

"Did you know that your lips move when you draw? And that working in a club with music that gives your kidneys St. Vitus dance is excellent training for lip reading?"

Cuinn's jaw dropped. *Oh, bungee fuck me.*

Tiernan was leaning back in his chair, cleaning his nails with the tip of his dagger, eyes glinting shards of blue from under his brows, one thin gold ring catching the light from overhead. "You going to tell me who's giving the last Loremaster orders?" The softly accented voice was quiet, almost uninflected. "Who's pulling the puppetmaster's strings?"

Cuinn pushed the little computer back across the desk-top, his eyes narrowing. "I have no strings to pull, your Grace. I answer to the Pattern. When I fucking well feel like it."

I can't intervene before it ends. But before it starts?

On the thought, he Faded.

Chapter Eighteen

"Why won't you scream?"

The question was completely reasonable, but all Garrett did was stare at him, his eyes glazed and reddened. Even when Janek yanked his head back by the hair, and a hank of the scorched blond curls tore off in his hand, it didn't do more than jar the breath from him. *Stubborn little shit.*

Maybe a little sweet reason would help. "The bitch is really happy with you right now. All she needs to be happy is for you to bleed." Yeah, his inner goddess was creaming her panties over all the blood. Which meant she was creaming Janek's. Which made him want to puke. Only she wouldn't let him. "But you're going to be doing that for a long time. Make me happy, and maybe I can make it stop." All right, not so much sweet reason as total fucking lies. But whatever. "All I need to be happy is for you to sing for me."

Janek reached down with his gloved left hand—and finding work gloves big enough for his swollen hands had been one bitch kitty of a job—grabbed a hank of the razor wire that bound the little girlyboy, and twisted it tighter. Breath hissed through clenched teeth, and more blood streamed down Garrett's arms and chest, but that was it.

And that was enough to stoke the bitch even more. *All I want is a taste, Meat.*

"Fuck that shit," he growled. "I know you. If I give you a taste, you're going to have my face in it till he bleeds out."

I could always let my male aspect ride you. The voice was a purr, but a poisonous one. *And you know what he would do.*

"I haven't been able to hold a hard-on in months, no matter who's in charge." But the thought made the bile rise in his throat. No way was he going to put up with being forced to fuck this bloody, mutilated, broken piece of shit.

"I have never... in my life... met anyone... as purely bugfuck crazy as you are." The southern drawl in Garrett's voice was more pronounced, the more pain he was in. Couple of times over the last hour or so, it had been hard to understand him. Those had been good times. Janek wanted more of them.

"You have no idea." Janek let go of the twisted strands—the barbs were sunk so deep that they'd stay buried in muscle even if he cut the damned wire—and crossed behind Garrett to the barrel half-full of burning planks. A wood fire wasn't anywhere near hot enough for what he needed, of course, but it was the best he'd been able to do.

He used one of the iron rods stuck into the hot coals to stir the fire, and grinned as Garrett turned his head away. Earlier applications of the rods had left stripes of tight flesh, blisters, and weeping, suppurating wounds in all kids of interesting places, including the cheek the little assfuck was showing him now.

159

"You really look like hell." Which was saying something, since he, the mostly late Janek O'Halloran, was probably the world's leading expert on looking like hell. "And you don't smell so good, either." That was, of course, a guess, since his sense of smell was as nearly dead as the rest of him, and the odor of his own rotting flesh probably overwhelmed the scent of burns and blood.

Garrett's blistered upper lip curled in what he probably meant to be a sneer. "I suppose it's too much to hope that I offend you—"

Pretty brown eyes rolled back in the dancer's head as Janek whipped the red-hot iron rod out of the barrel and jammed the tip into his nipple. He didn't stop until he saw curls of smoke rising. At which point he threw the rod against the wall with a curse, because the little shit still wouldn't scream. Body jerking like a hooked fish, razor wire shredding him, bit right through his God-damned lip, but no screams.

When did your tastes become so refined, Meat?

"Shut the hell up—"

Janek roared in pain and buried what was left of his face in what was left of his hands as the bitch rewarded him for his wiseass response with a couple of seconds' worth of blinding headache. *The next time you forget your place, there will be no warning*. The voice was so cold, it smoked like the dancer's tit.

"Even the voices in your head don't like you."

Janek's ungloved hand clenched into a fist and hammered like a piledriver into the side of the little fucktard's head. Which head bounced like a ball against a bloody shoulder and then lolled, rolling like the kid couldn't hold it up.

160

Don't be more of a fool than you must. The female's voice was withering. ***The catamite needs to be alive and recognizable when his Fae arrives.***

"It might be a little late for recognizable." Between the bruises, the burns, and the blood that still trickled from a cut on the kid's forehead and one corner of his mouth, it was unlikely even Garrett's own mother would be able to pick him out of a lineup.

Just leave a few of those pretty blond curls. That will be enough. Fuck, he hated that purr. But she had a point.

"Why do I have to keep him alive?" Garrett was groaning, and the right side of his body started seizing up in a sort of spastic tic. The groans were a good sound, not quite as good as screams but still enjoyable. "Once the Fae gets here, it's all over, right?"

The female laughed. Oh, look, you've frightened him, Meat.

"How can you tell?" Well, the kid was wheezing more loudly, and it looked like he was trying to open his eyes wider. Maybe that added up to scared. "And you didn't answer my question."

He could have sworn he felt the creature inside his head shrug. ***Does it matter?*** A pause, weighing, considering. ***You might be happier if you were less curious.***

Janek laughed, a harsh, barking sound. "The list of things that make me happy is very short. News flash, having no fucking clue what you plan to use me to do isn't on it."

The bitch sniffed. ***If you insist. This Fae is a healer. He is capable of filling you, or anyone, Fae or human, with magick, without causing pain. His toy***

161

will be your hostage, to make sure he fills your body with all the magickal energy either of us can hold.

"Whatever." Janek carefully kept his voice flat and I-don't-give-a-shit, and hid his thoughts away in the space in his mind that belonged only to him. *It's already said it needs a Fae to get more magick. But if I'm turned into a God-damned walking supercharged hoodoo battery, it's not going to need a Fae any more. Which means I don't get Guaire.* "Just tell me I get to kill him when it's over."

I wouldn't dream of disappointing you, Meat.

The fuck you wouldn't. Another thought to keep very, very close.

Garrett coughed, and a fresh trickle of red seeped from one corner of his mouth. His head fell back, almost like a dead weight; he coughed again, choking, then slowly started trying to raise his head.

Janek caught himself holding his breath, wondering if the little whore was going to manage to pull his head all the way up. Then he laughed, resisting the urge to stick out a finger and push the wobbling head back again. As much fun as it would be to fuck with him, it was even more fun to have those reddened eyes trying to focus on him and then rolling back in the kid's head when the two of them finally made eye contact.

No reason not to enjoy himself while he worked out a way to make sure his obscene passenger gave him what it had promised him, all those hellish months ago. "Ready for another round, beautiful?" Janek interlaced his fingers, and stretched his arms out in front of him. Instead of pleasantly stretching and cracking, the bones and tendons bent. Kind of like stiff rubber. But he was used to that by now.

The kid didn't flinch away from the sight of him this time. Maybe he couldn't. Gingerly, he licked his lips, making a face, probably at the taste of blood and snot and the shit that was oozing from the broken blisters. "You... let that thing... use you. You like it?"

"What the hell are you talking about?" Janek knew perfectly well, of course, but if he didn't come up with something to say quickly enough, the bitch was likely to jump in and twist his throat around to get it to say what she wanted.

Blood-matted blond curls barely moved as the whore shook his head. "Whatever it is... you hate it... don't you?"

Oh, fuck. He couldn't afford to have the monster's attention called to that little detail. Not right now. He bent and picked up one of the longer scraps of razor wire that coiled around his feet and made patterns in the dirt and mouse turds on the floor. Then he shoved the little shit's mouth shut and wrapped the wire a few times around his head, under his jaw and over the top of his head, and pulled it tight until the gasps changed to teeth-clenched moans. One of the barbs bit into the dancer's cheek, starting a fresh flow of blood.

Janek snarled as the bitch took control of him, bent him over, and swiped his tongue over the hot line of blood. The barb cut his tongue, too, but did the monster give a shit about that? Hell, no, it was too busy rolling its eyes in pleasure at the taste of blood. Though how it was tasting anything with the dead meat that passed for his tongue was beyond him.

More. Now.

Chapter Nineteen

Pants might have been a good idea.

Cuinn shook his head. Bare feet were all right. They were quieter than his boots, and quiet was a necessity if he hoped to get anywhere near his quarry. The rest of him, though, was feeling the predawn chill intensely. Fae had a greater tolerance than humans for extremes of temperature, which was odd considering that snow and scorching heat were both rare events in the Realm, but all the same, black silk boxers weren't an ideal choice for prowling. Granted, he'd left the hotel room with no clear notion of what was ahead of him, but Fading back for the clothes he'd left behind would be hard to explain to the triplets. Not to mention profligate of magick.

He grimaced, head tilted slightly and lips parted, the better to listen. He'd gotten out of the magick-conserving habits of the last couple of millennia, and considering how long the fabric of the Realm had taken to recover from his last few replenishments of energy, it was probably past time he got back into them. Which also ruled out simply going back to Greenwich Village and getting dressed, or even whipping up a poncho. Damn.

The sky overhead was still and black as the sky in a city ever got, so the only light in the narrow alley came from the bulbs left burning over the back entrances of a few of the shops that gave onto it, or from the stairwells of apartment buildings, shining through the latticework of fire escapes. For most of its length, the alley was barely the width of a small panel truck; there were small open spaces in between buildings, though, and it was in one of these that he presently stood, heightened senses trying to sift the sounds of the waking city to hear one Fae seeking his own death.

"Ca'fuil thu, grafain?"

Where are you, wild one? The hoarse murmur was somewhere on this block. Within a few buildings, if Cuinn was lucky. He eased around a battered Volvo, out of the parking area, toward the sound, hugging the bricks of the wall. The cold bricks. Fuck.

Now he could hear a rattling, the sound of a door in a frame. *Shit, if that place has an alarm rigged, we're screwed.*

I have to stop him. Somehow. If the *Marfach* got its human proxy's hands on a Fae—any Fae—there was no way to be sure the Pattern and the Realm weren't at deadly risk. An unShared Fae was in danger of direct attack and being taken over, his magic, or hers, warped to the foe's unspeakable evil; scores of Loremasters had ended their own lives in the battle before the Sundering to avoid that fate. A Shared one... well, such a one might be safe from a direct onslaught, but apparently a threat to a Fae's human *scair-anam* was also a threat to the Fae's mental stability.

Of course, Cuinn's only business was the threat to

the Realm. The Loremasters didn't give a meticulous shit about Lochlann's happiness, or even his sanity. What mattered was keeping the Realm safe. And Cuinn seeing what the Loremasters thought he needed to see while it happened.

Fuck them. All of them. Unpleasantly.

Cuinn eased forward, peering around the corner of the building into the next dark recess. Lochlann was bent over the knob of some business' back door, evidently trying to hear what, if anything, was going on inside. A single bulb over the door cast the other Fae's face into deep shadow, except for jeweled aquamarine eyes blazing out of the darkness, intent for the moment on trying to stare a hole through the door and oblivious to Cuinn's approach.

"*Chara.*" Cuinn stepped around the corner, with a murmur faint enough that a human couldn't have heard it. If the *Marfach* was actually on the other side of that door, hopefully it wouldn't either. Though if by some damnable chance it were, no doubt the two of them would be hearing the human's moans by now.

Lochlann's head snapped up, and the anger in the other Fae's crystal gaze didn't abate one bit at sight of Cuinn. "Get the hell out of here. Now."

Cuinn shook his head. "I can't. You have no idea what you're trying to walk into."

"Fine. Give me an idea, and *then* get the hell out." Lochlann shot one last disgusted glare at the door, then turned back to Cuinn. Feet settled squarely, he crossed his arms and rolled his well-muscled shoulders slightly, giving the impression that any hand laid on him would be very efficiently broken into its constituent pieces.

"*Magairl a'Ridiabhal.*"

One dark brow arched. "I'm not sure I heard that right. You don't strike me as the type to be impressed by either the humans' Satan or his balls. Unless you're speaking from first-hand knowledge, in which case please forgive me."

Cuinn fought down a snarl. "Damn it, Lochlann, can you forget you hate me for just five minutes?" Hopefully that would be enough time to save the fucking stubborn asshole's life.

"Short answer—no. Long answer—I don't have five minutes. Not while that monster has Garrett."

Lochlann's hands were clenched into white-knuckled fists, and if it were actually possible to kill the *Marfach*, Cuinn was willing to swear he was looking into the eyes of what would be its death. Under the circumstances, though, it felt a little like watching a kitten glare defiance at a rabid Rottweiler. "You do remember, this is the thing that over a thousand mages barely managed to banish?"

The slight twitch of Lochlann's shoulders might have been a shrug. "The fact that the human world is still more or less intact would seem to indicate it isn't quite as powerful as it once was."

"You have a point. It was living in the ley lines, even though it couldn't really feed on the raw form of magickal energy, and it took the first chance it got to escape. So it's living in reduced circumstances right now." Cuinn fought the urge to wrap his arms around himself against the cold, and settled for a stance mimicking Lochlann's. "But it's looking for a Fae to move into. Which is why you can't get anywhere near it. Theoretically, your SoulShare shields you from magickal attack. But theory has been shown to suck as a predictor of events." He thought about adding *and we have no fucking clue what happens if the* Marfach *offs your human,* but decided against it.

His pronouncement earned even less of a lift of Lochlann's brow than his cursing *as'Faein* had. "So you say. I'll take it under advisement." A brief pause. "I took it. Now, kindly get the hell out of my way."

"You are the most fucking iron-headed mule-assed obstinate Fae since—"

"I am a Fae whose *scair-anam* has been taken from him." Lochlann's voice was low, even, and more dangerous than Cuinn had ever heard it. "You cannot imagine what it felt like for me to find Garrett. To hold him, just for a few minutes, and then have him stolen. To find my magick, but lose my soul." The dark Fae's throat tightened around those words. "And if you could imagine it, you wouldn't be trying to stop me."

No. Cuinn couldn't imagine being forced to love someone. He could imagine fighting that kind of compulsion with everything in him, but he couldn't imagine giving in to it the way Lochlann apparently had. But he didn't have to imagine friendship. He only had to remember it. Even when the friend rejected it. "And if you had seen what the *Marfach* can do to a Fae, or to anything with living magick in it, the way I did, if you had seen fellow mages twisted into living weapons and Loremasters a thousand years old willing themselves dead rather than feel that touch, maybe you'd have some fucking sense."

"Sense has nothing to do with how I feel right now." Lochlann was looking at him, but Cuinn was pretty sure the other Fae wasn't seeing him at all. "I need to get Garrett back. And if you were ever truly

Deep Plunge

my *chara*, you will stand aside and let me do it."

"Not a fair argument."

"Look in my eyes, and ask yourself if they're the eyes of a Fae who gives a shit."

He's gotten harder. Cuinn wasn't sure why he was surprised; it had been over two thousand years, after all. Judging from what some of the poor bastards who had followed in Lochlann's footsteps had endured, maybe the wonder was that the other Fae had been willing to hear him out at all.

Still, if this was a war of stubbornness, he was going to come out on top. "Granted, I've had no practice at friendship for the last couple of millennia, but even so, it would be a fucking poor friend who would stand back and let you walk into the kind of death the *Marfach* has planned for the first Fae it can get its hands on."

Lochlann's aquamarine gaze froze him in place. "Then how fortunate for us both, that that's exactly what you are."

Cuinn stared, stunned, as the color swiftly drained from Lochlann's form, and then even the outline dissolved into nothingness.

Son of a BITCH.

Go looking for him again? Hell, no, this time the other Fae would be warded like a Royal's virgin daughter. And every minute Cuinn spent looking was one more minute the fucking suicidal maniac had to stumble onto trouble he would never find his way out of alive. Either that, or he, Cuinn, would find the *Marfach* himself, and be personally responsible for the ending of two worlds.

Wait.

169

There's another answer.

One Fae living, this side of the Pattern, could take on the *Marfach* head to head. Heads. Cuinn grimaced, fixed a location in his mind, and Faded.

Twinklebritches was going to hate to be interrupted.

Chapter Twenty

"Have I put you to sleep, girlyboy?"

An hour ago, Garrett might have managed a curse. Even though saying anything would have meant pain—when Janek sounded mostly human, he got off on making Garrett hurt. When the stinking behemoth sounded like a bad drag queen, he was all about blood. If the former bouncer wasn't already dead, which was doubtful, he was going to be eventually, with as much of Garrett's virus-laden blood as he'd wallowed in and tasted. *Sorry I won't be around to watch you die of AIDS, motherfucker.*

Now, though, he was saving his energy for things other than cursing. Like breathing. And not moving. He had razor barbs in more places than he wanted to think about, and every time he tried to move anything, he opened a new vein. But if he didn't do something, Janek was just going to try harder to wake him up.

Slowly, he hauled his head upright. The movement made him dizzy; doing his best to ignore the pain, which ran the gamut from throbbing to searing to screaming, he concentrated on trying to balance his skull on the top of his neck. Just like ballet class. *Hold your head up, look proud. Elegant. Don't let the fuckers think they're getting to you.* Well, the last part wasn't like ballet class. No, that was his battered, split-lipped younger self talking.

He tried to open his eyes. Not that he wanted to see anything—*fuck, no*—but seeing was better than being blind. *If I'm going to die, I want to see it coming.* One eye opened easily enough, though the lashes were heavy and crusted with blood. The other one... shit, it hurt even to try.

He actually suspected that his left eye might never open again. He'd heard the poker sizzling when the bastard laid it across the lid, crisping the swollen flesh that nearly hid it. Hadn't felt much when it happened, though. Which was a blessing. He was finally starting to find his way back to the numb place, a little at a time. The place he'd learned to make for himself when he was a kid getting the shit beaten out of him. *You just crawl into yourself, so deep you forget the way out.* It was a lot harder now, though. The clotted pool of his own blood on the floor and the smears of it on the walls kept reminding him of the way out, whenever he opened the one eye he could still open.

Garrett's whole body jolted as Janek kicked the chair. The movement reopened a half-dozen wounds and threatened to topple his head again.

"Stay with me, babycakes. I'm nowhere near done with you." Janek's nightmare of a face loomed in Garrett's field of vision, leering in what might have been meant as a smile. Garrett tried for a sneer, but about all he could manage was a twitch. His mouth had been beaten, bruised, burned. And kissed, once, when the female thing had hold of his captor. That was the one time he'd puked.

172

I have to live through this. I'll be damned if that's the last kiss I ever get.

"Your fucking Fae is taking his time coming after you." Janek disappeared from Garrett's view. He knew where the rotting hulk was, though, he could tell by the sound of a hand rummaging around in the bucket of knives and other implements sitting on the floor beside the oil drum with the fire and the pokers. "But that's all right, it means I get to take my time getting you ready for him."

Lochlann. The weight of need, of feeling riding the single word drew a groan from Garrett, a groan that turned into a tearing cough on its way through his abused throat. *Stay the hell away.* The thought of this walking obscenity getting his hands on the Fae, the crawling red horror that lived in half of Janek's face touching him, came closer to breaking him than anything Janek had tried yet. *If I have to die to stop that from happening, then, God, let me die. Now. Before he sees me like this.*

A sudden chill skittered over Garrett's bare skin. *Yes. Let it happen. Before he tries to rescue me and ends up like me. Or worse.* His biceps cramped viciously, thanks to his arms being bound behind him at the elbows, and barbs bit deep as his arms jerked.

How profoundly did it suck that he finally found one man he could trust, one man whose promise, whose hope, was worth holding on to, only to lose him, and the trust and the promise and the hope, without sharing any more than kisses and the touch of a hand? *And a soul... I guess that counts.* His eye closed briefly, and for an instant he caught a glimpse of Lochlann. Coarse unruly dark hair, soft full lips, vivid blue-green eyes. *I trust you, I love you... and I've lost you.*

It was time to make that happen. Before it was too late. "So how does it—" Garrett's voice caught, and he coughed, feeling like someone was flaying his throat from the inside. "How does it feel to be used, like that thing's using you?" If he had to provoke Janek into killing him quickly, this seemed like his best chance.

"Shut the fuck up." Janek shoved the chair again, nearly toppling it, and continued rummaging through the bucket.

"You'd like that, wouldn't you?" It was hard to talk through a clenched jaw and broken teeth, with cheeks stiff with blood and pierced by razor barbs, but he had to do it. "Don't want Master hearing how much you hate him. Or is it Mistress?"

"God damn it, I said shut the fuck UP!" The words came out in a roar, accompanied by a hellish noise as the former bouncer kicked the metal bucket full of knives and sent it flying into the far wall with a crash, its contents spilling all over the filthy floor.

Then Janek moved faster than Garrett thought a mostly dead man could, coming up behind him, putting him in a hammerlock and bringing a rusty butcher knife around to rest the point against his cheek, right under his one functioning eye. He could see tight blond curls stuck to the blade with blood, and by that he could tell that it was the same knife the motherfucker had used to cut off his boxers and shave his pubes a while ago, leaving him raw.

Blinding him wasn't going to get him what he needed, though. "What's the matter, won't it let you kill me? Or do you just not have the balls?"

Swollen, putrefying knuckles went white on the handle of the knife.

Lochlann, damn it, I'm so sorry.

"Grafain!"

A door rattled violently. Garrett saw the back door, wedged shut and chained, shift in its frame. At the sound of the clatter of the heavy chain, the knife withdrew, and Janek grabbed Garrett's hair and pulled his head up just enough to let him place the razor's edge of the blade against his throat.

Oh, Jesus, no. Lochlann. No. Garrett held his breath, trying not to groan or move or bleed. *Go away. Please.*

"*I was beginning to think you weren't coming*." The laughing voice was Janek's, but it wasn't. It was the creature riding him, twisting his vocal cords to its own purposes, its voice easily as loud as Janek's more human bellow. "***What kept you?***"

The door shook from an impact, as of a body being hurled against it. The makeshift chain held, allowing only a hairline crack from top to bottom. Again the door shuddered in its frame, and again the crack appeared. This time, though, the weight stayed against the door, the chain held taut.

"Oh, shit." Garrett's lips moved soundlessly as the air just inside the door began to change. No more than an outline of a figure at first, then an outline filled with a faint wash of color. An outline with brilliant blue-green eyes. Janek's fingers slowly clenched into a fist in his hair, pulling tight, and Garrett could feel that fist trembling. Not with fear, he was sure.

The rest of the outline filled in, suffused with color and form. "Garrett..."

175

Somehow, Garrett knew his SoulShare wasn't even seeing the monster behind him. The aquamarine gaze, the raw pain in the Fae's voice, those were all for him. "Don't look," he whispered, swollen lips barely moving.

Garrett choked as his head was pulled back, the blade set more firmly at his throat.

"I'd advise you to look very carefully, healer." The flat of the blade stroked Garrett's throat, almost lovingly. *"You have a choice to make. Give me the keys to the prison your race made for me, or watch what's left of your pretty dancer die."*

Chapter Twenty-one

He wants to die.

The most terrible sight before Lochlann as he took form in the precious sliver of space he saw through the crack in the weathered, battered door was not the knife at Garrett's throat. Nor was it the enormous creature holding it there, or the part of that creature's face that he couldn't look at directly without feeling his mind try to shut down. Not even the ruin inflicted on his lover's body, his all but unrecognizable face. No, the worst of it was Garrett's aura, seething with his determination to die. Lochlann had had the foresight to will his empathic sense to silence before entering what he knew to be a trap, but he'd forgotten about the auras.

"Don't look," Garrett whispered. The human's lips were split, swollen, and bleeding, his words no more than a breath, and when Lochlann remembered that mouth on his, the pleasure Garrett had given and received in a simple kiss, his own determination to murder rivaled his human's death wish.

Garrett's head was yanked back, the rusted and bloody blade placed directly over the pulsing vein.

"I'd advise you to look very carefully, healer." It

was the voice he'd heard through the door, and the voice he'd heard on the phone. The flat of the blade stroked Garrett's throat, the edge caught flesh and sent a trickle of red sliding down the wide blade. The Fae had managed to block out the blood scent, but now it assaulted him. Not just the hint of blood on the knife, no. There was a pool of blood around the chair to which Garrett was bound. And blood everywhere, floor, walls, even the ceiling. And the stench of carrion, thick enough to make him gag. *"You have a choice to make. Give me the keys to the prison your race made for me, or watch what's left of your pretty dancer die."*

"What makes you think I have those keys?" Garrett was bound with razor wire. Barbs were embedded deep in blooms of bloody and ragged flesh from his head to his ankles. Looking at those forced Lochlann to see all the rest of what had been done. Suppurating burns, skin stretched tight over grotesque swellings that spoke of broken bones and a ruined kneecap, still-seeping abrasions where pubic hair had been carelessly shaved. More slashes and hacks and stab wounds than he could bear to catalog. So damned much blood.

"You forget, I know you. Lochlann the exile. Lochlann the healer."

Lochlann tried not to look at Garrett's face. He failed. He tried not to flinch. Mostly, he succeeded. He would never turn away from his *scair-anam*. But he knew there was no hiding the rage that promised death to the monster responsible for what he saw. To the extent there was still any life in it to take. "Your host is dead. No one can heal death. And healing won't set you free. It won't gain you the Realm."

"Not entirely dead. My meat wagon needs no

healing, he serves me well enough as he is. The monster laughed. Or at least that's what it probably thought it was doing. ***"As for the other matter, magick is magick. I need all the magick of a Fae to unmake the Pattern and regain the Realm. You will give me yours."*** Garrett's head jerked back, the knife at his throat moved just enough to let the hellish firelight gleam on the blade. ***"Or we will see how well you survive without the other half of your soul."***

The only sounds in the shell of a storefront were the crackling of the fire in the battered metal barrel beside Garrett's chair, the monster's thick breathing, Garrett's rapid, shallow panting, and a muffled dripping. Garrett's blood, trickling from a barb buried deep in his arm, running in a thin stream down his forearm, dripping from one slack finger to splash on the warped wooden floor.

The devastation caused by the last battle between the Fae and the *Marfach*, in the Realm, was still with Lochlann. He could see it any time he closed his eyes, the silent land black and burning from horizon to horizon, dying mages bleeding the last of their life back into the land. But now, over that image was laid his ravaged lover, and the steady patter of his blood.

Choose between them?

"I'm going to have to touch you." Lochlann was amazed at how steady his voice was. "I can't do this from a distance."

"Lochlann, don't." Garrett's breath whistled in his throat, where a bruise betrayed a cruel blow. "I'm dead anyway. You know that."

"Not by his hand, you're not, *grafain*."

"By all means, lasihoir. Touch me." The

179

creature's attempt to sound seductive, while using the stolen voice of a massive male corpse, made Lochlann's guts wrench. ***"But this blade stays where it is until you have emptied yourself of your magick to my satisfaction."***

Three steps closed the distance. Three short steps. Forever. Long enough for Lochlann's rage to build to a killing heat as his boots splashed in a pool of Garrett's clotted blood.

Long enough for a plan to form.

Lochlann knew he couldn't look at the creature's face; the glimpse he'd gotten of red crystal and decaying flesh had been more than enough to remind him that the sight of the *Marfach* was enough to drive a Fae mad. Instead, he placed his hand on the thing's arm; the *Marfach*'s meat wagon had been heavily inked while he was alive, and black and red patterns had now decayed to gray and something like spoiled liver. "Brace yourself. This shouldn't hurt, but I can't guarantee you won't feel anything."

As he spoke, he rested his other hand lightly on Garrett's shoulder. He could feel blisters under his palm, and his fingers were wet with blood. Muscles twitched under his hand, as Garrett fought not to flinch. *I swear to you,* grafain, *it will pay.*

Magick blazed up in him, as he set it free. How long, since he had been able to do this? Much more than six hundred years, since the last time he'd had enough magick to channel. The sensation should have been one to glory in, but there was no time for that now; he drew a deep breath, and started the slow process of emptying himself into the *Marfach*, and its host.

And into Garrett.

The former human holding the knife to Garrett's throat grunted, and averted his eyes as much as he could. Lochlann's bemusement quickly gave way to astonishment, as a perceptible aura flickered to life, barely rising above the surface of the tattooed and decaying skin he touched. Pure, unadulterated hatred. And it wasn't directed at him, or at Garrett.

You didn't like being made to look at magick? A small, cold smile touched Lochlann's lips. *Poor human. I can work with that.* Carefully, he diverted some of the power he drew out of his core into the surface of his own skin. To the *Marfach*, and to its human thrall if the *Marfach* was riding his senses, he glowed like an arc light with magickal energy.

"What the fuck are you doing, asshole?" The voice was all human, suddenly, with no trace of unearthly female. "Turn it the hell off."

"Sorry, can't. That's just what happens when I channel." The human had no way of knowing that Lochlann was lying, and he fervently hoped the *Marfach* didn't either.

"Shit. **Continue**."

The sudden shift in tone made Lochlann shudder. He could almost feel sorry for the pathetic human. Almost. If he were capable of feeling sorry. And if he didn't want the fucker dead in agony quite so badly.

First things first, though. It was going to be a few minutes before there would be enough magick in Garrett's body for Lochlann to start shaping it into the massive healing that was going to be necessary, but for now he could let the flow of power ease his *scair-anam*'s pain, wherever it touched. Down his arm, to the gashes torn by the barbs in the wire that bound him; across his shoulder, to his neck and the dark bruises there; down his chest, to the hideous burn over his nipple. Garrett jerked under his touch, moaned softly through clenched teeth, but quieted as Lochlann tightened his grip.

"***What are you doing?***" The female voice sounded reserved, even suspicious.

Curses *as'Faein* echoed silently in Lochlann's mind. "You demanded the magick of a healer, this is what you get." He kept his face locked down, cold, but inwardly he seethed. *Shit. I can't heal just one.* The thought of being forced to give respite to the behemoth who was surely at least partly responsible for Garrett's torture made him feel physically ill. But what had to be, would be. At least until Garrett was healed enough that Lochlann could safely release him, and start figuring out how to turn the gift of life into the gift of death.

"Lochlann."

It was the barest of whispers, but it was enough. Lochlann made the magickal light flare brilliantly, blinding the human's eye and the monster's, and looked down into Garrett's eyes. The one eye that could open met his gaze, lines of pain deep in the corner of it, lashes singed and crusted with blood. But the deep amber gaze was clear, and steady, like a jewel glimpsed through a window into hell.

"Hold on, *grafain*." Lochlann's low murmur was accompanied by a gentle squeeze to Garrett's shoulder, and a barely camouflaged wince as a burn blister broke under his touch and wept clear, red-tinged fluid.

"I wish we could have had—" Garrett coughed, a

sound like his throat was tearing. "The joy. One more time."

"We will." Probably a lie, but its beauty was necessary. Something to hold on to in this charnel house with greasy smoke for air.

Garrett tried to answer, but the man-mountain yanked on his hair and pulled his head back, choking off whatever he'd been about to say.

Lochlann shot the decaying bastard an icy glare, just before his outward emotions shut down altogether. To hell with slow and careful. He reached within, opened the floodgates, and let the magick pour out.

He was going to have to be very careful. If his healing became visible, if Garrett's bruises faded, his slashes healed over, even something with a mostly rotted brain would notice something was going on. *Have to save that for last. When I'm ready to...*

Shit. He had no idea what he needed to be ready to do.

That deer can be hunted once it's grown. Garrett and his captor were both starting to glow, now, as seen with his magickal sense. The light was blessedly clean, free from the death-taint of Garrett's aura, the sullen hatred in the half-corpse's, and the promise of the humans' hell in the flickering firelight.

Being careful with unbound magick was nearly impossible, especially while it was still rushing into both males, and Lochlann felt a thin film of sweat forming on his forehead as he grasped the wild power and started to shape it. Willing it to become the image of health, of life, from the inside outward. For both of them. Unfortunately. Of course, there was only so much magick could do, for the one who was essentially dead.

The behemoth grunted, and turned to glare at Lochlann. The Fae turned quickly away to avoid having to look at the baleful red crystal. He held his breath, trying not to let the unruly magick escape his grasp, and trying not to look like he was trying not to lose control. Waiting.

Until the thing turned away again, the dull purplish-red aura of hatred clinging to tattooed, decaying flesh like scum to the surface of a muck-filled pond. *The sadistic son of a bitch truly hates the* Marfach. Maybe that was the window he needed, where a wedge could be driven. Somehow.

Lochlann dared another look at Garrett, and his breath caught in his throat. The bruises and the burns were still there, the cut that had at some point poured blood into his one open eye. But the lines of pain around that eye were gone, and the amber gaze that met his was clear. A wave of relief swept over him, so intense he needed to lock his knees so as not to fall to the bloody floor. His gift hadn't deserted him. This part of what he needed to do, at least, was going to work.

"More."

The single word drove a deadly chill bone-deep into the Fae. The voice was a cruel parody of the human's own, not male, not female. Something that embodied the death the human's decay only hinted at.

Something that grasped at Lochlann's magick, within itself, and began to pull.

Lochlann staggered, cursing violently. He had been pouring out his magick; now it was sucked from him, by an insatiable evil. He snatched his hand from Garrett's shoulder. *It's not getting the magick I've already given him.* There was time for that thought, and time to reach in desperation for the last of his magick, as it disappeared into the seething red maw he dared not look at.

"***This is not everything.***" The voice seemed to come from somewhere deep within the human; decayed lips barely moved as the gut-churning sounds issued between them. "***Fool. I have devoured Fae whole. I know how much magick you bear within you.***"

"You took it all—"

Garrett cried out. His head was yanked down and back, the blade in the human's hand indented his throat.

"***The rest of your magick. Now.***" A thin red line appeared along the edge of the blade.

Panic gripped Lochlann in fanged iron jaws. *I have to give it more. Have to find more.*

Only hours ago, the proto-magick of the ley lines had reached out to him, found him, filled him. He needed it now. And he found it. Called to it, with all the emptiness in him. Teased out a tendril, from the glowing stream below his feet. Grasped it and drew it into himself, feeling the power rush into him. Changed it, his body refining raw power into living magick.

"***Now I will feed.***"

Chapter Twenty-two

"I know you're only humoring me when you let me do this, you know." Josh smiled down at Conall, tugging gently on the scarf that bound his left hand to test the knot; satisfied, he moved on to the right hand, trailing the length of silk across Conall's bare chest before starting to tie his other wrist.

Conall shook his head. His heart was racing pleasantly, and he was already well on the way to a full erection, purely from anticipation. "I'm trusting you, *dar'cion.* There's a difference." He hissed softly as his *scair-anam*'s tongue caressed his wrist, his palm before knotting the scarf around it. "I won't Fade unless you tell me I may. You know that." What had been born of necessity in the nexus chamber under Purgatory—the need to arouse the Fae as much as possible as quickly as possible, so he could tap directly into the ley lines and banish the *Marfach*—had become a special delight for both of them. Josh insisted over and over he was no Dom, and Conall supposed he himself would make the worst sub in the history of ever, but the freedom of being bound was like nothing he had ever been able to imagine. And the pleasure it gave them—both of them—was seismic.

Josh's answer, for the moment, was a hot trail of licks and kisses, running along Conall's arm to his shoulder and up his throat. Then he straddled Conall's spread-eagled body and raised himself up, to give Conall the good long look at his ink that he knew Conall always wanted. *Dar'cion* was his pillow-name for his partner, 'brilliantly-colored' in the Fae language, and damn, was that an understatement. The Fae's fingers twitched with the need to stroke the beautiful designs on Josh's strong biceps, smooth over the hawk inked on his chiseled chest; his back arched, seeking the human's solid warmth, and he groaned as Josh easily avoided him. "You're a fucking tease, you know, lover."

"I learned from the best."

"Don't you two ever quit? The sun's coming up, for fuck's sake."

Reflexively, Conall channeled Air at the intruder, slamming him hard into the bedroom wall and pinning him there, his bare feet a good six inches off the floor. Then he saw it was Cuinn, considered, and decided to leave him where he was.

"Cute, Twinklebritches. You want to put me down?"

"Not particularly." Conall paused to give Josh a reassuring kiss on the cheek; the human had dropped to cover him as soon as the insufferable Loremaster had opened his mouth. "But because I was in a reasonably good mood until you barged in here, I will let you try to explain what the hell you're doing here before I banish you." He considered. "Greenland sounds good."

"Oh, fuck me oblivious."

Cuinn strained to release himself from his bonds, but Conall wasn't having it. He was aroused, the magick was flowing, and the Loremaster had pissed him off. "Yes, that's a large part of the issue. And my good mood is dissipating rapidly."

"Shit." Cuinn took a deep breath. "Look, it was actually an accident. My showing up here, I mean. I knew you two had moved into one of the two apartments over Raging Art-On, but I didn't know which and I had to guess when I Faded. And I had to Fade without knowing where the hell I was going because we have a fucking emergency on our hands. Lochlann's human has been taken by the *Marfach,* and the idiot Fae is out there trying to find him on his own. Begging to be taken over and turned against the Realm."

A whispered word released the Loremaster, who slid down the wall and landed on the floor on his ass. Conall ignored him, his gaze going back to Josh. "I did promise I'd ask," he murmured.

"What? Oh. The bonds." Josh turned an appealing shade of red, but at the same time he smiled, the smile that transformed his face. "Yes, you can Fade. As if you really had to ask."

Quickly, Conall left the bonds hanging limply from the four bedposts, and re-formed sitting on the edge of the bed, facing Cuinn, who had apparently decided to stay on the floor for the time being. "Does Lochlann have any idea where to look?"

"I was able to get it down to an area a few blocks on a side." Cuinn's eyes narrowed. "Would you mind putting something on? I don't normally have any problem with hot male nudity, but you really distract me for some reason."

"*Se an'agean flua, a'deir n'abhann.*" Conall shook his head, but channeled himself a pair of jeans, sighing as the fabric settled in and formed to him. "And envy's an ugly thing, incidentally."

"What does that mean?" Josh looked from Conall to Cuinn and back again, his expression one Conall recognized from marathon sessions of Animal Cops as being about thirty seconds from reaching for the tranquilizer gun.

Conall's "The ocean is wet, says the river," was only partly audible over Cuinn's "You're too funny by half, Twinklebritches."

"You could stand to cover up yourself." Conall arched a brow at the boxer-clad Loremaster.

"I'm not like you, o mighty mage. Some of us can't replenish our magick from the ley lines, you know. Waste not, want not."

"That's true, you can't. Not until you're *scair'ainm'en.*" Conall reached back blindly with one hand, and closed his eyes to enjoy the sensation as Josh's hand closed around his. After three centuries of not daring to let another touch him, the slightest touch from his SoulShare was bliss—it didn't even have to be sexual. "All right, for the sake of Lochlann's SoulShare, I'll ignore your crass bid for attention. What do you propose we do about this? And why didn't you just go after Lochlann yourself?"

"Several reasons." Cuinn counted off on his fingers. "One, because it's the motherhumping *Marfach*, and as you've never tired of pointing out to me, I can't take it on alone. Two, because it told Lochlann that if he didn't come alone, his human was dead, and I tend to believe it. And three..." Cuinn looked distinctly uncomfortable. "I tried. And he essentially told me to go fuck myself."

"And this surprised you why, exactly?" Conall tilted his head, studying the disconcerted Loremaster. "Although now that I think about it, you seem to care a great deal about what Lochlann thinks of you. You might want to get that affair wound up before it causes trouble. I doubt Garrett's going to be interested in sharing."

Cuinn flushed, and started to get to his feet, and if the look in his eyes wasn't murder, it would do until murder came along. "Lochlann is my *chara*, since two hundred years before the fucking Sundering, and if you're still having trouble getting that through your head I'll be glad to find a brick and help you."

Conall shook his head. "You could try. It might be entertaining. But until you find one, maybe we could think about what we can do to help Lochlann."

"I've already had a few thoughts along those lines." Maybe Cuinn thought his expression was earnest, but if he did, he was surely the only one. Loremasters were born devious, according to the old tales, and apparently things only got worse from there. "Once we find him, and once he's found the *Marfach*, you're the only one with any chance to get near it without being detected. Though what you do is so fucking dangerous, it gives me the shakes."

"Not to me, it isn't." Conall shrugged. Travel by Fading involved one brief instant when a Fae technically didn't exist anywhere other than in magick. One brief instant was all most Fae could handle. Keeping oneself almost totally incorporeal, right on the edge of dissolution, for any length of time, was one of the most hazardous things a Fae could do. Any Fae other than him. "I think something happened to me, when I melted down the Greenwich Village nexus, something that lets me ride that edge safely."

"I think something else happened to you, too. One of the most hazardous things a Fae in the Realm can do, and you use it as a fucking sex aid."

"Bite me." No point in asking how Cuinn knew; the Loremaster had his sources, and refused to discuss them. "And a little focus here? We already know it can't detect me when I'm Fadewalking." Josh had chuckled at his name for what he did while his physical nature was thinned almost to nothingness—*it sounds like something from a really bad horror movie* had been his comment—but it fit. "But I can't channel at all when I'm not corporeal, I need to be in Josh's body in order to handle the energy."

At least he no longer risked killing his *scair-anam* every time he channeled; six months of practice had nearly accustomed his human to the inevitable overflow of magickal energy that resulted from the initial flaw in their bond. Though Conall wasn't particularly inclined to call it a flaw, any more, not when practice sessions usually involved steel shackles, a leather blindfold, and a vibrating ass plug, all in the name of achieving the necessary level of arousal for a major channeling. *The things I suffer for the sake of my magick.*

"Does it have to be Josh's body?"

Startled out of his distraction, Conall would have laughed, but Cuinn was eyeing him like a cat at a mousehole. Suddenly, he didn't feel like laughing. "Tell me you're joking."

"Why should I be?"

191

It was a distinctly strange sensation for a Fae of the Demesne of Air, possessed of the gift of languages, to be without words. Conall didn't care for it. "Okay. Start with how intimate it feels when you're inside a lover, or he's in you."

"It doesn't, particularly." The other Fae smirked.

"Fuck. Can you pretend for a minute?" Conall grimaced. "Just imagine that there's something special about it. Then multiply that by a thousand, and you have some idea of what it feels like when I'm sharing a body with Josh." A shiver rippled through his body as he remembered the sensation. "It's almost as intimate as the SoulShare itself."

"Wouldn't know about that either." Cuinn tried to scratch a hard-to-reach spot on his back. "But this is an emergency. Capital-E Emergency. Think you could maybe get over yourself long enough to use Lochlann instead of Josh and catch the *Marfach* with its pants down, you should pardon the unfortunate mental image?"

'Let me drop my trousers so you can kiss my—"

"What the *hell* is wrong with you two?"

Startled, Conall turned to Josh. Despite the fierce impression his lover's extensive ink tended to give people upon a first meeting, he was one of the most warm-hearted individuals Conall had ever known. Certainly more so than any Fae. Which was why his anger now was so startling. "*Dar'cion?*"

Josh's brows were making one long, stern line. "Lochlann is out there looking for something that rips worlds apart for fun. Garrett has been kidnapped by that same thing, and God knows what's happening to him. But you two—" He looked pointedly from Conall to Cuinn—"seem perfectly happy to sit here and bitch at each other until sunrise rather than help either one of them."

Conall considered Josh's words, and his anger, puzzled by both. "I suppose it seems odd to a human." *Shit. Share a body with a total stranger?* The notion of fidelity was odd enough to a Fae; feeling strange about contemplating infidelity was even odder. Still... "I'll do it, I'll help. I may not know Lochlann, but I do know what it feels like to have a *scair-anam* at risk." He rested a hand on Josh's well-muscled thigh, trying to reassure himself with the solid strength of it. Memories of his own battle with the *Marfach*, when every use of his magick risked his SoulShare's life, were still entirely too fucking vivid.

"And I'll do what I can." Cuinn left off glaring at Conall to turn to Josh. "I let Lochlann down once." The other Fae almost looked serious. "I'll be damned if I do it again."

"Are you *sure* the two of you aren't having an affair?"

"D'orant!"

How Josh managed to turn a pillow name into a rebuke, Conall wasn't quite sure. But he definitely felt stung. "What did I do this time?"

Josh's hand rested over Conall's, on his thigh, gentle despite the human's irritation. "Maybe Lochlann can take care of himself while you two make like a couple of tomcats, but what about Garrett?" Ink danced as Josh shuddered. "I doubt he can take on even the *Marfach*'s human host."

Conall didn't blame his SoulShare for the shudder. Not at all. He wasn't looking forward to having to deal with the former Janek O'Halloran himself, much less the horror that rode him, not after what he'd had to do to them the last time they'd all met. Still, that was between him and the monster. "Maybe he can slow it down a little. Delay it, whatever its plans are. I'd imagine he'll at least try, and the more time he can buy me, the better."

"Slow it *down* a little?" Josh stared, aghast. "Garrett's alone with a world-killing nightmare and its pet zombie, and all you care about is whether he can stall it for you?"

"Oh." Conall cleared his throat. "This is one of those empathy things." He shook his head ruefully. It had been something of a shock to Josh when he discovered his Fae partner's attitude toward humans other than himself. Humans who weren't immediately useful, anyway. He'd been trying to educate Conall, and Conall for his part had been trying to understand the concept. "*Dar'cion*, if I were any good at empathy, I'd be a human."

"Not true. It just doesn't come naturally to you, that's all." Josh squeezed his hand. "You do fine with me."

"You're different."

Cuinn whistled loudly. "Hello? Time is of the essence, and all that ponderous bullshit. Are you in or out, Twinklebritches?—because I think you going in undercover is the only chance we have."

"Could you possibly be even a little more irritating?" Conall's lip twitched in the beginning of a snarl. "I'm in. But I need to go downstairs and tap into the nexus first." If he was going to have any chance of keeping the *Marfach* from taking Lochlann and turning him to its own use, without being in direct contact with the ley nexus under Purgatory as he fought the monster, he was going to need to be full to glowing with the raw magickal energy before he set out.

The other Fae snorted. "You are such a fucking horndog."

"Don't make me hurt you." Yes, he needed to be aroused in order to touch the nexus. It would be the same for any SoulShared Fae—which was why Tiernan had so thoughtfully created a playroom directly over the place where the ley lines intersected—but it was especially true for him, since he could channel so much more of the energy than any other Fae. Including, probably, the irksome Loremaster.

"How do you know I wouldn't enjoy it?"

"Christ, Cuinn, give it a rest, will you?" Josh put his arm around Conall's shoulders, drew him back and down to lie beside him, surrounding him with his beautifully-inked body. "You want him to risk his life, shut the hell up and let him do what he needs to do."

Conall smiled as he fitted himself to his *scair-anam*. "You teach me humanity," he whispered, nipping at Josh's earlobe. "But I'll make a Fae of you yet."

He let Josh's soft laughter fill him, center him, calm him as he closed his eyes and reached outward, seeking the nexus more than two floors below. Space didn't necessarily matter to him, in dealing with the raw power of the ley lines; it was important for him to know where the lines were, where they ran and where they intersected in physical space, but once that was known, he could sense them inwardly, without being in direct contact. He'd learned neither Tiernan nor Cuinn could do this, not at a distance; there were times, apparently, when it helped to be a freak of nature.

"Oh, shit," Conall breathed.

"What is it, *d'orant?*"

"Please don't tell me this is fucked already."

Conall ignored Cuinn entirely, opening his eyes and focusing on Josh instead. "Lochlann is drawing on the ley energy, somehow. I can feel it when I sense the nexus."

He closed his eyes again, to focus on the flow of power, as Josh's arms tightened around him. The lines that met under Purgatory came from four different directions, and he could sense a disturbance in one of the four lines, like a tease in a strand of silk. The healer was doing the impossible, drawing directly on the ley energy without touching the nexus. *Son of a bitch.*

Cuinn didn't take well to being ignored. "Can you tell where he is?"

"Yes. I can get fairly close, at least." The eddy in the bright current was like a stone in a boot, precise, uncomfortable, and impossible to ignore.

"Then go. Now." Cuinn's voice was tight, urgent.

Conall's eyes narrowed. "You want me to Fade blind?"

"No choice, we're out of time. I didn't think it was fucking possible to draw on the ley energy anywhere other than at a nexus, and if he's doing it, it has to be because he's found the *Marfach.*"

No shit. "I still need to go downstairs and replenish—"

196

"If Lochlann's tapping the lines, you can do it through him."

Conall's nostrils flared as he drew in a deep breath. Cuinn being in the right, even partly, was a seriously irritating experience, one he preferred to ignore in favor of resting his head on Josh's beautifully-inked shoulder. "I know I have to do this. But I don't like leaving you behind." He could deal with the danger to himself, from touching the ley energy directly without being prepared. He could even face the prospect of going a second round with the foe that had once, in its more potent form, nearly destroyed his entire race. It had to be done, and he was the only one who could do it. But alone?

"Don't worry about me. Well, try not to." Josh's low murmur and soft laughter were at odds with the tension Conall could feel in his partner's body, but they were exactly what Conall needed. "I'll go downstairs and set up the playroom, for after you're done."

"I love you—"

"Could you please haul ass?" Maybe Cuinn didn't *realize* he was being ignored. "I doubt the *Marfach* is waiting for you to get your groove on."

Conall looked over Josh's shoulder at the Loremaster, the snarl on his lips unexpectedly fading at sight of the other Fae's distress. *It's more than fear for the Realm that drives him. Who would have thought?* "Keep my *scair-anam* safe, *Mastragna*." 'Master of wisdom,' the ancient *as'Faein* title of the Loremasters. "Don't fail me. Or you'll wish you'd tried to do this yourself, because the *Marfach* would be a hell of a lot kinder to you than I will be."

Green eyes blazed. "I'll hold up my end. You take care of your own."

"Go, *d'orant*." Josh's hand smoothed down Conall's back, soft lips brushed his brow. "I'll be waiting." A chuckle rumbled against his body. "I make a hell of a lady sending her knight off to battle."

"I'm not your knight." Conall reached within himself, touched the magick at his core, and set it free; found the eddy of power that was Lochlann and his battle, and let it draw him. "I'm your Fae."

Chapter Twenty-three

"Fool."

Lochlann staggered, nearly fell into Garrett and his captor, clutching desperately at the magic flowing into him and through him. *Could I possibly have fucked this up any worse?* The *Marfach* had a savage grip on the ley energy, and was determined to suck in all the power of the line that ran under their feet. It was a deadly serious tug of war. Real war.

A war Lochlann was going to lose, eventually.

For the last minute or two, or forever, he'd almost managed to hold his own. Holding on to the magick was like tightening a fist around a rope of fire. Only the fist was everything he was, and he would have given anything for Garrett's pole gloves. His heels were dug in, figuratively speaking, but he was being dragged forward, inch by inch, even as he was abraded raw by the power that flowed through him. Closer to the vortex of pure evil he could sense even with his eyes closed. *If I let go, it gets the ley magick. If I don't, it gets me.*

"Why are you fighting? It will all be the same in the end." Low, thick laughter sounded close to Lochlann's ear. Too close. *"Let me have the power, and I will release you. Once I have it, you are nothing to me."*

"Fuck off and die."

"Death cannot die."

Hold on just a few more seconds, Doran. Whatever you do, don't let go.

"What the *fuck*?"

Mouth shut, eyes closed, death grip on the ley energy, there's a good lad. The voice was in Lochlann's head, it was almost his own voice, but not quite. *I'm almost in you, this is slow going. What the motherfornicating hell did you do?*

More of the monster's laughter greeted Lochlann's blurted words. *Start by convincing me I'm not raving mad.* Which would not be an easy task, not when he was pretty damned sure he was talking to himself at a time when he needed to give everything he had to fighting the *Marfach*.

Lochlann was sure he heard a sigh. *I'm Conall Dary. The only Fae capable of cleaning up this mess. I hope. I'm Faded, I'm going to share your body and deal with the* Marfach. There was a pause, and Lochlann wasn't sure, but he thought he could feel something moving inside him. *Shit, what were you thinking, giving it direct access to the ley energy?*

Conall Dary. Lochlann remembered the name from his conversation with Tiernan, another SoulShared Fae. *It was going to kill my* scair-anam. *I wasn't thinking. You're Shared, you understand.*

Hell, yes.

Yes, Lochlann was definitely feeling something moving in him, and it was creeping him the fuck out. Yet sharing a body, sharing thoughts, had its advantages; he suspected an actual physical conversation would have taken much more time than they had to spare. Even so, there was no time to waste. *What are you going to do?*

That depends in part on what's going on. But I'm the only mage who's been able to go mano a mano with the Marfach, *in its present limited embodiment. Once I'm situated, I can use your body to channel the volume of magick I'm used to working with, and get rid of the fucker. Somehow.*

It would have been nice to have a god to believe in, as so many humans did, just to have someone to thank. *You might be able to work with the fact that the human seems to be clinging to life purely out of hatred for the* Marfach. *And is probably healthier than he's been since whatever he went through to turn into this thing. I had to heal Garrett from the inside out, which meant healing him, too. He looks like shit, but other than that he's doing as well as a dead human can.*

There was a moment of inner silence, followed by just a hint of wild Fae laughter. *Oh, yes. I can use that. I know just how I can use that.*

Garrett groaned, and Lochlann's eyes snapped open. He still didn't dare touch his human—he refused to risk any kind of connection between Garrett and the *Marfach* forming through him—but he met Garrett's gaze as strongly and plainly as he could. *Not much longer,* grafain. *Hold on.*

So strange.

What's strange?

Lochlann felt the equivalent of a shrug. *Feeling that kind of connection second-hand. I know what I have with Josh, but it's different this way.*

Garrett stirred, winced, and Lochlann was abruptly out of patience. And on the brink of losing control of the magick, into the bargain. *If you have a plan, tell me what it is.*

I do. You release the energy, and let me take it up. Once I have it under control, I'm going to supercharge the Marfach, *and at the same time break its connection to Janek. Its human host. It'll be temporarily overwhelmed, and unable to control its ride. Then I should be able to banish it.*

Lochlann felt a chill. *Do we really want it supercharged?*

It won't be able to do anything with the magick. It needs a body it can control. Kind of like me, in you, at the moment. Once I deprive it of control of Janek, it's nothing more than a rock full of magick, sitting in a mostly dead dickhead who hates it. The laughter sounded again. *Just like disarming a bomb.*

If you say so. The ley energy surged in him, maybe in response to Conall's evident eagerness, and Lochlann cursed fervently with the pain of trying to contain it. *Just do it, will you? I don't think I can hold on to this much longer.*

Give me a second. The inner voice was sober, now. *I've never tried to channel the ley power without being aroused. It's going to be interesting. Which is to say, I could blow us all up if I fuck it up.*

Conall fell silent, and Lochlann concentrated on slowing the rush of the power, on ignoring the pain. The *Marfach*'s unseen presence loomed over him, gloating, drawing him nearer, the more tightly he clung. *You're not getting either one of us*, Cruan'ba. The ancient name given by Fae of the Demesne of Water to the *Marfach*, the Drowner.

"**Let go, Exile. Betrayed One**." The voice was

female once again, and it trickled over Lochlann's skin and into his ears like rancid oil. "***This burden should never have been yours to begin with.***"

A chill rippled down Lochlann's spine. "I told you to fuck off."

The *Marfach* ignored him. "***You were tricked into sacrificing yourself. You need do so no longer. Just let go.***"

Do it, Doran. I'm ready. Let go.

Lochlann barely stifled an actual, physical cry of relief as he released his hold on the ley energy. It blazed up in him for one, beautiful, terrible instant, as overpowering as it had been when it first invaded him as it returned to him. Then he watched, in wonder, as it was focused to an inner-eye-searing intensity, a laser of magickal light, and blasted straight at the mass of crystal Stone that housed the *Marfach*.

The creature's agonized, ecstatic roar shook everything around it. Lochlann still dared not look at its face directly, but he could see the body of the enormous human—Janek—convulse, before Conall used his hands to grip its upper arms with a magickally-augmented strength.

There was a dull clatter, as something metallic fell to the wooden floor. Followed by a choking sound, a horrible not-quite-liquid gurgling. Beside him, he could feel Garrett thrashing, heedless of the razor-barbed wire that bound him.

"***This was your choice, healer.***"

Lochlann looked down. He got only a glimpse, before Conall control jerked his head back up, but the glimpse he got was seared into eyes and mind and soul. The *Marfach*'s tool had cut Garrett's throat, with a ferocity that left the slashed pinkish-white of the human's trachea bare over a cascade of red that flooded down over his chest and pooled in the crease where torso met thighs, before pouring down in a river to the floor.

I can heal him. I can. Lochlann clutched at the torrent of magick—

—and was shoved away. *I can't let go.* Conall's voice within him was taut, strained. *The* Marfach *is still too strong for me. If I let up on it for an instant, it'll have me. It'll have us both.* The brilliant magickal light continued to batter the monster, and Lochlann could feel Janek's body jerking in his hands.

Do you think I give a shit? Lochlann struggled to look down, but Conall kept his gaze locked where it was. He could feel the tremors of Garrett's body against his own, though, and hear the wet whistling of air through a slashed windpipe. *Give me the magick back. Or you'll be next, I swear it.*

I can't. The other Fae's voice within him was anguished, but resolute. The magickal onslaught continued; the *Marfach* used Janek's voice to howl, to scream. But never loud enough to drown out the soft, desperate sounds of Garrett's life hemorrhaging onto the blood-soaked floor.

Then, abruptly, the screams stopped. *I just broke their connection. Janek, and the* Marfach. Conall sounded breathless, even though he had no need to breathe. *Now to get rid of them both. The* Marfach *has left part of itself somewhere else—I can send the rest of it there and it can't stop me.*

Waste one more second telling me and I'll cut your throat myself. Lochlann struggled to reach out a hand, to touch Garrett, but Conall kept his grip locked on Janek's arms. He felt Conall nod once, tightly, and the focus of the ley magick changed.

"...sorry. To leave..."

The whisper reached him in the moment before Janek started to howl again. Lochlann felt the rough tingling of magick in his hands, where they gripped the human monstrosity; flesh started to give way under his hands, becoming less substantial.

"*Spiraod n'Draoctagh...*"

The murmur was, impossibly, Cuinn's. Not that Lochlann gave a fuck. Not when Garrett had stopped trembling against him.

There was nothing in his grasp.

The ley magick flooded him as Conall released it.

Lochlann bent, cupping his palms around Garrett's face, heedless of the razors that sliced deep. Turned his *scair-anam*'s face up, poured magick into him. Healing magick. "Stay, *grafain*. Stay with me. Don't leave me. Don't."

The amber light in Garrett's eyes flickered. Died.

Chapter Twenty-four

"Spiraod n'Draoctagh..."

Cuinn breathed the oath, even before Josh had stepped through the rift from the Realm behind him. *Spirit of Magick...* not that magick cared what a Fae might want, or plead for. Lochlann clung to Janek, Fae and human alike glowing in magickal light almost too brightly to look at. Lochlann's human was bound to a chair in front of them, his head lolling back; it took Cuinn a few seconds to realize that Garrett wasn't draped in a crimson sheet, that it was his life's blood that covered him and poured onto the floor.

The form of light that was the *Marfach* and its host flared and went dark, sucking its afterimage with it into nothingness.

Lochlann caught Garrett's head, raised it, held it; he bent, his dark hair tumbling down and hiding the human's face from Cuinn's view. Now the human's body filled with light, with power. Yet it was still, terribly still.

The light went out.

"Grafain..."

Cuinn had seen Fae weep before. Fae wept in frustration, in anger, in despair, when deprived of something they cherished. But no Fae's voice had ever carried the weight of sorrow in that single word. Lochlann fell to his knees beside Garrett's chair, his arms around his *scair-anam*'s body, his clothing and flesh catching on vicious barbs that jutted from the wire binding the human. His face buried in Garrett's chest, he shook with the force of his almost-silent sobs.

I failed him, after all. Again.

At the edge of his field of vision, Conall took physical form. Josh instantly wrapped his arms around the red-haired Fae, murmuring, even as he himself shuddered. Astonishingly, Cuinn could hear Conall weeping as well. "I had no choice, *dar'cion. M'anam-sciar.*"

Just because there's no choice doesn't mean there are no consequences. His own words, chiding his fellow Loremasters for leaving him out of the Pattern, out of their master plan, echoed in his head. He hadn't had a choice himself, about bringing Josh here. Conall would have made him wear his balls for earrings if he'd let anything happen to the human.

Words, even inward words, abruptly failed him, as Lochlann's body blazed to magickal life once again. Garrett's followed suit, wounds closing, wire snapping and shattering and falling away, bruises fading. One of the healer's shaking hands cradled Garrett's head, and the edges of the gaping slash in the human's throat knit themselves together.

But the now-perfect body showed no sign of life, no spark. Cuinn stepped forward, rested a hand on Lochlann's shoulder. It was like touching a statue, cold unyielding marble. "It's done, *chara.*" He made his voice as gentle as he could. But if Lochlann had to lash out at someone, better him than someone else. He was the one who deserved it, after all. "Even you can't heal death."

Lochlann's head whipped around, coarse and blood-soaked black hair nearly hiding the flaming blue-green of his eyes, upper lip curled back in a snarl. He looked for all the world like a painted Pict, only instead of blue woad his skin was stained a gory scarlet, streaked with white where tears had fallen. "How do you know what I can and can't do?"

Before Cuinn could answer, Lochlann turned back to the body in the chair, resting his head once again on Garrett's chest. Cuinn had to acknowledge the perfection of the dancer's body, the beauty of his face; maybe he could understand Lochlann's tears, at that. Any Fae would weep, deprived of a plaything so fair.

A third time the magickal light flared. For the first time in his life, Cuinn was simply unable to comprehend what his magickal sense was telling him. A thin, brilliant stream of what had to be the ley energy spiraled up from below the floor, wrapping itself around Lochlann; hastily, Cuinn jerked his hand away from the other Fae's shoulder and stepped back, unwilling to risk the kind of meltdown Conall had accidentally caused in New York.

But the stream soon vanished; while Cuinn had been mesmerized, Lochlann had somehow himself *become* a flow of magick, and the ley energy simply joined the channel he was. None of the paradoxes a Loremaster or a mage had to accept in order to work with magick encompassed what he was seeing. In one sense, the dark Fae was still corporeal, kneeling beside the chair to which his dead SoulShare was still bound. But in another, he was only a vessel, through which magickal light poured.

Aine's shaping burned in his mind. *YOU NEED TO SEE WHAT LOCHLANN DOES. HOW MUCH HE CAN CHANNEL, NOW THAT HIS MAGICK IS RESTORED. WHAT HIS LIMITS ARE.*

Fuck you all until you bleed, if you've brought Lochlann to this just for the sake of my seeing what happens—

The visible Lochlann held tighter to his human, trembling with his effort. The Lochlann that was magick poured into Garrett and vanished, like a stream sucked dry by a desert. The magick responded, becoming a torrent. Lochlann's visible eyes opened wide, then closed tightly as he whispered his human's name, over and over, a mantra.

Fuck me senseless.

Lochlann's visible self was being washed away. There was no other way to describe it. The magick battered at him, swept over and through him, carrying off his substance. Washing it little by little into Garrett, where it disappeared along with the magick.

"Damn it, Lochlann, don't you fucking *dare!*" Cuinn's voice was hoarse, as if long unused. "You can't cure death!"

Lochlann's physical self slowly raised his head and turned to Cuinn, opening piercing faceted eyes washed clean of all color. "Watch me." His lips moved without sound.

Magickal light flared, and Cuinn flinched back, shielding his eyes. The magick was all there was of his friend, beautiful and terrible.

And then, abruptly, it was snuffed out. The only light left in the charnel house was the flickering firelight, playing over two lifeless bodies.

Chapter Twenty-five

Garrett stared resolutely at his feet. As long as he watched them, his bare toes buried in the soft loam of the forest path, they didn't move. Looking at the trees that lined the path worked, too. The trees were beautiful, leaves and flowers of every color he could imagine, stirring in a soft breeze. But if he looked up, he risked seeing some of the other people traveling the same path, and every time he did that, he found himself walking along with them, whether he moved his feet or not. Nobody seemed to mind the fact he was naked, their eyes were all fixed on the light further along the path.

The light. Shit. Even thinking about it started him moving again. He glared at his feet again, to make himself stop. At least he knew better now than to try to turn around and go back the way he'd come. It wasn't impossible to turn around, but it was extremely unpleasant. Almost as unpleasant as what he went through in the hours before he...

Died.

He was dead.

He'd thought he was going to die alone. He was still surprised at how much that thought had hurt. He'd been ready to die before Lochlann found him. He'd wanted to die then. But it didn't work out that way. He'd looked into Lochlann's eyes, felt his touch, and even before the healing had started, he'd known hope. He'd actually let hope in.

Then Lochlann had turned away. And then came the knife. *No, don't remember the knife. Don't remember what it felt like, the blade pulling, sticking in your windpipe, your head falling back, everything open to the air, not being able to get a breath.* And the worst part, staring up at a Fae who never looked down.

It hurts a thousand times worse to have hope taken away than it does to refuse it in the first place.

But sometimes you choose to hope anyway.

He'd been left with his head lolling back, able to see nothing but the rotting hulk who had just killed him, and Lochlann gripping that hulk, white-knuckled. Some kind of energy passing between them. Or maybe that had just been him, hallucinating as he bled out. But he hadn't hallucinated Janek vanishing. And finally, at the very end, a hand cradled his head. Lochlann bent over him, looked into his eyes in time to be seen before everything got dark. *At least the last thing I saw was him.*

Garrett shook his head, turning to look off into the cool depths of the forest, trying to clear his head. How fucking weird was it, to be thinking like this? Remembering his death, remembering what it felt like to die.

Trying not to be any more dead than he already was. He didn't feel dead, not at all. Warm, breathing, could use a shave. But he knew what the light was ahead of him, trying to draw him in. There wasn't any way *not* to know.

Nobody else around him seemed to mind knowing, or being drawn. Some of the others on the path were even hurrying, eager to pass that final boundary. But not him. He wasn't going. Not while missing Lochlann felt like the goddamned knife was still stuck in him.

Not while he still wanted, needed his SoulShare. Yes, needed. Everything he'd been through, hours of living hell, and he still refused to let go of life because he needed to feel Lochlann holding him again.

Cursing, he snatched his hand away from his throat. He didn't want to keep touching it, running his fingers along the line the rusty blade had left. He wanted to forget everything about it. *Shouldn't you be able to forget that kind of shit after you die?*

Although he kind of suspected if he forgot that, he was going to forget all the rest of it, too. All the rest of being alive. Music. Dancing. And a lover who held him as if he mattered and kissed him like his pleasure, his happiness, was the most important thing in the world.

Damn. He couldn't die. Not without trying to make it right with Lochlann first. Make up for rejecting him, for treating him like another anonymous trick. He needed to give the Fae something real, something he hadn't given—or pretended to give—to anyone else. Part of himself. Yeah, the hand job had been stratospheric, but it had happened mostly because he'd been trying to keep Lochlann at a safe distance. Stupidest thing he'd ever done. He wanted to be closer. Damn it, he'd never known intimacy before, and to have it dangled in front of him and then yanked away was completely fucking wrong.

Just once. Let me love him, just once.

Who the fuck was he kidding? Once? He wanted the rest of his life. And not the one that had ended. *I need to go back.* Tears burned his eyes.

His feet moved, entirely against his will, toward the light, and he clenched his teeth against a cry. Deep down, he knew hope was futile, there was no way to stop what was happening to him. Maybe he could hold on a little longer, a few minutes. He *would* hold on. But he knew the truth. He was going to die. *Really* die. Forever.

"Grafain!"

Garrett was so sure he was dreaming that for a second, he didn't even turn. But then he did, and the pain of trying to face back the way he'd come dropped him to his knees. Doubled over, the first thing he saw was a pair of worn black leather boots. Then arms went around him, his head was drawn to a hard shoulder, fingers plunged into his hair. Lochlann's body shook with sobs, just as it had right before Garrett died; the Fae held him so tightly, he could feel each catch of breath as if it were his own.

Garrett couldn't think of a single thing to say. Not one fucking thing. Nothing could carry everything he felt, anyhow. Bewilderment, joy, sorrow, anger, need. Fear. *I wanted to be alive, not to have him be dead too.*

And love. *God, yes.* Love.

"I love you," Garrett whispered against Lochlann's chest. Yeah, that came close to covering all of that. "I wish I'd said it sooner."

Gently, Lochlann urged his head up. Garrett got a glimpse of translucent blue-green eyes before those eyes closed and he found himself on the receiving end of a kiss that carried a whole heart with it. It wasn't just the receiving end for long, though; by the time they both came up for air Garrett's lips were chafed and tender from the Fae's growth of beard and his heart was racing.

"*S'vrá lom tú, m'anam-sciar.*" Lochlann looked more feral than Garrett had ever seen him, yet at the same time more impossibly beautiful, coarse coal-black hair falling around pale faceted green-blue eyes. Easy, now, to believe his lover wasn't human. "That means I love you, by the way."

"How the hell did you get here?" Garrett's voice caught. "Tell me you're not dead too."

Lochlann frowned. "I don't think so. But I'm not sure." One hand cupped Garrett's jaw, the thumb stroking his cheek. "I was trying to heal you. Even after it was too late, after I knew you were dead." The Fae's voice broke on the word, and his throat worked as he swallowed before going on. "I can channel more magick now than I could before I lost mine. But not that much." Lochlann's lips brushed Garrett's forehead. "I called up the ley energy, and I couldn't control it. I poured so much into you, through myself, that I think I lost myself. And now I'm here." Without moving his head, Lochlann glanced around. "Wherever here is. Is this your human heaven?"

"I don't think so. But whatever's in that white light might be. Don't look at it." Garrett drew Lochlann's head down to his shoulder. "It pulls you in if you look." His fingers played in Lochlann's hair. He never wanted to let go. Wasn't going to let go.

"It doesn't pull me." Lochlann smoothed a hand down Garrett's back. "Maybe it's not meant for Fae.

We don't have gods. Maybe we don't get a heaven."

"If you don't, then I'm not going." Garrett almost laughed at himself, the way he sounded like a petulant child. But it was true. "Grand'Mere Toinette used to say, Heaven is where you can never lose what you love. And if you're never going to be there..." *Then it can't be Heaven,* he would have said, but his throat closed up around the words. *Idiot. Your last few minutes with the man you finally figured out you love, and you're going to waste them dictating Hallmark cards?*

"Wait." Lochlann tensed against Garrett. "Wait a minute. It doesn't pull me." He turned to look back down the path, the way he had come, something Garrett couldn't even contemplate doing, then dipped his head to kiss Garrett again, hard, a promise. "I'm going to get you out of here."

The lump in Garrett's throat was painful. "I can't go back. I tried, believe me." He wanted to bury his face in Lochlann's chest again, make this strange and beautiful and sterile place go away, but any second with his lover might be his last, and he couldn't make himself look away from brilliant faceted eyes. "I can't take even one step back the way I came. The best I can do is stand my ground, and if I let my guard down I can't do even that much."

"I'll help you." Gentle fingertips touched the places where razor barbs had bitten deep and iron had burned; a kiss fell lightly on the lid of the eye that had been seared closed. "Because I'm not going back without you."

Chapter Twenty-six

"You pick a hell of a time to ask me to hope."

Lochlann felt Garrett tense; the tightness of his *scair-anam*'s voice made him wince. *No one should hurt like that here.* He stood, and reached down to help Garrett up. "It's not hope I'm asking for. I'm not going to fail you."

Garrett shook his head, then bent and brushed away twigs and grass clinging to his knees. "Maybe Fae get some special dispensation when it comes to death. If you're human, dead is dead."

"*Grafain.*" Lochlann kept his voice soft, but he couldn't keep the steel out of it. "Would you willingly go on from here without me?"

A long silence followed the question, during which Garrett kept his gaze down. "No. Not willingly. But the light's drawing me. I can feel it, even when I'm not looking at it." Finally he looked up, and there was fear in his amber gaze. "How much longer am I going to have a choice?"

"Let me help you." Letting go was a wrench, but he couldn't think of any other way to do what needed to be done. He stepped back, holding out a hand. "Let me try."

Garrett stared at Lochlann's offered hand, then slowly put out his own and clasped it tightly. Lochlann stepped back, away from the light, his own grip firm.

Fuck. Garrett might as well have been one of the trees that lined the path, for all he was able to move; he leaned forward, but his feet stayed rooted where they were, leaving him tilted toward Lochlann at an impossible angle.

"Son of a *bitch*. I can't even fall down in that direction." Garrett struggled to pick up one foot, then the other, holding even more tightly to Lochlann's hand. As if the Fae were a rope, pulling him out of quicksand. Except that he wasn't coming out. "Pull harder."

"Maybe pushing would work better." Lochlann let go of Garrett's hand and stepped around to stand behind him.

He realized his mistake too late, as Garrett cursed, covered his eyes with his hands, and vanished. Suddenly, he heard his lover behind him; he spun to see Garrett fall to his knees, facing back toward the light, with nothing at all between him and the beckoning brilliance. And moving, somehow, toward the light, until he went to his hands and knees and dug his fingers into the soft ground. The human was breathing in soft, panting gasps; his head was bowed, and he glared at the ground. "Shit. I can't even *look* back where I came from."

Lochlann growled under his breath and stepped to stand between Garrett and the light, pulling his shirt out of his jeans and ripping a strip from the soft fabric. "Close your eyes, *grafain*." He tugged gently at Garrett's golden curls, urging his head up, and quickly tied the makeshift blindfold. "Here, let's see if this helps."

"If it does, you're a genius." Garrett let Lochlann help him to his feet, alarm giving way to a wry smile. "And I'm a fucking idiot."

"I'd have to disagree with both." Lochlann turned Garrett to face up the path once again, noticing for the first time the steady stream of humans who passed them by with no more than a mildly curious glance. Young, old, hale, feeble, injured, whole—all kept their eyes fixed on what lay ahead of them, those who were able quickening their pace. Only his *scair-anam* had halted on the path. Only Garrett's face was streaked with tears.

"You *are* a genius." His human's beautiful smile flared briefly, before turning to a frown. "Except that I still can't move."

"*Magarl lobadh.*"

"What does that mean?"

"Loosely translated? 'Rotting testicles.'"

"Do I want to know the exact translation?"

"Only if you're a medical examiner looking for details for an autopsy report." *Even now, he tries to make me smile.* Lochlann looped his arm around Garrett's waist. "Here, lean on me."

Lochlann had never paid much attention to the difference in height between himself and his SoulShare, but it was impossible to miss now, with Garrett's head resting against his shoulder. There was a reason the best male dancers tended to be short, he remembered reading. Something about a lower center of gravity. He didn't care. Garrett was perfect, and it didn't matter why. His arm tightened, and he started forward.

Once again, Garrett stood as if rooted to the spot, and Lochlann growled. Instinctively, he reached for the magick he knew he still had left; he'd been drained and battered after the ley energy left him, but that was mostly the aftermath of the overwhelming rush of power that had carried his essence off after Garrett's. There was still magick left within the body he had left behind, and if whatever he now was could call on it, there was hope. He held his breath, opening himself; let out a great sigh of relief as the magick welled up within him, filling him until his skin tingled faintly. "Now, *grafain*."

He felt Garrett startle, at the touch of magick. The human lurched forward, one step, and another. Straining for a third, muscles taut and trembling. Lochlann, too, strained, sweat trickling down his temples and into his eyes, lips set in a silent snarl of frustration. There was no ley energy to be had here— he was lucky he had his own store of magick to rely on—and just as it was when he was in his physical body, when he was exhausted, the flow was maddeningly slow.

Unless...

Garrett gasped as Lochlann's mouth settled over his own. Lochlann breathed in the gasp, and darted his tongue between Garrett's parted lips, teasing at Garrett's until the human moaned softly and responded in kind, the stud in his tongue an insistent delight. Arousal was protection against the loss of sense of self that could occur when a Fae opened himself to channel magick. *And the joy of the SoulShare goes beyond that, to let me handle the extra load of the ley energy.*

That insight could wait until they got out of here,

though. Lochlann slid his hand down the perfect curve of Garrett's back, feeling the play of muscles under the skin as Garrett shifted to fit his body closer to Lochlann's, cupping his hand around the delicious firm concave ass that bespoke ballet training.

"Just to be clear, this isn't a complaint." Garrett only pulled back far enough to be able to whisper, and Lochlann could feel the human's lips moving against his own. "But why now?"

"Arousal calls to magick." Even in this strange place, even now, it was so easy to let himself fall under Garrett's spell. Yes, spell. Channeling was for the Fae, but his human needed none of that sort of magick to hold a Fae. "The more aroused I am, the more magick I can channel, and the more magick I can channel, the more easily I can bring you back." He caught Garrett's lip between his teeth, tugged gently on it. "Given my usual reaction to you, I predict a wind sprint."

Garrett laughed, a breathless chuckle that arrowed straight to Lochlann's cock and set it to straining against the zipper of his jeans. "Are we going to do it standing right here in the middle of the path?"

Lochlann's fingertips skimmed the makeshift blindfold, moved down to Garrett's cheekbone, traced the curve of his ear until the human shivered. "Let's save the exhibitionism for Purgatory after we get back. I'm not going to risk losing you if the blindfold slips."

"Thank you."

"For what?"

"Assuming we're going to get back." Garrett reached up, felt his way up Lochlann's arms and along his shoulders to bury his fingers in the Fae's hair and draw his head back down into another passionate kiss. "I needed to hear that." The words were rushed, breathy.

"I love it when you can't get your breath after you kiss me." Lochlann took Garrett's arm and steered him toward the edge of the path, keeping him as far from the light as possible while avoiding rooting him to the spot. "Let's work on that."

"Lochlann..." Garrett put his hands out in front of him, trying to feel his way, as soon as they were off the marked path and into the undergrowth. It was almost startlingly dark, after the diffuse brightness of the path and the brilliance at the end of it, and even Lochlann, with his enhanced senses, had to be careful about picking his way.

"Yes, *grafain?*" The Fae slid his hand up his human's arm, delighting in the smooth, unmarked feel of it, stopping him, turning him, and taking him into a loose embrace.

"I. Uh. Shit, I don't know what to say." Garrett's forehead rested briefly against Lochlann's chest, before the human's face turned up to his, and even though his eyes were covered, Lochlann could still somehow feel the weight of his lover's gaze. "I just died. About as badly as it's possible to die." Color rose in Garrett's cheeks. "I can't just forget that. I would if I could. You need me to. And I'll try. I do want you. That's what I've been holding on for. But I can't get rid of..." A shudder rippled through his body. "I can't stop remembering what the knife felt like. There's no healing to take that away."

Outwardly, Lochlann went very still, very quiet. Inwardly was another story. The Fae race had always believed the *Marfach* could never die. Maybe it couldn't. But it would not enjoy his attempts to prove common knowledge wrong. And its human host, the one who had wielded the rusty blade, could be made to finish dying. *Would* be.

"You're right. I can't heal that memory. Any more than I can heal the one I have of standing helpless next to you while you bled your life out, because my magick was needed somewhere else." Lochlann bowed his head, his rough cheek brushing Garrett's smoother one. "But I want to give you ten thousand reasons to leave that moment behind." To a Fae, a *galtanas deich meloi*—a promise of ten thousand—was a small thing, a matter of a hundred years to fulfill, sometimes less. But to a human, a hundred years was a lifetime. And what Fae had ever promised to put a partner first? Even once? "Please, *grafain*. Let me try."

Hesitant arms went around him; Garrett tiptoed and fitted himself to Lochlann, slowly and deliberately. "Ten thousand, huh?" The small smile that curved Garrett's lips was the sweetest promise the Fae had ever seen. "I think I'll give that a try myself." Teeth caught Lochlann's lower lip, worried it gently. "One."

Lochlann breathed in the whispered word, then took Garrett's mouth hard as he turned him to lean against one of the smooth-barked trees. His hands smoothed down his *lanan*'s sides; perfectly muscled ribs rose and fell with each panting breath, and he could feel the pounding of Garrett's heart. Again and again he stroked, gentle but firm, until he was rewarded with a shiver.

"Do you have any idea how good that feels?" Garrett's voice was barely a whisper.

"I'm starting to." He browsed long, slow kisses across Garrett's cheeks, enjoying the rasp of the soft blond stubble against his lips. Down his throat, lingering only for a moment where the knife had slashed. Lochlann's mouth traveled slowly down Garrett's body, pausing to caress, to taste, to explore. Tugging on a nipple with his teeth, kissing the hollow at the base of his lover's throat, teasing with his tongue at the golden down under one arm and drawing a startled grunt and a smile that looked nearly bashful.

"You like that?" The Fae recognized the first sweet tingle of SoulShared joy, and his laugh became a purr. "Don't be embarrassed. I want to know what every inch of you feels and smells and tastes like. *Every* inch. And I have such plans for finding out."

Garrett's body shifted against his, and Lochlann could feel the stirring, the growing heat of the human's arousal. Straightening for one more kiss, he dropped to his knees and curled his hand around Garrett's semi-erect cock. There was no trace left of the botched shaving job the man-monster had done, only tight dark-gold curls surrounding the base of a cock impressive even when it was mostly at rest. Pausing briefly to tease the curls with lips and tongue, Lochlann gripped the rising warmth and raised it to let him see the thick stainless-steel ring that pierced the underside.

"Lochlann..." Garrett's voice was strained, his body suddenly tense. "Are you sure this is... oh, fuck, it feels ridiculous to be asking a question like this here, but the goddamned virus..."

"You're healed. Completely." Lochlann browsed his lips across the smooth skin on the inside of one of

Garrett's thighs. "Believe me, I wasn't stopping to heal one thing at a time. This would be safe even if we weren't both wherever here is." He licked, long and slow, for the pleasure of feeling Garrett shiver against him. "Let yourself be pleasured."

"Do you have any idea what that means?"

"Yes." The Fae nosed at the human's golden curls, teased them with his lips. "I know what it feels like to get my life back. Thanks to you." Garrett's cock stirred against his cheek, lengthened; he cupped his hand around it and held it to his face, chafing it gently against his stubble.

"Oh, *shit*." Garrett groped briefly before finding Lochlann's head, working his fingers into his hair. "I want to see, damn it."

"Just feel, *grafain*." Lochlann licked over the piercing, a long, slow, flat stroke, tasted the metallic tang of it. "Imagine how this is going to feel in me." He took the head into his mouth, sucked gently; his tongue swirled over the smoothness, teasing the slit at the tip until he was rewarded with the first drops of clear fluid, smiling at the groan that greeted him when he let Garrett slip from his mouth. "I'm sure as hell imagining it."

Lochlann's breath caught sharply with the sweet pain of an erection straining to get out of his jeans. He *was* imagining what it would feel like, cool metal being heated deep in his ass and his lover moaning in ecstasy with every thrust; he shuddered once, sharply, one hand dropping to his groin to try to grip and stroke through denim stretched taut. He was hard enough to drill rock, he was sure. And his magick was stirring, ley power transformed by a Fae's body to living magick, quicksilver eddies that rose up from deep within and left him tingling where they flowed. And as if that wasn't enough, there was the joy. Pure SoulShare joy, welling up in him.

Garrett's hips moved in short, tight jerks, as if he fought to restrain himself; his hands fisted in Lochlann's hair, his breathing was hoarse and harsh. "I need you—I need to bring you. With me. *Damn.*" The human's cock was rising, thickening; the scent of his need was stronger with every second that passed. "*Please.*"

Lochlann knew, at last, what had to happen. *I need his pleasure, he needs mine.* He swiped his tongue through Garrett's nether curls once more, then reached up, circled his human's forearms with his hands, and urged him down, a smile of anticipation touching his lips.

"What are you—oh, yes. *Yes.*" Garrett let Lochlann draw him down, felt his way down the Fae's body, deliciously awkward. His mouth was busy even before he could fumble Lochlann's jeans unbuttoned, unzipped, nipping at the insides of denim-clad thighs, teeth closing over the outline of the Fae's cock straining against the crotch of his jeans.

Lochlann, for his part, drew one of Garrett's legs up, to use a beautifully-muscled thigh as a pillow while he took first one ball and then the other deep into his mouth, suckling, releasing, licking. He groaned, equal parts relief and sweet torment, when his zipper finally went down and his aching cock was taken into his lover's hands, and then his mouth. He was never going to be able to get deep enough into Garrett for his own tastes this way, and the position

Fae called ninety-six was always just a little awkward, but thinking of what he was going to be able to do for Garrett damn near brought him off on the instant.

"How long has it been?" He gave the underside of the human's cock a slow reverse lollipop lick, head to balls. "Since you let yourself come in a man's mouth?"

"Oh, God."

Lochlann felt and heard Garrett's groan, and sank his fingers into his human's ass just in time to keep him from pulling back. "No need for that. Remember?" He leaned in and placed a half-ring of soft, wet kisses around the base of Garrett's shaft, feeling the pulsing of a vein under his lips. "Now, how long has it been?"

"Fuck." Lochlann felt a sudden heat, trickling through his dark bush of hair, and knew it for his *scair-anam*'s tears. "Too long."

Without a word, Lochlann took Garrett deep into his mouth, down his throat. As deep as he could, until he felt a hot trickle at the back of his throat and his lover's Prince Albert at the base of his tongue. Garrett mirrored him, sucking hard and moaning like a human in the throes of fever. Lochlann dug his heels into the soft ground, trying to find some kind of purchase, arching into Garrett. Needing to be close, needing intimacy as much as he needed arousal.

Silence fell, broken only by the ethereal trills of birds in the trees overhead, and the grunts and moans and wet hungry sounds of the two males wrapped around each other on the forest floor. The magick was building under Lochlann's skin, and in some remote quiet corner of himself he knew he was going to have to move fast once his pleasure peaked. He couldn't count on the surge of power from orgasm to last for long, and if he spent it too quickly trying to get himself and Garrett the fuck out of here, he might not be able to get it back a second time.

But that was too much like thought, and what his lover was doing to him had nothing to do with thought. Garrett's tongue wrapped around his cock, and when the stud in it found the sweet spot under the head, Lochlann's whole body seized up with the sheer pleasure of it. *Damn. I never really understood the point of a tongue stud. I do now.* His body refused to relax from its tense arc, wouldn't risk slipping out of his human's mouth.

How do I make this as good for him? He teased with the tip of his tongue at the base of Garrett's shaft, stirring the curls there, breathing in his scent. As mind-blowingly good as Garrett's ministrations felt, it was even better, his own pleasure was even more intense, when he focused on making his *grafain* buck and moan. *And why has it taken me more than two thousand years to ask that question?*

The answer to that question, at least, was simple, as simple as the thrill of joy that raced down his spine.

Without warning, Garrett sank two fingers deep into the Fae's ass, and took his cock so far down his throat that Lochlann saw stars when the human swallowed. Cursing ecstatically, he wrapped his hands around Garrett's erect shaft and started to squeeze, in a rippling wave that mimicked what he planned to do when the human took him at last. When they were out of here. Garrett's piercing was still visible, and Lochlann lashed it with his tongue, then licked away the clear stream that flowed from the tip. *"Thar lom, grafain,"* he whispered. *Come with me.* He took the swollen brick-red head into his mouth and suckled, moaning in anticipation as he felt Garrett's cock curve hard in his hands. *Free the magick.*

Garrett's hips jerked hard—and so did Lochlann's, in near-perfect unison. Liquid heat raced down his spine, pooled in his balls; the twin globes grew deliciously heavy even as they drew up tight. He felt the first pulses of his human's orgasm in his hands, his mouth flooded with salt and musk, and he felt Garrett's cry around his cock the instant before everything whited out in a storm of pleasure, and joy, and magick.

One jet of hot clear fluid after another shot straight down Garrett's willing throat. Lochlann himself was less neat about receiving the thick white ropes Garrett pumped out, but the hot splatters on his cheeks and throat when he let Garrett's cock slip from his mouth only made him come harder.

The pleasure never ebbed, never faded into sweet exhaustion. It merely changed, feeding the joy, and feeding the magick that now chased itself in translucent eddies over Lochlann's skin. For a second, Lochlann stared in wonder at his own hands, gloved in swirling energy as beautiful and fragile-seeming as a soap bubble, yet humming with power.

"Come on, *grafain*, we have to move. Now."

Chapter Twenty-seven

"Right now? You don't ask much, do you?" Garrett laughed breathlessly.

He could hear Lochlann rising, the soft sounds of clothing being settled into place. The loss of contact left him feeling bereft, and made him want to stay right where he was and pull the Fae back down with him. *Later. If there is a later.* Lochlann's hand around his upper arm urged him to his feet; he felt a strange, exhilarating tingle where the Fae touched him, one that spread rapidly through his whole body and settled in bone-deep.

Lochlann held tightly to his arm, until the underbrush disappeared from around them and he could feel his feet on the soft, smooth path once more. The Fae's hand slid down his arm, caressing, and clasped his hand tightly. Then a fierce kiss, leaving Garrett's lips rasped by stubble, and then the hand in his was pulling, urging him to run.

Strangely, Garrett didn't feel unsure of his footing at all. The blindfold didn't matter. He just had to trust the hand he held. It was like dancing, when everything came together and the music told him what to do.

"So strange."

"What is?" He could hear Lochlann's footsteps, just barely, ahead of him and to the right.

"The light. It's getting brighter as we run away from it. But we're the only ones casting shadows— none of the humans going toward it have one."

"I'm going to take that as a good sign." Garrett shivered, though, at the eerie picture his mind was making for him. "Hell, I'll take anything as a good sign right now."

Lochlann's hand tightened around his. "I'm not letting you go into the light, *grafain*." There was steel in the Fae's voice. "Not happening."

I love you. "How much farther do we have to go?"

"I don't—oh, fucking A."

Lochlann stopped so suddenly that Garrett ran into him. "What is it?"

"Nothing. Literally. Nothing."

The flatness of Lochlann's tone made the hair stand up on the back of Garrett's neck. With a curse, he tore off the blindfold off and threw it aside. He found himself staring, transfixed, at a rectangle of pure blackness barring their way. It absorbed all light, even the unearthly light of the portal shining on it from behind them. No, it didn't absorb the light. It devoured it. "Son of a bitch."

"That sums it up. I can't even see into it. Fae senses are better than human, but there's just nothing there to see."

This was what death was supposed to look like. Not the white light that he could still feel playing over his back. Compared to this soul-sucking darkness, the light was almost seductive. Calling to him. Caressing him.

Fuck, no. "I'm not giving up." Garrett looked up at Lochlann, letting the Fae's gemlike eyes distract him from both light and dark. "After everything I've been through, I'm sure as hell not afraid of the dark."

He turned and stepped into the darkness, pulling Lochlann in after him.

Oh, shit. The blackness was utter and enveloping; no light followed them into the darkness, and when he craned his neck around, there was no gap in it, no way to tell where they'd entered. In fact, he quickly ascertained that he could not even see his own hand when it was an inch from his face.

"Grafain?"

"You don't sound so good."

"Fae... we, well... we have this... it's a claustrophobia issue." Garrett wasn't sure, but he thought he could hear Lochlann's heart pounding. "I'd thought I was over it. I've had long enough. But it's genetic. And right now, it's bad. *Really* bad."

Having no clue what else to do, Garrett slipped his arm around Lochlann's waist and drew him close, holding him tightly. "Does this help? I won't let go, I promise."

He felt Lochlann's cheek rest against his hair, heard the Fae draw a deep breath and felt the breeze of it stir his hair. "It helps." Soft, nervous laughter stirred his curls. "At least I don't feel like running in a blind panic. Pardon the expression."

"Can you do something with your magick?" *And I didn't think of that before why?* Well, maybe because the thought that he had a lover who could work magic on him of *any* kind hadn't had time to sink in yet.

"I'm not much for light, but I can try." There was

a brief silence. "The magick's there, but I can't see a thing. Shit."

"Conall! I found him!"

A voice echoed through the darkness. *But that's impossible.*

"What was that?"

"A... friend."

Garrett wondered at Lochlann's hesitation, but let it go.

"Can you hold the link? Do you have enough magick left?" Another voice, naggingly familiar.

"I can if you cut the talk and start some action, boy wonder." There was strain evident in the first voice.

"I think I prefer Twinklebritches."

Something caught hold of Lochlann, yanked him off his feet and to one side so hard and fast that Garrett's arm slipped from around his waist. Lochlann's hand shot out and grabbed Garrett by the wrist, locking around it. More magick poured into Garrett through that fierce grip, and Garrett wasn't sure, but he thought he felt something cold and metallic wrap around his arm and Lochlann's hand, an instant before Lochlann was hauled away, and Garrett with him.

"Shit, that was close." Lochlann's voice was unsteady. "If we'd gotten separated in here..."

The Fae didn't finish the thought. He didn't need to. *To get this close and then be lost. Lost forever, without even a chance at the light.*

"What's going on?" Anything to get his mind off that thought. He was starting to feel kind of claustrophobic himself, and welcomed the feel of his hair being blown back from his forehead in the wind of their passing. At least he could be reasonably sure they were going somewhere, and not just floating in some sadist's idea of a sensory deprivation tank. Which was his own newly-minted notion of hell.

"It's a Summoning. A way to get someone to come to you. Usually they're suggestions. Sometimes compulsions." Lochlann laughed, a harsh staccato sound nothing like the low, rich sound Garrett had only heard a few times. "I've never had one yank me off my feet before. But Conall's no ordinary mage."

There was light ahead, the barest hint of a glow, but in this blackness it might as well have been a searchlight. The two of them were being drawn toward it. The sensation of flying was stronger now, and the light was reaching out to them. Warm, welcoming, the light of home. Nothing like the light he'd fought against. Maybe those other souls had sensed a welcome waiting for them, on the other side of that light. Not him. Never him. As impossible, as ridiculous as Garrett would have known it was even to hope for what he now had, only a few days ago, he knew he could never be at home, be at peace, anywhere Lochlann wasn't.

Lochlann's laughter startled him out of his own thoughts. The Fae was looking at his own hand, where he gripped Garrett's arm, so Garrett did too, and saw the metal he'd felt in the darkness—a gleaming silver-blue chain wrapped around their wrists, binding them together.

"Bondage?" His eyebrow went up, he couldn't help it. "Any other quirks you haven't told me about?"

God, he loved Lochlann's laughter. Now all they

had to do was get themselves alive again, so he could keep hearing it. "It's truesilver. Metal that knows the purpose it was forged for. I guess my subconscious knows what it wants."

Right there, in the middle of the laughter, Garrett felt his heart lurch. Sex with Lochlann was all wrapped up in joy. And love, apparently, was made sweeter and stronger by laughter.

He looked ahead, at the light bearing down on them. *There aren't any guarantees. Even now.* He met Lochlann's gaze squarely, looking into shimmering blue-green eyes. "If this doesn't work—or if it only works for you—thank you. And I love you." He could feel himself turning red. "And I'm sorry I was such an asshole."

Lochlann drew Garrett into his arms and cradled him close, one hand made awkward by the chain around their wrists, his body curving around Garrett's as if trying to shield him from the impact only moments away. "This has to work. Because those are *not* going to be your last words, *grafain*—"

The light that flared around them was so brilliant, Garrett's eyes squeezed shut and tried to roll back in his head. *Is this what the other light would have felt like?*

As quickly as the light had blazed up, though, it was gone.

It took pretty much everything he had to crack an eyelid. The first thing he saw was the play of firelight. The second was Lochlann's body, slumped over his. He was still sitting in the chair to which Janek had bound him, though he couldn't feel any barbs in his flesh or the tightness of burns. Not that any of that mattered. Not when Lochlann wasn't moving.

Son of a bitch. "Lochlann." He was waking up from the dead, back from the other side, and what the fuck did it matter if his lover didn't wake up with him?

The faintest tingle of magick stirred against his skin, where Lochlann's body touched his. *Damn it, I don't need it any more. Keep it. Use it. Wake the fuck up.*

Lochlann stirred. Went still. And Garrett's patience officially ended. He reached to bury his fingers in Lochlann's hair, and felt cool metal slide down like water to clatter to the floor as the chain fell away. Working his fingers into Lochlann's hair, he drew the Fae's head up. Aquamarine eyes opened, as if answering his will; sensual lips curved into a faint smile.

Garrett wasn't in any kind of mood to wait. He took his lover's mouth, in a kiss that started slow and ended hot and sweet and spiced with promises.

"That's two," he murmured. *What a fucking amazing thought, a promise of ten thousand.* "Nine thousand, nine hundred ninety-eight to go."

"Cuinn needs you over here, healer. Right fucking now."

Chapter Twenty-eight

The sharp retort Lochlann was ready to deliver died on his lips. Cuinn was slumped against the nearest wall, his eyes half closed, his breathing rapid and shallow. Conall knelt next to him, his hands hovering over the other Fae as if he didn't have any clear idea what to do with them, and a gorgeously inked human Lochlann vaguely recognized from Purgatory rested a hand on the mage's shoulder. Both Fae knelt or lay in blood. Garrett's, from the look of it. "What the hell happened?"

"That Finding took a lot out of him." Conall sounded exhausted, himself. "It's a damned good thing he knew that particular channeling, because I don't. And I don't know anyone else who could have followed you that far."

"I'm not quite dead yet." Cuinn struggled up to one elbow. "And conversations in third person bore the shit out of me."

"It really does have to be all about you, doesn't it?" Conall rolled his eyes.

"All the good stories are." Cuinn's tone exuded his usual fuck-you-very-much, but he couldn't put any volume behind it, and it sure as hell didn't match his pallor or the sweat trickling down his forehead. "Was that a compliment you just paid me, by the way, Twinklebritches?"

Lochlann growled. "Cuinn, put an apple in its mouth and shove a spit up its ass." He staggered to his feet, every muscle protesting the sudden movement.

"I recognize them." Garrett spoke softly, looking up at Lochlann, clear amber eyes still shadowed by the confusion of resurrection. "From Purgatory. Josh, the tat guru, and his partner. The other guy's a regular, I don't know him. Are they Fae, too?"

"Josh, no. Conall and Cuinn, yes."

"Are you all this crazy?"

That startled a laugh from him. "Probably. Sometimes, anyway." He shrugged out of his coat and wrapped it around his *scair-anam*'s shoulders, holding him for just a second before turning back to Conall.

And to Cuinn. *Do I owe him my life? And Garrett's?* Not long ago, he had vowed to give the male's eyes to the crows, and his heart to the wolves. His soul...

Cuinn had nearly lost that, himself, into the endless dark. To try to bring Lochlann back from it.

Sometimes, *a'gár'doltas* was satisfied short of death.

His attention went back to Cuinn when the Loremaster tried to gather his legs under himself enough to sit up. It didn't work. "Well, fuck me tremulous."

"Still not interested. I may not need to kill you any more, but that doesn't mean I plan to get intimate."

Cuinn smirked, but the smug expression didn't

reach as far as his eyes. *Message received*, the level gaze said. And that was all the acknowledgment Lochlann was likely to get.

"So, what happened? What did this to you?"

"Are you sure that's a purely professional interest?"

Lochlann sighed. Even a *chara* could be a pain in the ass. "Do you want a healer's help, or don't you?"

"You can't do anything for me. I'm not injured." Cuinn's skin went a shade grayer; he pushed sweaty hair off his face with a trembling hand.

Lochlann stared at the hand, and at the way Cuinn didn't seem to notice the way it shook. Six-hundred-year-old memories became restless and started to murmur. "Are you hungry?"

Cuinn looked at him as though he'd suddenly grown an extra head and the head was on backwards. "What kind of a stupid question is..." He cleared his throat and glared at Lochlann. "Now I am. Thanks, *chara*."

Oh, shit. "I think I know what's happening to you."

"Care to share?"

"Not long ago, I would have called it poetic justice. Now?" Lochlann started to shrug, but thought better of it. "I think you've nearly lost your magick."

The sandy-haired Fae had been pale before, but that was a riot of color compared to the paper-white he went at Lochlann's words. "I can't. I fucking can't."

"It's survivable. I lived through it, you can too." *Maybe it* is *poetic justice, at that.*

"It's not a question of surviving." White showed all around Cuinn's pale green irises. "I have to be able

239

to get back to the Realm. I can't regain magick by way of the ley energy, I'd fry every nerve in my exquisite body."

"You really do never stop," Conall muttered. "So let Lochlann give it back to you. He can do that without harming you, remember?"

Before Cuinn could reply, Lochlann shook his head. "I'm low myself. Almost out. I could heal, at least once, before I'd need to replenish, but there's not enough left in me to make any difference, not to that kind of need."

There was movement off to his side; Garrett, coming to stand beside him, barefoot and wrapped in his black pea-coat. Josh looked up at this, and the two humans traded a look Lochlann, at least, had no idea how to read.

The nearness of his SoulShare, though, triggered a host of thoughts. A few of which had nothing to do with taking that coat off him and celebrating his resurrection properly. "Wait a minute. I can call the ley energy. I might not be able to help calling it, in fact, at least when I'm this tapped out. There's a line near here—"

"Shit." Cuinn managed to push himself away from Lochlann, in the process pushing himself further up the wall, until he was sitting more or less upright. "Don't even think about that. I can't let raw ley energy get anywhere near me. Not while I'm unShared."

"Why not?"

Cuinn's pale green gaze unfocused; he frowned slightly, shook his head, as if he struggled with his own thoughts.

Conall answered for him. "I found out the hard

way what happens when a Fae who hasn't SoulShared touches the ley energy. I nearly got myself killed, and took out a whole lesser nexus doing it." His human's hand tightened on his shoulder, and Conall rested his own hand over it. A few days ago, Lochlann would have found it strange for a Fae to want to touch, and to be touched. Now, of course, it was perfectly understandable.

"What did you mean, you might not be able to help calling it?" Cuinn's focus was back, and his brilliant eyes and palsied hands made him look like a human running a killing fever. In fact, the intensity of his gaze was fucking unnerving. "Do you think you're bound to it?"

"Bound?" The idea took Lochlann by surprise. "I don't think so. I was able to channel without calling it. It was only when I needed more—when the *Marfach*'s tool told me he was going to kill Garrett unless I gave more, and I'd already used everything I had to start healing Garrett—that I called the power, and it answered."

"So it's your choice. Why does that not make me feel any better?"

One eyebrow arched. "I have no idea."

Cuinn grimaced, coughed. "Can you channel more magick now than you could back in the Realm? Before you spent all your own magick?"

"Hell, yes. I could never have handled a concentration of power like the one in the lines." Lochlann's eyes narrowed. "Why the interrogation?"

Cuinn's head fell back against the wall, his eyes half closed. "You remember what I told you, that night at the Lincoln Memorial?"

241

"About why you watch us?"

"Yeah." The other Fae's head came up, his pale gaze transfixing Lochlann. "I think I've started to figure out why I'm supposed to be watching you in particular."

Lochlann didn't have to look, he could feel Garrett bristling beside him. He wrapped an arm around the dancer and drew him close. "Why?"

"You're showing me where I'm meant to go. I think you have been all along."

A chill ran through Lochlann, one he couldn't attribute to the dying fire.

Abruptly, Cuinn gestured, and Lochlann stared as the air tore apart beside the Loremaster, creating a ragged-edged window into a world he had left behind more than twenty-three centuries ago. In contrast to the slaughterhouse around them, the world on the other side was so beautiful his eyes ached with the sight. They would have ached no matter what, though, he was sure. He caught a glimpse of a crystal waterfall, the scent of flowers that grew nowhere in the human world. Heard the full-throated song of a bird, almost enough to take the memory of screams out of the air.

Almost.

"I can't hold it." Cuinn's whisper was barely audible. He was strangely transparent; not Faded, just insubstantial. "Fuck." The edges of the window started to blur, to run.

Lochlann fell to his knees beside the Loremaster, dizzy from the sweetness of the air that rushed through the portal. Air that had never been misted with blood or choked with his lover's cries. "Here." He rested his hands on Cuinn's bare shoulders, letting the last of his own magick trickle into the other Fae, feeling him stiffen. "Don't worry, this is all mine."

"I guess you really do forgive me."

"You're still alive, right?"

Cuinn laughed softly. "For now. *G'ra ma agadh*." The edges of the window solidified again. "Let me go."

Lochlann took his hands away. Between one blink and the next, Cuinn was gone, and the window with him.

Garrett knelt beside him, gingerly. Reluctant to kneel in puddles of his own blood, no doubt. Golden-brown eyes searched his face; a hand rested briefly on his cheek, stroked the roughness of it, pulled away.

"What is it? What's wrong?" Lochlann cupped Garrett's jaw in his hand, savoring the male's softer blond stubble against his palm.

"That place. The one I saw through the hole. It's home, for you, isn't it?" Garrett's whisper was choked. "It's beautiful."

"Beautiful, yes. Home, no." Lochlann kissed his human, hard. "*This* is home."

Chapter Twenty-nine

"How long is that asshole going to stand there in the shower?"

Until I'm fucking ready for him to come out. The male voice had achieved a level of pissed off that until not long ago would have had Janek desperate for some way to hide from the thing inside his own head.

But now? Things were different. Thanks to the motherfucking Fae.

Janek sat on the toilet, elbows on knees, dripping pinkish water all over the bathroom floor. At least he hadn't been shredded this time. But feeling like he'd been sucked through a straw and then blown back out of it somewhere else wasn't a hell of an improvement.

He raised his head and looked into the shower. Easy to do, the door was open and water was spilling all over the floor, because when he'd materialized inside a small shower with Bryce Newhouse, they'd both fucking panicked and Janek had smashed the shower door out of its tracks.

A few seconds of water hadn't done shit to get the dancer's blood off him. Newhouse was probably going to piss himself when he saw what was happening to his anal-retentively clean bathroom.

Once the monster decided to let him piss himself, anyway. Right now it seemed happy to let him stand under the shower head and stare at the wall. He was probably drooling, too, although with all the water there was no way to tell.

Why can I control him, and not you, Meat? He could feel the female twitching. More than that, he could feel it trying to make *him* twitch, and failing. And it must really be desperate to be admitting that it couldn't control him.

"You're asking me? The meat wagon with the rotted brain?"

Not true. Not any more. Oh, he was still basically dead. All it took was one look at his discolored skin, or stamping his feet to know he couldn't feel them. But he didn't stink any more. Nothing was in danger of falling off. His brain, what was left of it, was working fine. Most important, the *Marfach* wasn't pulling his strings any more. He could hear its thoughts, but it couldn't hear his. It couldn't force him to move or to speak.

And it was seriously pissed.

It must have been the Fae. Janek could feel the monster trying to grind his teeth together. ***When he went from filling us with magick to using sympathetic magick—***

"Wait, I've heard of that." Janek shook his head, and was immediately sorry he had. *Guess things aren't quite settled after that little hellride, after all.* "Voodoo dolls, and shit like that? I didn't think Fae did that."

They don't, you moron. The female wanted him to get up, wanted him to pace—as if anyone his size could pace in this fucking closet with bloody water all

245

over the floor. He didn't budge. *Somehow, that Fae knew part of my substance was somewhere else. And he was a strong enough mage to make the magick in that small part attract the magick in the rest of me.*

"Us."

Don't flatter yourself, Meat. You were along for the ride, nothing more.

"You're not talking like something that's totally fucking helpless without its meat wagon." Janek laughed out loud. How long had it been since he'd done that? Since he'd felt like doing it? "Maybe you should try being nice to me."

I am not helpless. Even though Janek was sure the monster couldn't get at him, the third voice still reached into him and made his gut wrench. *The dark Fae filled me with far more power than Guaire could have.*

"Yeah. But without me, all that power is sitting on a toilet for as long as I feel like it." Which could be a very long time. One thing about being a zombie, he'd developed one hell of a tolerance for boredom.

Janek imagined he could feel the thing in his head throbbing with rage. At least, he hoped he was imagining feeling it. If it was actually throbbing, he was going to creep the fuck out. *You are not indispensable. My other lackey can discipline you if you make it necessary.*

Janek guffawed. "That pissant in the shower?" It took him a while to get this bout of laughter under control—he didn't have much of an imagination left, but what little he had was having a field day with the thought of the slack-jawed tool in the shower trying to put hurt on him.

The *Marfach* said nothing as Janek got hold of himself. *Maybe it realizes I'm right.* "And even if he had the balls to do anything but slap me and burst into tears, you don't want him to damage me. You're fused to me. If I die, maybe you do too. And even if you don't, you're stuck with a corpse."

Perhaps there is room for negotiation. The female was back, syrupy sweet. *I admit to having been... sidetracked... from your desires. I can remedy that situation*.

"Guaire's head?"

On a platter, if you wish.

"I'll settle for a dumpster."

Chapter Thirty

"Holy shit." Garrett craned his neck to look up at the façade of the small hotel. All three stories of it. A pocket hotel. And the smaller the hotel, the more expensive it was likely to be. "You didn't tell me you lived in a place like this." He slowed, stopped walking.

"The subject never had a chance to come up."

Lochlann's arm tightened around Garrett's shoulders. Between his SoulShare's embrace, and the Fae's heavy wool coat he'd worn wrapped around himself since the two of them left the makeshift slaughterhouse, he almost felt warm. Almost. "I can't even afford to breathe in there."

"Please don't worry about that, *grafain*." Lochlann urged him forward, reaching around him to open the door. Staying close, because they'd discovered just how much Garrett hated to be alone when Lochlann had made his brief expedition to Garrett's apartment to get clothes for him. By the time he'd returned, Garrett had been shaking uncontrollably, his back to a wall and a poker clutched in one white-knuckled fist.

A lanky, silver-haired man came out from behind a small mahogany desk in one corner of the lobby.

"Mr. Doran! I'm sorry, sir, I didn't see you go out."

Garrett hadn't thought it was possible for him to feel any filthier than he'd felt when he and Lochlann made their way out of the boarded-up store. The understated luxury of the Colchester's lobby showed him how wrong he'd been. He wrapped his arms around himself and tried to step carefully, minimizing his presence.

Lochlann frowned down at him and held him closer. "That's all right, Gerald." The Fae barely glanced at the concierge as he steered Garrett toward a small elevator at the far end of the lobby. "Could you have breakfast sent up? Maybe in a few hours?"

"Of course, sir. Anything in particular?"

"Two of everything."

The door slid open soundlessly, and Lochlann urged Garrett inside. Not that Garrett really needed the urging, although the elevator was just as immaculate as the lobby and the sight made him groan. Looking back out into the lobby as the doors slid closed, he half expected to see a trail of bloody footprints across the plush pearl-gray-and-rose carpet.

"*Grafain*." The low murmur came from behind him; he felt Lochlann's lips brushing his ear, Lochlann's arms enfolding him from behind. He wished he could stop shivering, just to let the Fae know he'd noticed and appreciated the gesture, needed the closeness. Instead, he settled for resting his hands on Lochlann's forearm and gripping tightly.

The door chimed softly and slid open. Lochlann let go of Garrett and ushered him out, down a narrow, immaculate hallway to a heavy wood-paneled door with a modern lock that looked very out of place.

Lochlann reached into the pocket of his coat, the coat he'd put around Garrett's shoulders, took out a key card, swiped it, and opened the door wide.

Jesus. Garrett closed his eyes after his first glimpse of the little suite. *The rooms are worse than the lobby.*

"Welcome home, *grafain*." He heard the door click shut, felt Lochlann's breath warm against his ear. Hands rested briefly on his shoulders, moved to take away the heavy coat.

Garrett gripped the heavy wool, pulling the coat more tightly around himself. "I'm still cold. Do you mind?"

Lochlann's hands fell away, but only for a second; Lochlann turned him, tilted his face up, waited silently until his eyes opened. Frowned, as Garrett flinched. "What is it? You don't want to see me?"

"You've got it backwards." Garrett swallowed, loathing the coppery taste in his mouth the scent of his own blood had left there. "I hate the thought that you're seeing me."

He hadn't really expected the Fae to nod, but he did. "Just healing your wounds wasn't enough, was it?" Lochlann cupped his chin, his palm brushing lightly over Garrett's soft growth of beard—which had, apparently, been restored by magickal healing, since Garrett distinctly remembered that part of his face being ministered to by a red-hot iron poker at some point. "You're more than just your body."

Garrett rested his forehead on Lochlann's shoulder, unable to think of anything to say that wouldn't sound idiotic.

"I think it's time to start healing the rest of you."

"Do you have magick for that, too?"

Fingers worked into his hair, turning his head so his cheek lay against Lochlann's chest. Lochlann's thumb played with his ear. "Not the same kind as the other, but yes, I think I might."

Lochlann kissed, him, hard, but not nearly long enough; gasping, Garrett let the Fae slip the coat off his shoulders, this time. It fell to the floor. Lochlann caught Garrett's hand, and led him away from it toward a door that stood ajar.

I should have suspected the bathroom would be as luxe as the rest of the place. Garrett hung in the doorway, watching Lochlann cross to the cream marble bath set into one corner of the small room, turn on the taps, and add what looked like a couple of kinds of bath salts and oils.

"I'm a bit of a hedonist," Lochlann offered; he didn't turn, but Garrett could hear his smile.

"No, really?" Garrett managed a smile of his own, one that grew wider as Lochlann rose, shucked out of his shirt, and reached for Garrett's just as Garrett started to do the same.

"Let me do that." The Fae's tone was light, but his gaze was piercing. "Please. Let me make it good for you. All of it."

Oh, Jesus. Garrett sucked in a breath at the sensation of Lochlann's hands sliding across his abs, gripping the sweatshirt he'd fetched from Garrett's apartment. A shirt quickly gone and forgotten, and Lochlann was unbuttoning Garrett's jeans, reaching around behind him, hands sliding in to cup and grip his ass and slide the jeans down.

Garrett leaned into Lochlann as he toed off the

sneakers Lochlann had brought him. He didn't need help balancing. He needed to feel Lochlann's solid warmth. This close, the Fae's ink was mesmerizing, a beautiful pattern in bluish silver, maybe tribal, maybe Irish or Celtic or whatever, slanting across his chest. He didn't even realize he was tracing the design with a fingertip until Lochlann laughed softly.

"I like that." Lochlann bent and nipped lightly at Garrett's ear. "Feel free to continue."

The jeans pooled around Garrett's ankles; he stepped out of them and kicked them aside, then watched as Lochlann divested himself of jeans and boots. What floor space there was, was soon covered with discarded clothing

Lochlann drew Garrett close, and with nothing between them, Garrett was sure his Fae lover's keen senses could pick up both the hammering of his heart and the thin film of sweat that slicked him.

"*S'ocan, grafain.*" Lochlann's hand smoothed down Garrett's side, his flank; curved around, gripped his buttock and fitted him against the much taller Fae. "Peace." The whisper was barely audible over the rush of water into the tub.

"I'm trying," Garrett whispered back. The whisper caught hard in his throat.

This kiss lasted long enough for him to moan into it, to part his lips to a questing tongue. To damn near melt, holding on to Lochlann's hard shoulders to keep from staggering. But no, he couldn't melt. If he did that, he wouldn't be able to get into the bath with Lochlann.

Lochlann broke the kiss with a parting nip at Garrett's lower lip and a feral sound that might have been a purr, or might have been a growl. Whatever it was, it brought Garrett to full and rigid attention. The smile that followed nearly finished him off. And when Lochlann slid one arm down behind him, swept him up, and set him in the tub? Utter bliss, shot through with a vein of the pure joy he'd tasted in his dressing room, in his apartment, and wherever it was he'd gone after he died. He tipped his head back and let out a sigh, smiling as the water closed around him, scented and charged with whatever Lochlann had added to it.

Lochlann kissed Garrett again, one hand cupping his head and the other running slowly down his chest, gliding under the water, the open palm running over the ridges of his abs. Garrett's back arched, and he felt Lochlann's lips curve in a smile just before the kiss broke.

"I think you're ready." Lochlann climbed into the tub and knelt astride Garrett's thighs. Leaning forward, he braced himself with a hand on the rim of the tub, brushed his lips across Garrett's, and settled in for a long, scorching kiss. At the same time, his other hand closed around Garrett's erection, squeezing, thumb playing with the silver ring piercing the head.

Water sloshed as Garrett's hips jerked involuntarily. He heard and felt and could have sworn he tasted Lochlann's soft laughter. "I'm just getting started." The Fae interrupted his own words with tongue-play, licking and nipping at Garrett's lips and chin until Garrett moaned. Then the teasing moved downward, along Garrett's throat; his head fell back, and Lochlann accepted the accidental invitation, biting hard enough to make him cry out, and then groan with pleasure as the bite was soothed by the Fae's hot tongue.

Lochlann's hips shifted against him, in time with the slow insistent pumping of his cock. Even surrounded by the heat of the water, Garrett could feel the brand of Lochlann's erection gliding against his groin and abs, and managed to raise his head enough to look. The images rippled under the water, but there was no mistaking what he saw, Lochlann's hand working his length and Lochlann's own thick rod sliding over his tight blond curls. "Glad you didn't use bubble bath."

The Fae's laugh was erotic as hell. "I like to watch, too, *grafain*." Glancing down, he teased at Garrett's Prince Albert, and both of them groaned in unison as Garrett's cock pulsed gently in Lochlann's grip.

Garrett tried to sit up, to open some space so he could reach between their bodies and return the favor. But Lochlann shook his head firmly. "Relax." Strands of the Fae's dark hair were plastered to his temples, his forehead, with sweat and with the moisture that hung in the air, framing his faceted aquamarine eyes. "Just enjoy. I want to see you enjoy this."

"Oh, God." Garrett's head lolled back again, until it hit the high back of the porcelain tub. Lochlann was using both hands, now, still keeping to the rhythm set by his hips. They were both panting, and soft grunts of pleasure hung in the humid, scented air. As much as he wanted this to go on forever, Garrett couldn't keep his hips still, and Lochlann's firm grip around the base of his cock was just about the only thing keeping him from sweet release.

Then one of the Fae's hands vanished, and an instant later Garrett felt a hand between his thighs and insistent stroking at his taint. "Oh, *fuck*." His grip on the sides of the tub went white-knuckled.

"Oh, no, you don't. Not yet." Lochlann's voice rasped, his breathing was uneven. "Guide me. *Now*."

Garrett froze. Take Lochlann inside himself? But what if—

I can let him do this. It's safe. I'm *safe*.

Ignoring the tears streaming down his cheeks, he encircled Lochlann's thick shaft with his hand, pumping, making him ready.

"*Grafain*—"

"I'm all right. Do it." God, his lover's eyes were beautiful. "Take me." He swallowed hard. "I love you."

The joy, the laughter, blazed up in him, a clean fire driving out all memory of the torturer's fire. And from the look on his face, the sharp intake of his breath, Lochlann was feeling the same thing. *Yeah, that was the right thing to say.*

Water sloshed over the edge of the tub as Garrett and Lochlann hurriedly rearranged their legs, Garrett hooking his heels over the edge of the tub, trying to brace himself. Taking the Fae's hot shaft back into his hand, Garrett eased him to his entrance. *Damn, I wish my hands would quit shaking.* "Sorry."

Lochlann shook his head sharply. "No regrets." His hips swayed a little, just enough to let Garrett feel his blunt head probing. "I don't know if this is the first time for love, for you. And you don't have to tell me. But it is for me." The Fae's beautiful, sensual smile flashed. "My hands are shaking too."

Yes, the hands parting him were trembling. Garrett bit his lip, and groaned as his ring was breached. *Hell, yes, it is.* When he'd come to D.C., he'd been barely eighteen. A couple of wild nights in high school, never with anyone his own age, the wounds were too fucking deep for that. One all-nighter with his physics teacher, a bong, and a bottle of Jack, *God* what a night. But that had been the sum total of his experience before he started renting his ass out in order to pay the bills on a dancer's wages.

Now? Now the man he would have dreamed of if he'd ever let himself dream was sliding into him one mind-blowing inch at a time, looking down at him with eyes that were starting to unfocus with pleasure, whispering his name. Loving him.

Sharing a soul with him.

Garrett tried to move with Lochlann, but he couldn't do much in the tight quarters. Lochlann didn't seem to mind, he was panting for breath and moaning low in his throat with every thrust, but Garrett wanted, needed, to do more. He'd learned things, ways to blow a john's mind and get him the hell out the door, but nothing he knew was meant to prolong the experience. *I'm an encyclopedia of screwing, but I know fuck-all about loving.*

"Hold me." Lochlann's voice was as unsteady as his hands had been. "*Grafain, m'lanan*, please, hold me, hold on to me."

He'd heard that plea before. Or he thought he had. There was a memory like a dream, his lover being swept away by something, begging Garrett to hold on to him. Was he being swept away now? Garrett reached up, wrapping his arms clumsily around Lochlann's neck. He did his best to hold him inside, too, clamping down with his ring and working his inner muscles against the shaft that burned so sweetly on its way in and out of him.

Which was, apparently, exactly what his lover needed. Lochlann fell forward, sending water sheeting over the sides of the tub, sealing his mouth to Garrett's an instant before his body stiffened, his cock curved within Garrett. Garrett felt the first hard pulse pumping the thick clear seed of a Water Fae into his hold, heard Lochlann's low, almost breathless cry, before every other sensation gave way to the delight he remembered from his dressing room. He'd fought it then. There was no reason to fight it now.

He was being kissed. His face was being searched with kisses. And oh, Christ, he was hard. His cock was pressing up into Lochlann's abs, and his PA was pinned, digging into his erection in a way he'd never felt before.

"It's your turn, *grafain*." Laughter, SoulShared laughter, filled Lochlann's words.

"It's—*what*?"

"You didn't think I was going to leave you to take care of your situation all by yourself, did you?"

"What I'm doing right now has very little to do with thinking—*oh*, shit." Garrett's whole body jerked as Lochlann opened up just enough space between them to slip in a hand and grip his cock. "Lochlann…"

Lochlann tugged at Garrett's lower lip with his teeth, caressed it with his tongue, and finally kissed him deeply, stroking him the whole time with a dexterity that made him ashamed he'd ever thought he was an expert. He slid his hands down Lochlann's wet, slick body and sank his fingers into the firmest ass it had ever been his pleasure to grab, pulling him close and grinding against him, thrusting insistently into his hand.

Echoes of delight still rippled through him, and he laughed into the kiss when he realized what his body was doing. Lochlann pulled back, just enough to look at him quizzically, and this time he laughed aloud. "The next time I work the pole at Purgatory, I think the crowd is going to set a world record for the biggest simultaneous orgasm."

The Fae's guttural purr made Garrett even harder. His grip tightened, his undulations against Lochlann's body sent water splashing. "So. Damn. *Close*."

Releasing Garrett's shaft, Lochlann leaned back and pulled him forward, slipping out of him in the process. More sloshing, a foot nearly disastrously placed, a breathless apology, and Garrett found himself kneeling between Lochlann's thighs, his lover facing the twin faucets and holding on to the edge of the tub, looking pure, unadulterated fuck-me-now back over his shoulder.

"I've wanted to feel that ring in me since I first touched it." Lochlann rocked back against him, innocently lascivious. "Use it the way it's meant to be used, *grafain*."

"Shit." If anything, his hand was shaking harder than it had been before, when he was tending to Lochlann. He wrapped it around the base of his cock. Water dripped from the swollen tip, clung to the stainless steel ring, dropped into the dimple at the base of the Fae's spine. He'd been fucked so many times he'd lost count. But never since his diagnosis had he allowed himself the pleasure. Every so often, a john had wanted to take it, rather than dish it out. They usually laughed and called him old-fashioned, when he said no. Maybe he was. A few had been angry. He didn't give a damn. It hadn't felt right.

Now, with Lochlann teasing him, coaxing him with eyes and smile and ass and laughter, it was impossible for it to be any more right. Holding tightly to Lochlann's hip with one hand, he positioned himself with the other and sank himself deep, sucking in a breath as his Prince Albert cleared the Fae's tight entrance. And once he was fully seated, he took hold with both hands, spreading Lochlann's cheeks with his thumbs. He wanted to see, damn it.

Lochlann's back arched like a cat's when Garrett's piercing found his sweet spot. "Fuck. You're going to do it to me again."

Garrett's vision was starting to go, too, flashes of white coming thick and fast every time he drilled in. And he could barely hear Lochlann over the roaring in his own ears. But he heard. Letting go of one hip, he reached around, finding the hot, heavy truth of Lochlann's words and jerking on his cock with a desperate rhythm matching his own.

Lochlann's hand closed around Garrett's, tightening his grip.

Something—the feel of the veins and ribs and heat pulsing against his hand, Lochlann's unsteady cry, the splashing of the water as he thrust, a spasm of the Fae's inner muscles, all of it—stole the last of Garrett's self-control. Pleasure sleeted down his spine, turned to a hot weight in his balls, curved his cock rigid and quivering, and exploded.

He couldn't breathe. That was okay, he didn't need air. He just needed more of this. Blinding pleasure. Knowing he was giving Lochlann the same, as the Fae's cock throbbed in his hand and he heard Lochlann's choked moans. *Someday I'm going to make him scream.* Pure, white-light joy. At the prospect of giving that to Lochlann. At being buried to the hilt in a lover. At being free.

At finally, and forever, giving himself.

Garrett was slumped over Lochlann's back, rising and falling with it as the Fae tried to catch his breath. It took him a minute to recognize the pleasant heaviness making him reluctant to so much as lift his head. This was what being at peace with a lover felt like.

Letting go of Lochlann's softening shaft, he stroked the Fae's hard and still-heaving abs with his open palm, in ever-widening circles. Slower, slower, until he came awake with a little jerk. "Oh, hell."

Lochlann laughed softly. "No wonder you're falling asleep, after the night you had. Here, let me take care of you."

Garrett tried to protest, but it did no good. Somehow, Lochlann got them both out of the bath, dried him thoroughly with a towel that felt like a cloud, wrapped him in a robe made of the same stuff, and helped him to bed. Normally, Garrett would have hated to be helped, but in this case he counted it as a win, because he'd managed to talk Lochlann out of carrying him. Yes, he wanted to be in the Fae's arms. But not as an invalid.

"I don't want to sleep." This, as Lochlann came into the bed with him and drew a comforter up over them both. "I know I probably should. But I don't want to."

Slowly, deliberately, Lochlann entwined his legs with Garrett's, then wrapped an arm around him and drew him in close. "The healer says you should sleep."

Garrett sighed, and started to protest, but was stopped by a finger across his lips.

"Your *scair-anam*, on the other hand, remembers that he made you a *galtanas deich meloi*." Fingertips played in Garrett's still-damp curls. "I owe you ten thousand reasons for joy, if I remember correctly."

"I only need one," Garrett whispered. "And I have it."

Epilogue

Cuinn hadn't had the strength to place the damned rift properly, and his fall from ten feet above the ground was anything but graceful. At least he landed on soft earth and green grass, and not in the nearby rocky basin at the base of the waterfall, close enough for him to be dripping with cold water from the spray in seconds.

Not that he gave a damn about being wet. Or any of the other beauties of home he'd glimpsed before falling through the portal. His body was starving for magick, and he hugged the turf, drawing it into his body through every pore and with every breath, straight from the substance of the Realm. The ultimate storehouse of all the living magick that had been drawn out of every source in the human world, willing or not.

Shit. Is this what it felt like for Lochlann? He hadn't been around when his friend had finally lost his magick—which, in light of some of his recent speculations, he found more than a little suspicious—and hadn't felt comfortable bringing the subject up of late. But if his own experience was any guide, he completely understood the whole 'eyes for the crows, heart for the wolves' thing.

Magick trickled slowly back into his body;

262

slowly, no matter how hard he drew or how sharp his craving was. *Maybe if I'd been totally depleted...* He'd had to close his eyes against the brilliance when Lochlann was drawing on the ley energy. *Maybe a Fae has to be empty, before he can be the vessel for that kind of power.*

And the Pattern, the Loremasters, wanted me to watch that. They'd wanted him to watch a hell of a lot more, actually. Starting with Lochlann's agony, stuck halfway through the Pattern. Lochlann's increased capacity to channel, after losing his magick. And Cuinn had a sneaking suspicion he'd been meant to see what happened when his friend lost himself, in the torrent of magick it had taken for him to go after his SoulShare and find him wherever it was humans went when they died. *I was meant to see that. And I wasn't meant to see what it was like for a Fae to lose magick.*

He closed his eyes, one cheek against the dry and brittle grass. *I wonder how close I was meant to come to finding out for myself, up close and personal.*

His fellow Loremasters had always said part of what he needed to accomplish, in his role as bridge between the Realm and the human world, was to figure out his own ultimate role in the Pattern. He was starting to get an inkling. And it was one motherhumping ugly inkling.

The original Loremasters had walked, or been carried, quietly and voluntarily, to their self-immolation. If he'd been asked to do the same, then, Cuinn would have joined them. But he now had something his fellow Loremasters didn't have. Twenty-three hundred and some odd number of years of surviving.

He'd acquired a taste for it.

He didn't realize until he heard the splash of water nearby that he'd stopped hearing it a while ago. Curious, he pushed up, started to get to his feet.

Stopped, staring in horror at the ground on which he'd lain. Earth and grass alike were black, and not the rich black of fertile earth. This was a crusted, grayish, sterile blackness that put Cuinn in fear that it might crumble away under him. Carefully, he pushed up to a kneeling position and looked around.

A shudder rippled through his hard-muscled body. Everything around him, in a circle a hundred yards across, looked just like the patch of ground on which he knelt. *I was fucking out of control.* Fortunately, he was full of living magick again, he could feel his nerves humming quietly to themselves. *I don't want to have to do this again any time soon— this kind of damage is going to take months to heal.*

The splashing sound became more urgent, and Cuinn groaned at sight of the source of it. The waterfall that had soaked him upon his arrival was gone, the stone of the bluff over which it had tumbled was grey and cracked. And the basin into which the water had spilled was nearly empty, except for a small ink-black pool. The surface of which, impossibly, was rippling.

Black on black, the ripples became a shaping, one that held form for only a moment and then became illegible. *WHAT DID YOU SEE?*

Cuinn's jaw clenched tight as he reached inside himself for the magick to create a book. Something to shape on. Something to shape with.

NO. This splash was loud, urgent, and Cuinn had to wait for the pool to settle to make out the next shaping. *SPEND NO MAGICK UNNECESSARILY.*

"Well, then, what the fuck am I supposed to do?"
ONE OF US CAN HEAR YOU WHEN YOU SPEAK. NOT ALL. BUT THIS WILL DO.

"Aine?"

YES. QUICKLY, TELL US WHAT YOU SAW. WHAT HAPPENED TO OUR ENEMY? The Loremasters had always been reluctant to shape the monster's name, and small wonder, when the shapes of names were what made up the Pattern itself.

"Fuck if I know. When I got there, Dary was in Lochlann directing the channeling, and the *Marfach* and its life-challenged host were lit up in magickal light like the Times Square ball on New Year's Eve."

LIKE WHAT?

"Not important." *Not to you, anyway. Personally, I've made a point of making out under that ball every New Year's Eve since 1929, and I'd just as soon keep doing it for a good long time yet.* "Both of them were pumped full of living magick, Lochlann could tap straight into the ley energy somehow, even though the nearest line was a couple of blocks away. And then Dary... well, he made the bad guy go away again. Somehow."

The water was still. It might as well have been crude oil, and the thought made Cuinn feel queasy. Then, slowly, ripples formed. *SO THE ENEMY IS LOOSE IN THE HUMAN WORLD, AND FILLED WITH THE POWER IT HAS BEEN SEEKING SINCE ITS EXILE.*

Cuinn felt a chill that had nothing to do with his own near-nudity. A half-dozen wiseass comebacks died on his lips. "Yes."

DIRE NEWS.

265

No shit.

IT GETS WORSE.

"Not exactly what you want to hear from the closest thing your race has to a god." A very Fae sort of god, with no one knew how much power and just enough foresight to keep from driving the whole race headlong over a cliff.

One hoped it had that much.

NEVERTHELESS. A sigh seemed to pass over the surface of the water, calming it. *THIS SCAR ON THE REALM YOU HAVE CREATED IS NOT GOING TO HEAL.*

Cuinn stared at the water. It didn't reflect him. Didn't reflect anything.

THE END HAS BEGUN.

Which meant, the Realm's store of living magick was gone. Irreversibly. What there was, in the trees and the earth and the animals and the Fae, was all that was left.

And when it was gone, everything in the Realm would look like the blasted circle around him.

Once more the ripples smoothed, the water's surface went murky oily black. When they came, the ripples were slow, measured.

ONE HOPE REMAINS.

THE EXILED FAE NEED THEIR LEADER.

IT IS TIME, CUINN. TIME FOR YOU TO FIND THE PRINCE.

Following is the first chapter of Firestorm,
Book Four in the SoulShares Series

Firestorm

Prologue

The Realm
July 12, 1991 (human reckoning)

Cuinn would have clenched his fists in frustration, if
he'd had any. It was probably a bit much to expect the
new Queen of the Demesne of Fire to quit cooing at
the fussy bundle of hair-at-one-end-and-the-smell-of-
sulphur-at-the-other who had elevated her to the throne
just by being born. But she'd been doing it for going
on two hours, and if she didn't put the brat down and
find something else to do, he, Cuinn, was going to
miss a very important appointment. Either that, or he
was going to have to add regicide to the list of crimes
he was pulling off tonight, and he was reasonably sure
his friendly overseers in the Pattern would be unhappy
with his lapse in diplomacy.

As if kidnapping a baby stood much higher on
any moral scale than killing the baby's mother.

Cuinn shrugged. Mentally, anyhow. Hard to do
that physically when his physicality was Faded. *Come
on, your newly-minted Majesty. Put down the brat and
back away slowly. Or turn and run. I'm easy either
way.*

His fellow Loremasters had concocted a system,
more than two millennia ago, to ensure that the
elementals among the Fae kept breeding, and in so

doing feeding elemental magick into the Realm. While a chosen four thousand slept through the final battle with the *Marfach*, Cuinn's fellow Loremasters had, not to put too fine a point on it, fucked with their heads. When they woke up, they all recognized the formerly reclusive and rare elemental Fae as their rulers. Not only that, but the new rules of Royalty required the throne of each Demesne to have two occupants at all times, a King or Queen and his or her opposite-sex offspring. A single Royal, or a childless Royal couple, was just killing time, until a female gave birth and the offspring's sex determined who would be ruler and who would be Consort. So when Nuala, here, had popped out baby Rian, she had given herself one hell of a promotion. Hence, all the fussing and cooing and gurgling.

Well, the promotion to Queen probably had a lot to do with it, yes, but there was also that whole love-of-blood-for-blood thing the Fae had going on since even before the Sundering. Good thing he had lost all his own blood kin a long time ago. Not to mention the fact the squab's ensouling ceremony had been this morning, so no doubt Mama Queen was feeling even more maternal. Fae didn't suffer from illnesses, and wounds not mortal healed quickly, but more than half of all infants died, inexplicably, within two weeks after birth. So tradition said that a newborn Fae didn't receive his or her soul until two weeks passed safely. *Too bad this one's going to lose half of his so soon.*

Oh, fuck, not another lullaby. Cuinn tried to pace, but when he was in this condition, he could only drift. He was good for another three or four hours of this, but every minute he spent Faded increased the chance he would get careless and look into one of the many mirrors scattered through the palace to trap Fae foolish enough to attempt what he was doing. Royals were paranoid, all of them. Perhaps rightfully so.

The Queen made a lovely picture as she bent over her son, he admitted grudgingly. Her long blonde hair was done up, and fastened with strands of fire opals; her diaphanous scarlet gown moved as she swayed with the infant in her arms, clinging to her in ways that under other circumstances would have had Cuinn conjuring a bucket of water to soak her to that creamy skin. At the moment, though, all he wanted was to see her put her precious Rian into his cradle and tiptoe out of the nursery.

SIMPLE ENOUGH. He'd groaned out loud, reading the shaping that had sent him off on this idiotic venture. *ENTER WHILE FADED, TAKE THE CHILD, AND LEAVE BY THE NEAREST EXIT.* At least the other Loremasters had understood he couldn't just Fade out of the palace with the kid, not the way Royals had taken to warding their residences. Unless he wanted to be turned inside out. Which he didn't, particularly.

What the fuck had the other Loremasters been smoking, to come up with this? Not that immortal souls bound in a matrix of pure magick were likely to smoke anything, but still—

The Queen bent, carefully placing the swaddled infant in his cradle. She kissed his forehead, and Faded without straightening.

That's the last time she'll ever do that. The thought startled Cuinn. His conscience, such as it was, picked the damnedest times to rise from the dead. He

269

had an assignment to complete, and if he was lucky he could do his duty and be back in San Francisco before the bars closed.

Drifting out of the curtained recess where he'd been lurking, he took form. Just to be safe. Which was fortunate, because when he approached the cradle, he saw the mirror at the head of it even before he saw the sleeping baby. One last soul-trap. The Fire Royals were thorough, he had to give them that.

All their precautions weren't going to help them, though. Cuinn reached into the cradle and lifted out the infant, swaddling clothes and all. The kid would probably need the blanket, though Cuinn hoped the Pattern would drop him someplace where it was summer.

No, now was not the time to be thinking about what he was going to be doing to this helpless baby. Now was the time to be getting the fuck out of here before someone spotted him. Yet he lingered, looking at the child asleep in his arms. One thing he'd learned, over his twenty-five hundred something years of life, was that people who gushed about beautiful babies were, for the most part, either talking about their own children, or just being polite about someone else's. Babies all tended to look vaguely sinister to Cuinn, as if they weren't quite finished being formed yet and were looking around for some nice tasty life essence to absorb to fill up the corners.

This one, though, really was everything a proud new parent had ever bragged about. Perfect features, a fuzz of blond hair, one tiny hand curled up in a fist under his chin, and fuck if his lips didn't look just like a little rosebud.

Cuinn wished his conscience would shut the hell up. He was spending too much time around humans. Almost time for a sabbatical, back here in the Realm, anonymously banging everything over the age of consent that moved, and a few select things that didn't.

The baby's eyes opened. Rian Aodán had the bluest eyes Cuinn had ever seen, the blue faceted like a cut gemstone. Perfect blue topaz. He got the distinct impression those eyes were accusing him.

Cuinn grimaced, and deliberately turned his thoughts back to the route he'd taken to get to the Royal nursery. Shielding the baby with his arms—not that it would hurt him to be Faded by someone else, at least not until he came of age and came into his birthright of power, but dropping him now would be the textbook definition of a Very Bad Thing—he Faded to the closest window he remembered, a bay window set into the wall of a corridor, with a velvet-cushioned window seat.

Said window was set seamlessly into the stone wall. *Son of a syphilitic bitch.* Cuinn thought about trying to break the glass. Then he thought about trying to climb out of a shattered window over jagged shards of glass, unnoticed, carrying an infant. Not happening.

The next window he tried presented the same situation. The next one, too. Worse, his Royal Highness was starting to get restless, his face working as if he was about to either cry or fill the Royal nappie. Worse still, he could hear the voices of what sounded like a gaggle of servants heading his way. He'd been incredibly lucky so far. Maybe it was time to stop counting on luck.

There was a scullery entrance almost halfway

around the perimeter of the palace. He hadn't wanted to use it to get in, mostly because it was too damned far from the nursery and it would have taken him hours to drift incorporeally to his target. But the door had been open when he passed it yesterday, scouting the place out, and he'd caught a glimpse inside. Enough to let him Fade there without ending up half inside a stone wall?

I sure as shit hope so.

He could hear footsteps now, as well as voices. *Time to go.*

Holding the infant tightly, he Faded.

Taking form in the Royal kitchen, he found himself staring straight at what had to be the delivery entrance. All the way through the curtain wall, wide enough to allow for the unloading of a wagon, bolted with a counterweighted latch the thickness of a tree trunk. *It's a door. Good enough.*

"Who are you?"

The female voice came from behind him. Which meant she hadn't seen his face, or the Royal brat in his arms. Without turning, he made sure matters would stay that way, closing his eyes and drawing on his inner store of magick to channel a pulse of brilliant white light that would leave anyone, even a rapidly-healing Fae, blind for at least a minute.

The female screamed. Unfortunately, so did Rian.

Fuck me backwards. Too late to deafen the female as well. Cuinn sent the magick arrowing straight for the door, channeling the counterweight up, opening the double doors wide with a silent blast of power.

He was greeted by darkness. He caught a glimpse

of the yard outside, bare earth churned by the hooves of horses and the wheels of wagons, and the torch-lit wall of the enclosure around the postern gate, off to one side.

And the deep, angry baying of at least a half-dozen hounds. The Royal Fade-hounds.

Cuinn sprinted out the door into the darkness, the screaming infant clutched as close as he dared. The bellowing came from the area of the gate, so he took off running in the other direction.

He tore through the torch-lit darkness, not even daring to spare the magick to snuff out the torches as he fled, much less speed his flight or do something about the fucking dogs. Fade-hounds scented magick. If the hounds had his scent, they'd be able to follow him when he Faded. Which would mean an untimely end to his role in the Pattern's ultimate plan for the Realm, unless there was something he could do while each of his limbs was being carried off triumphantly by a different dog.

Rian squalled in his arms. Cuinn didn't dare spare a glance as he hurdled a watering trough set out for the cart-horses, but he was sure that perfect little face was screwed up like a monkey's and a brilliant shade of red. *Shit, could we possibly be any more obvious?* He had to get far enough ahead of the hounds to be able to spare the time to stop and Fade, and between the dogs and the brat, it was only a matter of time before the Royal Defense cut him off.

The rounded shape of a giant stone cistern loomed up ahead of him.

I am fucking insane.

Cuinn leaped to the tongue of a wagon drawn up

beside the cistern, and from there to the driver's seat. One more leap brought him teetering to the edge. His luck, such as it was, was holding; the basin had no cover, and it was nearly full. Looking down at the screaming baby, he clamped a hand over the tiny nose and mouth, drew a deep breath, and jumped into the dark water.

Fuck, I hope water kills magick-scent. Though it was a bit late for that particular concern. Rian kicked and wriggled in his arms as the two of them settled to the floor of the cistern. The instant his ass hit the stones, he reached within, found his magick, tapped it. One last Fade.

Water came along with the Loremaster and the infant Prince Royal, spilling away from where Cuinn sprawled on the floor, the baby still cradled against his chest. He heard a tiny cough, a gasp for air. A pause, as if to consider options. Then the caterwauling started up again.

Cuinn gritted his teeth and slowly, carefully got to his feet. The black floor gleamed under his feet like polished crystal, lit only by the moonlight from the single window over his head, and the silver-blue shimmering of the complex knotwork of lines under his dripping bare feet.

The lines changed, shifted into a shaping. *YOU'RE WET.*

"No shit." This was the only place in two worlds where he could talk directly to his fellow Loremasters, whose souls formed the matrix embedded in the Pattern. "The next time you decide a felony needs to be committed, you can fucking well do it yourselves. Or at least tell me if I need to bring drugged meat for the dogs."

The shaping under his feet ignored him entirely. Which was typical. *TIME IS SHORT. LEAVE THE CHILD AND GO.*

Rian was still crying, but the shrill, fingernails-down-chalkboard quality of most newborns—Fae or human—was gone. Babies this small were too young to weep, yet it seemed as if this one did.

But what the hell did he know about babies?

"You'll let me know where to find him on the other side?" Normally Cuinn didn't ask where a Fae was going, didn't really care. A lot of them didn't survive the transition. This one would—whenever the Pattern told him to get involved with a transition, the Fae involved lived through it—but there was usually no point to getting attached to a stray Fae. The infant Prince was making himself an exception, though, and the Pattern could usually find out if it tried.

NO. YOU MUST NOT KNOW. NEITHER CAN WE.

"*What?*" The edge to Cuinn's voice set Rian off again. "You expect me to just dump a newborn into the human world and walk away?"

YES. This shaping had the gentler curves that meant Aine had been delegated to handle the conversation. She was the one Loremaster who could usually get through to Cuinn. *YOU CANNOT TOUCH HIM, AND NEITHER CAN WE.*

"Why?" Cuinn was starting to get irritated. He wasn't going to lose sleep over this, given that even a newborn Fae would be immortal on the other side of the Pattern, but was a straight answer every once in a while really too much to ask?

THIS IS A PART OF THE PLAN WE HAVE

BEEN UNABLE TO FORESEE. The silver-blue light flickered, the Pattern's equivalent of a sigh. *YOU COULD REFUSE, OF COURSE. BUT IF YOU DO, YOU PUT AT RISK EVERYTHING WE HAVE ALL WORKED FOR. THAT MUCH, WE DO KNOW.*

Cuinn glanced involuntarily at the window. A shaft of moonlight shone in, the full moon nearly framed in the chamber's one tiny window. He had set this channeling up himself, twenty-three hundred years ago, his own little secret, a magick no one but him understood, creating a pathway between worlds that didn't draw on the Realm's ambient magick. All he had to do was put the baby on the floor in the path of the moonlight, and let the moon do its work.

Once again, Rian's crying was subsiding, though tears still stood in the corners of his eyes. Cuinn couldn't shake the feeling that they were angry tears, and that those faceted blue eyes were glaring at him. *Shut up, conscience. This is not my fault.*

He shifted the little bundle in his arms. Paused, frowned, feeling something small and hard and heavy in the blanket that wrapped the little Prince, something that hadn't been there before. Peeling back the blanket, his brows arched at a glint of gold, the color visible even in the pure white moonlight. The color meant it was truegold, formed of magick and possessed of a purpose all its own.

He reached into the blanket and caught up the object, just enough to see what it was. The Royal signet, the stylized *Croí na Dóthan*, Heart of Flame, carved deeply into the flat surface. He'd be willing to swear it hadn't been there when he took the child. Obviously, it had decided to come along, for its own reasons. Cuinn hoped it hadn't just vanished off the Prince Consort's finger. At least, not while its owner had been looking.

NOW, CUINN. The shaping flared, almost as bright as the moonlight.

Cuinn growled in response, tucking the ring back into the blanket. Rian was still glaring at him, fair winglike brows drawn together into a scowl. "I'm not stealing the damned thing. I couldn't if I tried."

Two steps took him to stand in the path the moonlight was marking across the wet floor. He bent and set down the infant, straightened.

Shit. The tiny chin was quivering, fists smaller than Cuinn's thumbs were flailing.

Cuinn looked down at the infant, surrounded by the intricate bluish-silver network of loops and whorls that made up the Pattern, and every single fucking memory he'd been trying to suppress since he Faded in here came back in a rush. Watching his best—his only—friend test the new-formed Pattern, only to be stuck halfway through, in utter agony. Testing it again, himself, after making changes to the channeling that powered it, and discovering that the agony was only slightly less when the damned thing worked the way it was supposed to. He'd had nightmares for months afterward, as had every Fae he'd ever seen pass screaming through the Pattern over the millennia since.

And he was going to do that to a baby?

GO. NOW. OR YOU WILL BE CAUGHT YOURSELF.

The circle of moonlight on the floor was brushing the finely stitched hem of the blanket that swaddled the Prince Royal. Around him, the floor was beginning to go transparent, the lines to brighten, to glint like the blades they were, keen enough to divide soul from soul. The baby stared up at him, silent, faceted eyes wide. Not pleading, it was as if he knew pleading was useless.

Memorizing. Remembering.

Rian Aodán was about to take Cuinn an Dearmad's face to hell with him.

Cursing, Cuinn Faded, and found himself leaning against the outside wall of the little round tower he had built himself, over two thousand years ago. Unable to stop listening, he waited.

Wind howled within the tower.

The baby screamed. Cuinn flattened his hands over his ears, but it wasn't enough to stop the sound. Nothing could be worse than the uncomprehending terror in that sound.

Nothing, except the silence that came after.

The following is a glossary of the *Faen* words and phrases found in *Hard as Stone, Gale Force,* and *Deep Plunge.* The reader should be advised that, as in the Celtic languages descended from it, spelling in *Faen* is as highly eccentric as the one doing the spelling.

Glossary

(A few quick pronunciation rules—bearing in mind that most Fae detest rules—single vowels are generally 'pure', as in ah, ey, ee, oh, oo for a, e, i, o, u. An accent over a vowel means that vowel is held a little longer than its unaccented cousins. "ao" is generally "ee", but otherwise dipthongs are pretty much what you'd expect. Consonants are a pain. "ch" is hard, as in the modern Scottish "loch". "S", if preceded by "i" or "a", is usually "sh". "F" is usually silent, unless it's the first letter in a word, and if the word starts with "fh", then the "f" and the "h" are *both* silent. "Th" is likewise usually silent, as is "dh", although if "dh" is at the beginning of a word, it tries to choke on itself and ends up sounding something like a "strangled" French "r". Oh, and "mh" is "v", "bh" is "w", "c" is always hard, and don't forget to roll your "r"s!)

ach   but

a'gár'doltas   vendetta (lit. "smiling-murder")

agean   ocean

amad'n   fool, idiot

anam   soul

   m'anam   my soul. Fae endearment.

aon-arc   unicorn

asling   dream

batagar   arrow

beag   little, slight

bod   penis (vulgar)

bodlag   limp dick (much greater insult than a human might suppose)

bragan   toy (see phrase)

briste   broken

buchal alann   beautiful boy

ca'fuil?   Where?

ceangal   Royal soul-bonding ceremony in the Realm (common alt. spelling *ceangail*)

cein fa?   Why?

céle   general way of referring to two people

   le céle   together

   a céle   one another, each other

chara   friend

cho'halan   so beautiful

coladh   sleep

cónai   live

croí   heart

Cruan'ba   The Drowner. Name given to the Marfach by the Fae of the Demesne of Water.

cugat   to you

d'aos'Faen   Old Faen, the old form of the Fae language. Currently survives only in written form.

dar'cion   brilliantly colored. Conall's pillow-name for Josh.

dearmad   forgotten

deich   ten

   deich meloi   ten thousand

derea   end

desúcan   fix, repair

dóchais   hope (n.) (alt. spelling dócas)

dolmain   hollow hill, a place of refuge

doran   stranger, exile

d'orant   impossible. Josh's pillow-name for Conall.

draoctagh   magick

   Spiraod n'Draoctagh   Spirit of Magick. Ancient Fae oath. Or expletive. Sometimes both.

dre'fiur   beloved sister

dre'thair   beloved brother

dubh   black, dark

eiscréid   shit

Faen   the Fae language. *Laurm Faen*—I speak Fae.

   as'Faein   in the Fae language. *Laur lom as'Faein*—I speak in the Fae language.

fada   long (can reference time or distance)

fan   wait (imp.)

fíor   true

flua   wet

folath   bleed

fonn   keen, sharp

fracun   whore. Comes from an ancient Fae word meaning "use-value"—in other words, a person whose value is measured solely by what others can get from him or her.

galtanas   promise

gan   general negative—no, not, without, less

   gan derea   without end, eternal

gaoirn   wolves

g'demin   true, real

g'féalaidh   may you (pl.) live (see phrases)

g'fua   hate (v.)

g'mall   slowly

grafain   wild love, wild one. Lochlann's pillow name for Garrett.

halan   beautiful

impi   I beg

lae   day

lámagh   shot (v., p.t.)

lanan   lover. Tiernan's pillow name for Kevin, and vice versa

lanh   son

lasihoir   healer

laurha   spoken (see phrases)

   related words—*laurm*, I speak; *laur lom*, I am speaking, I speak (in) a language

lobadh   decayed, rotten

lofa   rotten

magarl   testicles (alt. spelling *magairl)*

Marfach, the   the Slow Death. Deadliest foe of the Fae race.

marú   kill

Mastragna   Master of Wisdom. Ancient Fae title for the Loremasters.

milat   feel, sense

minn   oath

mo mhinn   my oath

misnach   courage

nach   general negative; not, never

n-oí   night

ollúnta   solemn

onfatath   infected

orm   at me

pian   pain

pracháin   crows

Ridiabhal   lit. "king of the devils", Satan. A borrowed word, as Fae have neither gods nor devils.

rochar   harm (n.)

savac-dui   black-headed hawk, Conall's House-guardian

scair'anam   SoulShare (pl. *scair-anaim*)

   m'anam-sciar   my SoulShare

   scair'aine'e   the act of SoulSharing

   scair'ainm'en   SoulShared (adj.)

scian   knife

scian-damsai   knife-dances. An extremely lethal type of formalized combat.

scílim   I think, I believe

sibh   you (pl.)

slántai   health, tranquillity

   slántai a'váil   "Peace go with you". A mournful farewell.

s'ocan   peace, be at peace

spára   spare

   spára'se   spare him

spiraod   spirit

súil   eyes

sule-d'ainmi   lit. "animal-eyes", dark brown eyes

sus   up

s'vra lom   I love (lit. "I have love on me")

ta'sair   I'm free (exclam.)

thar   come (imp.)

> *Thar lom.* Come with me.

tón   ass (not the long-eared animal)

torq   boar

tre   three

> *Tre... dó... h'on...*   Three.... two... one...

tseo   this, this is (see phrases)

uiscebai   strong liquor found in the Realm, similar to whiskey

veissin   knockout drug found in the Realm, causes headaches

viant   desired one. A Fae endearment.

Useful phrases:

...tseo mo mhinn ollúnta.   This is my solemn oath.

G'féalaidh sibh i do cónai fada le céle, gan a marú a céle.
   "May you live long together, and not kill one another." A Fae blessing, sometimes bestowed

upon those Fae foolhardy enough to undertake some form of exclusive relationship. Definite "uh huh, good luck with that" overtones.

bragan a lae   "toy of the day". The plaything of a highly distractable Fae.

Fai dara tú pian beag. Ach tú a sabail dom ó pian I bhad nís mo.
You cause a slight pain. But you are the healing of more.

Cein fa buil tu ag'eachan' orm ar-seo?   Why do you look at me this way?

Dóchais laurha, dóchais briste.   Hope spoken is hope broken.

Bod lofa dubh.   Lit. "black rotted dick". Not a polite phrase.

Scílim g'fua lom tú.   I think I hate you.

S'vra lom tú.   I love you.

Sus do thón.   Up your ass.

D'súil do na prácháin, d'croí do na gaoirn, d'anam do n-oí gan derea.
"Your eyes for the crows, your heart for the wolves, your soul for the eternal night." There is only one stronger vow of enmity in the Fae language, and trust me, you don't want to hear that one.

Lámagh tú an batagar; 'se seo torq a'gur fola d'fach.
"You shot the arrow; this wounded boar is yours."
The equivalent as'Faein of "You broke it; you buy
it." Often used in its shortened form, "*Lámagh tú an
batagar.*" (or "*Lámagh sádh an batagar*" for "they
shot". It's probably only a matter of time before
some Fae in the human world, taking his cue from
"NMP" for "not my problem", comes up with
"LTB".

*Tá dócas le scian inas fonn, nach milat g'matann an
garta dí g'meidh tú folath.*
Fae proverb: Hope is a knife so keen, you don't
feel the cut until you bleed.

G'ra ma agadh.   Thank you.

*Tam g'fuil aon-arc desúcan an lanhuil damast I
d'asal. G'mall.*
"May a unicorn repair your hemorrhoids. Slowly."
One can only imagine....

Magairl a'Ridiabhal.   Satan's balls.

Se an'agean flua, a'deir n'abhann.
The ocean is wet, says the river. The pot calling
the kettle black.

galtanas deich meloi
"promise of ten thousand". A promise given by a
Fae, to give ten thousand of something to another,
usually something that can only be given over
time. Considered an extravagant, even irrational
showing of devotion.

About the Author

Rory Ni Coilean majored in creative writing, back when Respectable Colleges didn't offer such a major. She had to design it herself, at a university which boasted one professor willing to teach creative writing: a British surrealist who went nuts over students writing dancing bananas in the snow but did not take well to high fantasy. Graduating Phi Beta Kappa at the age of nineteen, she sent off her first short story to an anthology that was being assembled by an author she idolized, and received one of those rejection letters that puts therapists' kids through college. For the next thirty years or so she found other things to do, such as going to law school, ballet dancing (at more or less the same time), volunteering as a lawyer with Gay Men's Health Crisis, and nightclub singing, until her stories started whispering to her. Currently, she's a lawyer and a legal editor; the proud mother of a proud Brony and budding filmmaker; and is busily wedding her love of myth and legend to her passion for m/m romance. She is the winner of the Rainbow Books Award. She is a three-time Rainbow Award finalist.

***Dee's Hard Limits: Book Two of the Masters of Cats
Series***
by Trinity Blacio

***Caging the Bengal Tiger: Book Three of the Masters
of Cats Series***
by Trinity Blacio

Made in the USA
Las Vegas, NV
26 November 2021

35301721R00164